Praise for *One Good Dog*

"Those who ate up *Marley and Me* will want to check out Wilson's novel, which follows a disgraced millionaire who finds a friend in a scruffy pit bull."

—*EntertainmentWeekly.com*

"A love story between man and dog . . . you'll cry at the end."   —*USA Today*

"*One Good Dog* belongs on the top of everyone's reading list."   —*Telegraph Herald* (Dubuque, Iowa)

"Nowhere can we see the potential for our own redemption more clearly than in the eyes of our dog. Susan Wilson illustrates this truth poignantly and beautifully in this story of second chances."

—Tami Hoag, *New York Times* #1 bestselling author of *Secrets to the Grave*

"Fans of *Marley and Me* will find a new dog to cheer for in Wilson's (*Beauty*) insightful heart-tugger. . . . Chance tells his story in his own words, which makes his mistreatment and return to the fighting pit powerfully disturbing. Combined with Wilson's unflinching portrayal of Adam's struggle to overcome his past, *Old Yeller*'s got nothing on this very good man and his dog story."   —*Publishers Weekly*

"[*One Good Dog*] is a finely wrought story of second chances and also of the power of the human/canine bond, the amazing and myriad ways in which dogs can touch and make better people's lives. As Chance himself so aptly puts it, 'What else could I have done? I'm only canine, I had to help.'"

—*Bark* magazine

"[*One Good Dog*] evokes both laughter and tears, but the ending assures you that humans and dogs are capable of redemption."   —*Library Journal*

"Susan Wilson's evocative and deeply moving novel reminds us that even the most unlikely human can also find redemption, sometimes, with a little help from a canine friend."
—Melissa Jo Peltier, *New York Times* bestselling coauthor of *Cesar's Way*

"*One Good Dog* equals one great book!"
—Rita Mae Brown, *New York Times* bestselling author of *The Purrfect Murder*

"*One Good Dog* will make you cry, will make you laugh, will make you feel things more than you thought possible—and it will make you believe in second chances."
—Augusten Burroughs, *New York Times* bestselling author of *Running with Scissors* and *A Wolf at the Table*

"*One Good Dog* is a wonderful novel of healing and redemption."
—Spencer Quinn, *New York Times* bestselling author of *Dog on It*

"Anybody who has ever loved a dog—or been 'a pack of two,' as Chance so aptly puts it—will love *One Good Dog*. . . . I hope Susan Wilson sits and stays—forever."
—Lisa Scottoline, *New York Times* bestselling author of *Save Me*

"*One Good Dog* is a terrific book that held me from beginning to end!"
—Iris Johansen, *New York Times* #1 bestselling author of *Eve*

"I was so moved by Susan Wilson's writing: her understanding of the lost, in the language of the wild."
—Luanne Rice, *New York Times* bestselling author of *The Deep Blue Sea for Beginners*

Don't miss Susan Wilson's next novel, *The Dog Who Danced,* coming in 2012

Nothing was ever handed to me. My old man taught me the value of never expecting kindness. My stepmother taught me that the only way you get to be first in life is to stand alone. I've managed. I've never gone hungry, or worn anything I was ashamed of because it was threadbare, at least not since I left home at seventeen and a half. I've never sold myself in order to eat; I've met women like that. It's true I've had living arrangements that might be looked at as nearly that bad, but that's only if you're looking in. I have done some things I'm not proud of, but each one was the result of wanting something I was willing to make a hard choice to get. And yes, I've made those "bad" choices along the way. Even if you don't grow up with religion, you still know right from wrong, and the difference between good and not so good.

My name is Justine Meade and in my forty-three years there have only been a handful of people that I have loved. No, that's an exaggeration. Two. Two that I lost because of stupidity and selfishness. One was my son. The other was my dog.

—from *The Dog Who Danced*

Also by Susan Wilson

Summer Harbor
The Fortune Teller's Daughter
Cameo Lake
Hawke's Cove
Beauty

One Good Dog

SUSAN WILSON

ST. MARTIN'S GRIFFIN

NEW YORK

This is a work of fiction. All of the characters, organizations, and events portrayed in this novel are either products of the author's imagination or are used fictitiously.

ONE GOOD DOG. Copyright © 2010 by Susan Wilson. All rights reserved. Printed in the United States of America. For information, address St. Martin's Press, 175 Fifth Avenue, New York, N.Y. 10010.

www.stmartins.com

The Library of Congress has cataloged the hardcover edition as follows:

Wilson, Susan, 1951–
    One good dog / Susan Wilson.—1st ed.
        p. cm.
    ISBN 978-0-312-57125-2
    1. Executives—Fiction. 2. Life change events—Fiction. 3. Community service (Punishment)—Fiction. 4. Soup kitchens—Fiction. 5. Pit bull terriers—Fiction 6. Human-animal relationships—Fiction. I. Title.
    PS3573.I47533O64 2010
    813'.54—dc22

                                                            2009040089

ISBN 978-0-312-66295-0 (trade paperback)

First St. Martin's Griffin Edition: February 2011

10 9 8 7 6 5 4 3 2 1

Dedicated, as always, to my family—with love.
And in memory of two good men, our fathers:
William Everett Hidler and Frank Gordon Gibson, Jr.

Prologue

He was a rough-looking thing. Big ears, wiry hair. His muzzle just beginning to grizzle. He looked like the sort who'd been living outside of society for a while, maybe never really been a companion. After a long parade of supplicants appearing before me, each wanting me to choose him or her, their noses pressed up to the chain-link fence that separated us, there was something in this one's deep brown eyes, not a pleading—pleading I can overlook—but something else. A quiet dignity, maybe even an aloofness, as if he really didn't need me or my kind being nice to him. Yes. That was it, a haughtiness that declared he needed no one's pity; he shouldn't even be here. Don't look at me; I'm only here by coercion.

Our eyes met and held, but then he turned away. Beta to my alpha. But in that brief gaze, I saw something I recognized. Maybe it was just that I saw my own independent streak, the one that has kept me on top. Or the eyes of a fighter down on his luck, but with memories of recent glory. Maybe I saw that underneath the rough exterior lay a heart, like mine, not entirely hard. You've got to be tough to live in this world, whether your lip is curled in real anger or fear aggression, you have to be willing to carry out the threat. This battle-scarred fella understood that, and on that basis I made my decision. He was the one for me.

So I wagged my tail.

Chapter One

"Sophie." Adam March doesn't look up from the rectangle of paper in his hand. His tone is, as always, even, and no louder than it should be to reach across his executive-size office, through the open mahogany door, and to the ears of his latest personal assistant. On the pink rectangle of a "While You Were Out" memo slip, in Sophie's preferred lilac-colored ink and written in her loopy handwriting, are three simple words that make no sense to Adam March. *Your sister called.* Not possible. Time and date of call: yesterday afternoon, while he was enduring what he hoped was the last of the meetings he was going to have to hold before today's main event. A meeting in which he'd given a combination pep talk and take-no-prisoners mandate to his handpicked team.

Adam flips the pink note back and forth against the knuckles of his left hand. This is a mistake. Sophie has made a mistake. Not her first. Lately he's been noticing these little slips of judgment, of carelessness, of Sophie's slightly less than deferential attitude. As if she's not a subordinate, but a peer. Too many late nights when the jacket comes off, the tie is loosened, and the sleeves are rolled up. Too many weary hours leaning over her as she works on her computer, struggling to make every document perfect. She's made a common mistake: Being in the trenches together doesn't mean that they are friends, that he will overlook sloppiness.

Adam closes his eyes, takes a deep breath. The most important day of his career and it's already started out badly.

His alarm hadn't gone off. Which meant he hadn't had time for his run around the gravel jogging paths of his gated neighborhood, which meant he had lost that thirty minutes of "me time" he needed so desperately before a day filled with meetings, conference calls, at least one confrontation with middle management, and, at the end of the day, a dinner party his wife, Sterling, had planned in order to befriend the newest neighbors, the Van Arlens, before someone else got them. The Van Arlens, it was believed, had connections to the best people. People who were useful to anyone interested in social advancement and really good schools for their children. Which basically summed up Sterling.

Adam had no objection to a get-to-know-you dinner; he just preferred not to have them on the same day as so much else was going on in his life. But then, if they waited until he had a slow day, they'd still be living in Natick and their daughter wouldn't be enjoying the connections that would serve her for the rest of her life. It was hard work, laying the groundwork for social/business/education/recreational pathways for a teenage daughter who greeted him with ill-disguised sullenness when he made the effort to show up for one or another of her endless sports in time for the final score.

When Adam thought about having kids, he'd pictured

himself the Ward Cleaver of his family—wise, loving, adored. Ariel hadn't been wryly mischievous like Beaver, or devoted like Wally. Adam hadn't heard an understandable phrase out of her mouth in years, every mumble directed at the table, or muttered behind her long blond hair. The only time he saw her face was when he attended her horse shows, when her hair was scraped back and under her velvet-covered helmet. But then she blended in with the other girls, all pink cheeks and tight breeches and blue coats. Sometimes he rooted for the wrong girl/horse combination. To say nothing of the fact that all the horses looked alike, too. To Adam, horse shows were a tortuous and endless replication of the same blue coat, black helmet, brown horse racing around the course, and then the girl crying when a rail was knocked or a time fault incurred or because the horse was crazy, lazy, lame, or just plain stupid.

Except for Ariel's drive to become some kind of horse-jumping champion, a goal at which Adam had thrown great handfuls of money, she was an enigma to him. Yet this is why he worked so hard. This and Sterling's four-carat dinner ring and her personal fitness gurus, one at each of the three homes they owned—Sylvan Fields, Wellington, Florida, and Martha's Vineyard—the support of an increasingly large staff and their illegal cousins; and the cadre of financial managers to make sure he didn't pay more taxes than he should. They, unlike most of the rest of the people he employed, were very, very good.

At age forty-six, Adam March had found himself, on this overcast morning, pressing his forehead against the bathroom mirror and wishing he didn't have to go to work. Not only had his alarm failed him but the housekeeper had failed—again—to have the made-to-order granola he needed.

Nowhere in the giant pantry could he put his hands on the imported cereal he preferred. All he could find was the crap Ariel ate. With a childhood fed on cornflakes, now he could afford the best in breakfast food, so was it too much to ask that he find his granola when he wanted it? The sheer cost of importing it from Norway had to be justified by his eating it every day. But beyond that, without it, his bowels wouldn't function, and if that system also failed him, Adam knew that he was in danger of really losing his temper, and it might be that this housekeeper would be the biggest loser once he was done with her. Which, of course, he couldn't even consider until after this dinner party. To fire the stupid bitch today would mean that Sterling's ire would overshadow his, until his temper and his bowels would shrink to a pipsqueak size.

Sterling, blond, whippet-thin, and sleeping the peaceful sleep of the person in charge of everything, was a force to be reckoned with, and Adam wasn't about to unleash that power on a day so patently important to her. Not for her own sake, she so often said, but for his sake. His advancement, their only child's advancement. It was social warfare out there, and Sterling provided the leadership of a general over her troops. "We have to be seen; we have to support the right charities." Their name even appeared as supporters on a PBS documentary series. "We need to attend the right concerts. If you intend to succeed, that's the price you have to pay." That was but one of Sterling's cheerleading themes. Some might say that Adam March had already succeeded. What more could he want? Some men might want strings of letters following their names, others the glory that came from leadership in the arts, the sciences, the political arena. Adam lusted after three letters: C E O. Chief Executive Officer. Such an achievement was no longer dependent on moving up in the ranks of promotions and cultivating years in the same company. It was more of a hopscotch of leaps across and over, one foot down, now two, from corporation to corporation, allowing himself to be seduced away from one major executive role to another. Manager, Vice President of Acquisitions or Division. A rise that came with a move to a bigger house in a better—read: more exclusive—neighborhood, another vacation home where he'd spend most of his time on his phone, too afraid to be out of touch for more than the time it took to use the bathroom, more BlackBerrys. More expense. Some days Adam felt like he didn't have two coins to rub together. All of his salary and bonuses seemed to be absorbed into this machine of ambition. Still, the ripe red cherry of the top post was just out of reach. But not for long. After today, Adam's elevation to the ultimate spot on the ladder at Dynamic Industries would be secure. President and CEO.

But this morning, all Adam had wanted for himself was a bowl of Norwegian granola and a fucking run through the contrived landscape of his most recent gated neighborhood. He wanted his "me time," thirty minutes to call his own, leaving the Bluetooth behind, keeping his head down and his eyes only on the path so that he didn't have to wave at neighbors or their help. His best ideas often came to him during that thirty minutes.

There was only one thing stopping Adam from just taking his run and going into work a bit late. He held himself and his staff to a rigorous standard of punctuality. Adam March entered his office at precisely seven-thirty every day. Not one minute before or after. It was a source of incredible satisfaction to him that people could set their watches by him. Adam believed that timeliness was an art and a science. Despite the ten-mile commute and all the variables of traffic, Adam arrived on time. And woe betide the staffer in his group who wasn't there to greet him. Adam required simple things of people, the sine qua non of his expectation: Be on time. The groups that wandered into the building here and there, untaxed by punctuality, smacked of a basic sloppiness he would not allow in his.

Adam stared at his reflection in the bathroom mirror, looking at an attractively craggy face, his morning shadow of dark beard firming up a jaw that had only just begun to soften. He stared into his own cold brown eyes, eyes that had earned him the nickname, "Dead Eye." A nickname he didn't find offensive, but grudgingly affectionate. A face with gravitas. A face suited to the take-no-prisoners deal maker he had become.

If there was a shadow of an angry, grizzled man in the mirror, Adam swept it away with a brushful of French milled shaving soap.

Adam runs a hand down his silk tie, tucks the strange note into his jacket pocket. Sophie is still AWOL. He stares at her empty chair and, for the first time in many years, wonders about his sister.

Sophie's armless secretary's chair is cocked at an angle, as if its occupant weighs more on one side. Her computer screen with the Microsoft logo drifting around speaks of her having been on the computer opening up the e-mails that she will either forward to him or to his underlings or delete as unworthy. It isn't enough that she's in the building. Sophie needs to be at her desk when he arrives.

Adam lays the offending piece of memo paper down and

opens up his old-fashioned top-loading briefcase. He can't remember what he's looking for. There she is, slinking back to her desk with a giant paper coffee cup in one hand, a pastry in the other. Even from deep in his office, Adam can see that she has a flake of icing on her chin. Now Sophie really is testing him. Instead of dropping everything and grabbing her notebook, she leans over her computer keyboard and taps the mouse. She is checking her e-mail. On his time. Outrageous. Sophie knows this is an important day. What can be more important to her than getting her marching orders from him? He's really getting tired of her insubordination.

Your sister called.

Chapter Two

Adam sits on the floor of a small kitchen. The floor beneath him is sticky, splotched here and there with stains so old, they are part of the geometric pattern of the linoleum. He plays with a Matchbox car, making car noises as he pushes it along and around the cracks in the tile. He is underneath the kitchen table. Four chairs are pushed in; only one has someone sitting in it. His father. Big feet in work boots, one lacing looser than the other. One foot tilted just a little on the rubber edge of its lug sole. Adam runs the little car up and over the feet of his father. His father shifts his foot away, removing the mountain. Adam putters his lips and propels his car around the perimeter of the defined space beneath the table. He can hear the clink of glass on glass, and the rustle of the newspaper being folded. They haven't had supper yet, and there are no sounds of it being prepared. A pair of improbably high-heeled vinyl boots appears. His big sister. From his lair, Adam can see her knees, pale, knobby protuberances peeking out over the top of the white boots, above them a long sweep of skinny leg to the hem of her miniskirt.

"Where do you think you're going?" His father's voice is low, tired.

"I'm going out. I told you."

"You are not. You need to start dinner."

"You promised."

Suddenly, his father scrapes back the chair and stands up. "Veronica." Now all Adam can see is his blue work pants, the too-long pant legs covering the tops of his black steel-toed boots. His sister's legs are obscured by their father's. "No, I didn't. You have responsibilities in this house."

"Fuck my responsibilities."

The sound of the slap is sharp, brief, startling, like the sound of his cap gun, and involuntary tears spark his eyes. His sister makes no sound. "Don't you talk like that, young lady. Who do you think you are?"

"I'm sick of this. I'm sick of you. I'm sick of being the unpaid babysitter. He's your kid; you take care of him."

Adam watches from beneath the table, watches his sister's long legs in those ridiculous boots stride to the back door. They live on the second floor; this door leads to the back stairs, to the dank hallway below with its clutter of empty cans and unused garden tools. She opens the door.

"Don't you walk away from me." His father's voice is authority, dominance, power. Adam is too young at five and a half to think in those words, but he recognizes the hollowness in his chest every time his father speaks. The hollow fear that the troll beneath the bridge is talking to him and that he won't have the answers.

From under his kitchen table cave, Adam watches as his sister's legs come back, coming closer, until her small feet in the vinyl boots point directly at him. He feels a little relief. She's back. She'll stay.

He leans out a little, to see past his father's legs. Veronica speaks, and what she says become the last words he'll ever hear from his sister; the last words he remembers. "Fuck you, old man." The door slams shut. And he is left alone with his father.

"Sophie." A little more insistent. He needs to stop this before it goes any further. Where is that girl? Why isn't she here standing in front of him with her little steno pad, her lilac-colored pen at the ready, waiting for his orders, waiting for his needs to be expressed and acted on. Waiting to hear him say that he, Adam March, has no sister and that whoever left that message should not be given any encouragement. He will not speak to her. Even before he can start the day's critical work, now he has to tell Sophie she's made a mistake, that despite those three innocuous words, despite what some woman has told her, he doesn't have a sister. Sophie needs to be smarter about crank calls.

In more than forty years, he's never had a word from her, not since the day she stormed out of the house, leaving him behind, alone with their widowed father. Veronica has been gone so long that he's never spoken of an older sister, not even to his wife. Why would he bother bringing up a faint memory, a vague recollection of sitting on the couch and sharing a bowl of popcorn, when Veronica's existence has nothing to do with him? With who he is. Who he has become.

Adam has not so much denied his history as created a whole new mythology—that of self-made man, his history beginning not with childhood, but with his summa cum laude graduation from the University of Massachusetts with his B.S., followed by his Harvard M.B.A. He has whitewashed the years of working as a Pioneer Valley Transit driver to pay for college.

He has downplayed his childhood as a virtual orphan, refusing to speak of his past with a firmness that implies a slightly romantic, yet painful experience, not the facts of a father who gave him up to the state. Or the series of foster homes. The degradation of a life in the system. Long ago, Adam March encapsulated his actual childhood as the body will encapsulate a splinter, forming a hard mass of cells to separate the foreign body and dissolve it. In its place, he found ambition. Adam is a man who always catches the gold ring.

Adam folds the pink note. *Veronica. "He's your kid." The sound of a slamming door.*

Adam feels a tiny squeezing of his heart muscles. Not pain, not angina. Something else. Tension. The tension that makes him the tiger he is in the boardroom. Adam closes his eyes for a moment, then opens them and rereads the note. *Your sister called.* That is all that is written on the paper. No number. No address. No name. As if he knew them already.

Certainly this is Sophie's misunderstanding, but what if it's not? What if, in some bizarre circumstance, some unimaginable turn of events, his sister has come back? If so, what does she expect? A tearful reunion? What does she want? Money? That makes some sense, and he makes a mental note to call his lawyer as soon as he can break free from the day's high-pressured activity. He opens the slip once more.

Your sister called. The shaky ground on which he has built his life trembles.

"Sophie." The name spoken in a flat tone, devoid of warmth, as if addressing a dog. A dog that is being disobedient. A dog that needs training.

"Be right there, Mr. March." Adam can see Sophie framed in the open office door as she bends over her computer, tiny dimples forming in the backs of her knees where her slightly too-tight, slightly too-short skirt slides upward in defiance of his dress code. Ties for the men and appropriate office wear for the women. Adam March does not tolerate Ally McBeal wear in his office. Sophie's ample backside wavers from side to side as she taps the keyboard with a response to whatever it is she's finding so amusing at his expense. His expensive time.

Suddenly, his mouth is dry and he is very thirsty. As he reaches for the carafe on his credenza, Adam suddenly feels his blood pressure drop, and with it a swooping dizziness, a sense of being outside of his own head. He touches the edge of his desk for solid contact, but his hands feel disembodied, attached to his wrists by threads. The momentary dizziness stops as his blood pressure begins scaling up, but not the sense of plummeting.

Outside of his office, Sophie laughs. Each note of her musical trill strikes him as increasingly taunting. Adam's thoughts are circling wildly, his razor-sharp thinking suddenly clouded with anxiety. He's got to get back on track; he has important phone calls to make. He doesn't have time for distractions. He doesn't have time to puzzle out what this means. Time for a sister.

Adam crushes the note and tosses it into the receptacle beneath his desk.

His sister, thinking to just walk back in, to pick up a relationship she abandoned when he was a little kid? Leaving him to be passed from one foster home to another? To jeopardize everything he's spent his whole adult life building?

Adam retrieves the note and tears the sheet into halves,

quarters, and eighths. Adam March has no sister. He has a business to run.

"Sophie." Adam says her name again as if it is a dead word, a word that is meaningless, invented. "Sophie." Harder on the second syllable. SoPHIE. Not imploring. Threatening.

The girl stands with her back to him, bending over her computer keyboard, her whole posture mocking his authority.

"Sophie." His voice gone from authoritative mezzo forte to forte, and still the girl doesn't come to him.

Still bent over the keyboard, Sophie raises one hand and waves back at Adam, a casual, dismissive salute, acknowledging his voice but postponing his wishes. Putting him off. Like Sterling puts him off. Time and again, when she stands in front of him in their bedroom, unabashedly naked, slowly lotioning herself, spraying the fine mist of her signature perfume into the air and walking through it, readying herself for whatever social event they are scheduled to attend or host. Untouchable. Her surgically enhanced body nearly unattractive in its rock-hard contours and artificially enhanced breasts, but invoking lust in him anyway. Lust that Sterling allows only afterward.

Waving him away like Ariel does, diminishing his importance in front of her teenage friends.

Sophie's dismissive hand lowers to the keyboard, the importance of her electronic friend subsuming the importance of him. She shifts, the dimples behind her left knee disappearing and the ones on her right deepening, little mocking eyes.

Too much has been invested in this day. This day's anticipated outcome. Too much of Adam's time, effort, reputation, and future is wrapped up in his almost eighteen months of careful analysis, planning, coercing of colleagues to see that he is right, that this takeover is the right thing to do. Too much of his life has been spent in building up to this moment; maybe his whole life has been lived in preparation for this glorious day. With today's launch, he will step into his rightful place as CEO designee, no longer lying in wait to take over Louis Wannamaker's position. The years of building upon the weak foundation of his boyhood, his years of achievement, will come to fruition as heir apparent.

Veronica. He called out her name, then and for years after she slammed through the back door.

And Sophie is seriously challenging his authority. She needs reminding. She needs to remember herself and her place in this corporate pack.

"Don't you talk back to me, young lady."

Your sister called. What idiot believed some raving madwoman?

Adam's mouth is bone-dry; his tongue sticks to the roof of his mouth. His pulse is pounding in his right temple, a curiously painful thumping that seems audible, as if he can listen to the rising of his blood pressure. He is out of breath. Behind him, the morning light casts a yellow square onto his massive black desk, his shadow like a keyhole in the center. He presses his knuckles against his leather blotter. A thin line of ragged pain arcs between his eyes for a single audible pulse beat. Adam presses his knuckles down harder, presses himself against the edge of the black desk, rocks a little to gain momentum, and pushes off. Coming around the wide desk, he knocks the regulation vase of fresh flowers askew; the foot of the fluted glass vase is suspended slightly over the edge, its balance held by the weight of the arrangement. A lily petal loosens and falls to the floor. Adam's shoe crushes it into the carpet, a pink stain like roadkill against the macadam-colored weave.

Even as he reaches the doorway of his office, Adam is amazed at just how angry he is. It is as if the anger is boiling up from some deeper region of himself than he knew he had, that it is transforming him, physically wrenching his bones into another shape, his skin into another species. Adam has known anger; he's shouted at his truculent daughter, at underlings, and even, rarely, at Sterling. But every time he raises his voice, he is reminded of his father, of his father's last words to his escaping sister. His father's voice is the only sound in his head right now. *"Don't defy me, young lady."*

"Sophie." A croaking whisper, as if the anger has him by the throat, squeezing his breath out. The pulse in his temple pounds, and for an instant Adam thinks he is going to faint.

"Fuck you, old man."

Sophie Anderson is riveted to her computer screen, reading through her e-mails, laughing at jokes forwarded from her pal in Consumer Affairs. She stands up only as she feels Adam's breath on her neck. Then his hand on her shoulder as he wrenches her around to slap her full in the face.

Later, those who witnessed the event would claim they didn't know who was attacking Sophie, that they all thought some crazed madman had gotten by security. It took four middle managers and two security guards to wrestle Adam to the floor. Like a beast, he howled. Corporate legend would tag Adam March forever as the Jekyll and Hyde of Dynamic Industries. A man primed for battle in the world of corporate take-no-prisoners management style had slipped his reason, like a steel bear trap sprung accidentally by the touch of a rabbit. Adam March lost his shit, as they said in cafeterias and cocktail parties for years to come. The high-and-mighty top dog was wrestled into submission and never seen again. But his legend, his incomprehensible act of wild self-destruction, lived on.

Chapter Three

I should explain a little about myself to you. A little bio. A thumbnail—or in my case, a dewclaw—description. I'm a little over three years old, still young enough to have to vie for position, old enough to go against only the best. I have good teeth, set in a strong jaw. One of my ears is sheered off at the bottom; the other hangs in a three-quarter break, and I keep it tight against my skull whenever I greet. My tail is as straight as a stick and I almost never let it rise above my back like some happy-go-lucky retriever. It's a divining rod of my intentions, a whip, a warning. Depending on my circumstances, I'm forty-five or fifty pounds. When I'm on the street, I might shrink to a mere thirty unless I suss out the best Dumpsters and get there ahead of my vermin brethren. I don't know what color I am; it's an unimportant characteristic among my kind. What is important is that my anal glands describe my authority, my education, and my living arrangements to any who encounter me—where I've been and where I'm going.

My urine marks a wide territory. I have no testicles. The first time I was nabbed, off they went. I'll come to that part of my history directly, but I will say that by that time I was fully masculine, and I have not given up my boyish ways except for the fulfillment of my genetic destiny. I can do it, but I'm shooting blanks.

From birth, my manifest destiny, as arranged by the young men who kept my parents in cages in a cellar, was to fight. My size and sex determined that I received the best of care from those who had no affection for the animals holed up in the inner-city cellar. I got fed. I got to wear heavy chains around my shoulders to bulk up my body into a mass of rock-solid muscle. I got strong enough that two of these callow young men, boys, pups of their species, had to hold me back. I rarely saw daylight. I was a creature of the night, shuttled from one cellar to another in the darkness, an ill-fitting muzzle all that was between me and their hands. I don't recall ever being touched by them in a nonbusiness way. All jerks and pulls and pushes; the end of a stick, the flat of a board. Had either of those two young men ever dared unmuzzle me and pat my head, I would have licked his hand. They were afraid of me, of what they had created.

As I say, I was born in an inner-city cellar. My parents, unusually, were both on-site, so I got to know them both. So many of my kind are not so lucky. My mom was a full-blood pit bull—whatever that may mean in the lexicon of swaggering young men—descended from a long line of dogs whose survival depended on their prowess in the fight arena. None of them particularly angry, but all able to be incited to destruction; all highly competitive when pitted, no pun intended, against an adversary. Like the gladiators of old, our adversaries aren't of our own choosing, but chosen for us by the men who employ us. Fighting is our livelihood. Our pre-determined career. A job. The hours aren't bad, and if you're good at your job, you get to live another day and do it again.

Mom, whom they called "Bitch-dog," was scarred along her lips, even to where there was a half-moon of missing flesh exposing her upper side teeth. Long retired from the pit, she'd become a breeding machine. Her dugs hung limp and wobbly; even after the authorities removed her from the cellar, her teats would never retract to their earlier tightness.

Now, we don't identify one another by the breedist notions of those who cause our creation, but everybody knows that our different shapes and sizes, smells, and tail carriage help us to identify ourselves to one another. So, for convenience sake, I will say Dad was a blend of several types of "breeds" that have power and stamina; Dad was a mix of pit bull and rottweiler or boxer, maybe a little old-fashioned bulldog. Dad's rottie parts gave him his height and bulk. His pit bull parts thinned out his back end but gave him a Bluto disproportion in his front end. He was a tough one in the ring, knew his game well, and he never gave ground. They called him "Fitty," after some rapper they admired. It seemed to me, even as a youngster, that calling a gladiator like Dad "Fitty" was a bit silly. Although Dad and I were neighborhood champs, our boys were not contenders on the real dogfight circuit; thus were able to pass mixed breeds like Fitty and me off on their equally ama-teurish friends.

Naming conventions have ever puzzled us. If we don't come when called, it's likely that the appellation assigned to us is unacceptable. In my life I've been called many things, some of them not polite. We know one another by the names shouted at us, but more intimately by our scents. I think of my mother not as "Bitch-dog," but by the warm scent of her particular skin, her particular odor nursing my less fortunate littermates. I was the big one. I was the one on the top teat. My lesser sibs perished in the boys' brutal effort at selective breeding, tossed like so many field mice into the training cage.

On the street, my friends, and I've had many, are untethered by spoken names. I can visit them, even if they are out of sight, by their markers. Ah, there's the tough little one. I see that the bitch who mates with big dogs has been hanging around the alley. Maybe I'll wait for her. A further snuffle and I realize that she is now pregnant yet again. I see her in my mind's eye, her teats swelling and her self-satisfied tongue lolling as she seeks out a safe haven for her nest. We think in pictures.

I picture the cellar in which I was born, comforted by the rich, warm scent of my mother's skin and hair; curious at my first whiff of blood, the sweetish scent of it coming to me beyond the partition that separated us from the makeshift ring; not knowing what it was, but equating the smell of it with the sounds that came to me, the sounds of combat. My senses prepared me for my own experience, so that when I first saw blood, first engaged in a fight, it was as familiar to me as if I had studied the textbook.

When it was time to put aside childish things, I left my mother's kennel and moved into isolation. I believe I may have howled on that first solitary night, but I was quickly quieted with a smack. Ever since, I have ducked my head at the sight of a fast-moving hand. My assailant tossed in a hard rubber ring, which I proceeded to gnaw, ingesting the slurry and vomiting in the night before I finally slept.

I picture the heavy chains that were looped over my head and onto my shoulders as I was paraded in the mean streets by the boys. They gave me a strong dog look, and I confess I might have swaggered a bit. I wasn't fettered by the chains; I was proud of them. Around my neck a perfect uniform of tackle suited to controlling an uncontrollable animal. A collar that when jerked pressed prongs of metal into my thick neck. A leather collar fitted out with pointed studs was my dress uniform, the one I got to wear on formal occasions, like when the boys took me out to show off to their crew.

By the time I had reached my full size, the boys had begun my training in earnest.

Though I most resemble my mother—longish body, muzzle like a shoe box, whiplike tail, I am big like Dad. The rottie parts are pretty thinned out, so I'll never weigh in at ninety pounds like those bruisers, but I'm in the heavyweight category for my sport. Fifty pounds, all muscle and bone and spit.

How do we know what to do the minute we're dropped into a pit? We don't. The first time, all we know is that our men expect something from us. Their sweat tells us that they are challenging one another; their voices are sharp, encouraging, cajoling, berating, fierce. In a few moments, we know what to do. We know what they want. We pick up on their agitation; we get into the trash talking. We engage. And, like those old-time gladiators, we know that defeat is not an option. This is what our men want. This is our job.

From the first time my boys put me in the ring, I understood what was expected of me. I fought out of fear. I'm not ashamed to say that. If you didn't fear getting your nose bitten off, you were as crazy as those boys. Be the aggressor and you might not get hurt, or hurt as much. I'll say something else: I didn't always hate it. When you're a little hungry, isolated, when you never get to meet your fellows in any sort of comradely way, your noses never touching the communicating part, only recognizing one another through the scents left on the fence posts, well, you get a little testy. It was my only outlet. I was pretty good at it.

I am and always will be a beast, a man-designed bag of sinew, bone, muscle, and teeth. My ancestors thought it was a good alliance between our kind and man, never dreaming that their physical shapes and proclivities would be so determined by another creature. I am made bestial by the job I was trained to do. Many of my species have lost that bestiality, replacing a heritage of scavenging around the firepit with an attachment to some human who will dote on them.

I never knew about that until the day my boys brought in a mutt from off the street, clean, toenails well clipped, uncollared, but a clearly attached *Canis domesticus*. This happened every now and then. When they'd run out of runts, the boys would bring in involuntary recruits for us to spar with. These draftees were not meant to be real challengers; they were generally short on muscle and low in stamina, often soft from good living. These naïve fellows arrive shamelessly tail-wagging, thinking they've found a new friend, and the next minute some tough-skinned, pale-eyed contender bites into their cheerfully upraised necks.

This one told me his story during the hours we had caged in the cellar of the house, his cage placed close enough to mine that we could talk so quietly that our voices didn't provoke either of the boys to shout down "Shaddup." His scent, even without my being able to sniff around his communicating area, was replete with good food and human touching. He told me that he had a person who took care of his every need, gently, even offering him treats for every silly thing he did. His job was not to roll around in a pit, but to walk without pulling on the leash. No, he didn't wear a collar like mine. His, which the boys removed, was of soft leather, two metal disks declaring who he was and to whom he belonged tinkling merrily from it. He missed the sound; he wasn't sure he could sleep well, not hearing the gentle ding of his tags as they touched while he circled for sleep. They and the collar were the badge of his service. And of them, he was quite proud. I was appalled. The idea of such submission sent an involuntary shiver along my back and I shook hard to rid myself of it. But I was curious, maybe even a little jealous.

I made short work of him in the practice pit, but he stuck in my mind as someone whose story was not singular, but indicative of a whole world beyond my cellar. The idea began to take hold. I spoke to others as we waited our turn, and, yes, they knew of these fellows who lived in houses, who didn't bite for a living. Fellows who owed everything they had to packs of humans. Fellows who were expected to submit at all times like puppies to a grown male, even up into their mature years. They'd seen them, and not just in the arena. They'd seen them as my competitors were walked down the streets of the city, being brought to me on their own chains, they'd seen these others attached to light, meaningless leashes, happily gazing up at the faces of those who held the ends. They were usually dragged away to one side as the gladiators lumbered by, the fear in their people telegraphing caution to those at the end of the leash. The occasional lifted lip, not in challenge, but in submission. They were a hoot. Can you imagine?

I could, and, increasingly, I did. I was good in the pit, but I knew that there would always be the day when I'd be beaten—either by another fellow or by my boys. Beaten as punishment for being beaten. It's what happened to Dad at least twice in my life.

But there was another sort of fellow that I met on a more regular basis, the one that lived an entirely independent life: the street dog. Usually more intelligent than the occasional leash dog, these street dogs were savvy. They understood the freedom of a life lived naturally. If they were often cold, hungry, and in danger of being run over, they lived their lives as they pleased. Unfortunately for them, they were also an easy target; put a plate of food out and, wham bam, they were snagged. Not just by my boys and their ilk but by the authorities, the men or women who made such dogs disappear in exactly the same way as my boys. One minute licking their hindquarters on the sidewalk, the next in a cage. But their stories were the best. High adventure, travel, frequent mating. Oh boy. It was rumored that the street dogs who were captured by the authorities only made it out if they were charming. Those who weren't charming didn't. But it's hard to know charming when your whole life has been directed toward being irascible. No one knew where they went, but it didn't take a standard poodle to figure it out. The odor of charring meat and bones that threaded through the miasma of scents that filled the city air was enough of a clue. Through the diesel and effluvia, doughnuts and wieners, the sweaty population and its overlay of artificial scent, working its way like a winding river of finality, the smoke of oblivion.

I was resting in my cage after a particularly challenging bout. My opponent had nearly prevailed, until by sheer bull force I pushed him over the line that demarcates winning. They thrust the breaking stick between my jaws and the game was over. I was sliced up pretty good, and one of the boys had made a squeamish attempt to stitch up the gash on my chest. The stitches pulled the skin together something like a badly made baseball. I licked at them, tasting the rough edges of my blood-crusted trussed skin, but I couldn't reach the worst of it. My opponent lay on a pile of newspapers, his head flung back like he was baying at the moon. There was still a light in his eye, so I knew he hadn't yet bled to death. I snortled an apology through the bars of my cage and he lifted his head. He snortled back, a kind of absolution for just doing my job. We're a brutish lot, but we don't hate one another. *If we had hands, we could break out of here.* He agreed, then laid his head down, and I watched as his spirit lifted away.

A pounding above our heads. Mom sat up, dispersing her latest litter onto the bottom of her cage. *The men. The men are here.* We'd heard about them, the men who come and our kind disappear. We'd heard they removed us to bigger cages, smaller cages; to fight us with other species, to simply cut our throats. Rumors of the men circulated most often after one of us died. A dime is dropped and things happen.

We heard the percussion of big boys' feet upstairs, dashing toward the back of the apartment, clambering down the back stairs. I knew that there was a door to the outside, to the square of dirt where we were allowed to defecate twice a day. None of the boys ever stepped foot out there in the field of shit. We who used the yard, trotting around the perimeter, sniffing out one another over and over again, raising our legs against one another's mark, we knew how to skirt the worst of the mess. If we lived on the outside, we'd be careful to place our business away from where we lived.

I heard the back door open; I stood and pressed my very sore nose against the wire of my cage and pricked my ears. I sniffed the air, an amalgam of our boys' pungent sweat and the scent of the men. The men and one female. Her female scent lightly mingled with her heat. My mother shoveled her brood against the back of the cage with her nose, a worried gargle in her throat. I shook myself, ready for anything.

Chapter Four

The one-bedroom apartment is his accountant's idea. "Until your lawyer straightens out the alimony and child support, you can't afford to go on living in hotels."

As the months rolled by, Adam had moved from one hotel to another, each one losing a star as the costs of keeping his almost ex-wife and child provided for, writing check after check to keep up with the billable hours of his lawyers fighting on the three fronts of his wife's complaint, Sophie's complaint, and what he determined was Dynamic's illegal firing, drained his nonrenewable resources.

"Get yourself a little place, cook your own meals. Economize a little, Adam."

"Afford?" For some reason, Adam is stuck on that word. It has been thirty-five years since the word *afford* and its ugly stepsister, *economize,* have been used against him, and then by one of his foster fathers with an electric bill in his hand. Not since the early days of their marriage had Adam expressed any concern about finances to Sterling. Maybe even never. By the time they met at a corporate retreat at which her father was keynote speaker, Adam was well on the way to self-made millionaire. A man whom her father, the all-powerful Herbert Carruthers, could admire.

Maybe he even encouraged spending, or at least did nothing to discourage the acquisition of possessions required of their place in life. For Sterling, it was the beautiful fashion-forward clothes, the legitimate designer accessories, the best and most current automobiles—gas consumption be damned—the home entertainment systems, and the luxury vacations. For Ariel, the increasingly more expensive horses, the promised Miata for her sixteenth birthday, and a guarantee that she would never suffer a student loan in her life. His little girl wants for nothing. His little wife had always wanted for nothing, and she intends to keep it that way.

Sterling knows what their marriage is worth and is scooping everything up with both arms. The houses, the portfolios, the cars, except his 2007 Lexus, a car that he would have been trading in this year as outmoded, time for a new one. The real estate investments. Her lawyers are really good. Words like *mental cruelty* are being lobbed at him; he is accused of being threatening, then is threatened himself with a restraining order. The documents chronicle the shadow of fear under which his family now claims to have lived. Adam knows exactly what threat he's levied against Sterling, the threat to her social standing. Her husband is the crazy man who struck his PA. He is the executive whose massive takeover campaign failed to launch.

She can no longer hold her head up in polite society. People like them don't strike underlings, at least not in public. People like them don't fail.

His helpmeet, his partner in life, his Sterling has turned on him.

Adam leans his forehead against the glass of the picture window that looks out onto the street. There are no curtains on the window, and the landlord has yet to install the promised venetian blinds. There is one bedroom, just big enough for his double mattress on its frame and a bureau that he liberated from the attic of the Sylvan Fields house. It might have belonged to Sterling's grandmother, or an aunt. Neither one could recall, and the possession of it was one of the rare moments of noncontention they have enjoyed in the last year and a half. A tiny bathroom with a puke green carpet on the floor opens into the living room. He has a futon, purchased from the same discount furniture place where he bought the mattress, a television on a pressboard stand, a hideous coffee table, a small kitchen table, now tucked against the opposite wall, and two folding chairs. The kitchen is a galley kitchen, barely big enough to turn around in, which makes it surprisingly efficient, especially as he uses only the microwave and the kettle.

The apartment is on the third floor of a four-story building in a row of four-story brick-faced buildings facing west. Not quite town houses, no bay windows or granite steps, these postwar buildings are utilitarian. A line of city trees soften the landscape, promise that this downscale Boston neighborhood is still inhabited by taxpayers who care.

Across the street, a line of small mom-and-pop businesses, a newsagent, a yarn shop, and a store with a jaunty rainbow of colors splashed in an arc across the plate-glass display window: A to Z Tropical Fish and Pet Supply. Little hand-painted fish gambol around the letters.

Standing at the bare rectangle of picture window, Adam stares down onto the early-morning street until he sees a light go on in the hole-in-the-wall paper store. He pulls on his pants, zips the fly but leaves the button undone. His two-day-old T-shirt hangs out, a small hole beginning under the right arm. Adam hasn't taken well to doing laundry. He hasn't figured out the rhythm of keeping a supply of clean underwear and is continually surprised to find none in his dresser drawer a mere week after having dragged his pillowcase of dirty clothes down to the Laundromat that anchors the fleet of businesses across the street from his place.

Adam roots around in his pants pocket for enough change to buy his daily fix of newspapers, *The New York Times*, which once simply appeared at his breakfast table, and *The Wall Street Journal*, which Sophie would leave on his credenza, important articles neatly highlighted in yellow. Nowadays, he adds the local rag to his pile as he scans for news about himself. His loss of control has become a metaphor for the rapacious greed of today's overcompensated executives. If time heals all wounds, the year that the court cases have taken has diluted the amount of coverage. He's old news now.

His sentencing is today. The final chapter for public consumption.

It's pretty amazing at how effective some lawyers can be. Cadres of them. Ranks of men and women in expensive suits, carrying bulky briefcases crammed with the weaponry of law, filing into and out of windowless conference rooms with broad tables and dry-erase boards scarred with the wrong markers. The heavy scent of the knowledge of the law emanating from their very pores. Red-painted lips closed over perfect teeth; rep ties stroked downward, inanimate pets. Adam dreams of them at night. The red lips of the women parting to reveal razor teeth. The rep ties becoming reptiles, hissing and forking at him. Sometimes the faces become those of his adversaries: Wannamaker, Sophie, Sterling. In his scotch-drenched dreams, Adam shrinks as they rise above him like hot-air balloons, and he feels the flames of their anger torch his skin.

The predawn air is thick with humidity, a vaporous scrim obscuring a rising sun that casts no shadow on the street in front of Adam as he crosses over to the newsagent's shop. It's gonna be another hot one. The weather this year has been an example of extremes—miserable cold, nonexistent spring and now a September heat wave that lends credence to the wails of the global warming alarmists he and Dynamic had contradicted with their own cadre of experts. Barely five-thirty, and already Adam feels the slick of sweat coat his underarms, and perspiration trickles down the back of his neck, sliding around in fat drops into the depression of his clavicle. A fast-moving car threatens Adam as he crosses midblock to reach the other side. Adam does not walk any faster, challenging the driver to go around him, or hit him. The car swerves, its honk an afterthought. Adam raises his left hand in comradely salute, a single rude finger extended. It's a gesture he hasn't made since undergraduate days, but it pleases him in some atavistic way.

A man is coming down the street, north to south. He is dressed in the full-dress uniform of a businessman, defying the crack-of-dawn heat with a summer-weight suit, a crisp white shirt that glows in the humid murk, a beautiful yellow print tie done up in a proper Windsor knot, and spit-polished tassel loafers completing his look. Adam sees this man every weekday morning, since he's begun waking so early, and assumes that he is walking to the T, perhaps the only physical exercise he can eke out of a busy day. Adam imagines that he works in one of the law offices, or for a management firm. Instead of a briefcase, he carries one of the modern soft-sided bags that laptops fit into, with a wide strap to carry it over a shoulder. He probably lives in one of the better neighborhoods that abut this one and is taking a shortcut. Not once has the walker acknowledged Adam's presence on the same sidewalk at the same time five days a week. He marches by, his eyes averted. Just the tiniest pursing to his lips to indicate he is aware of Adam standing at the doorway of the newsagent's; a slight acceleration in his pace.

Adam wrenches open the door of the shop, the old-fashioned clanging bell above the door announcing his arrival. There is an old man behind the counter. He perches his wide bum on a stool, an unlit cigar clamped into the corner of his mouth. His apron is newsprint gray, and his hands are black with it. His thin gray hair is highlighted with the ink, as if he's been drawing new hair on his head. He looks up from his crossword puzzle. "Mornin'."

"Mornin'." Those are the only two words of conversation Adam has had since yesterday morning at this same time. Except for his lawyer's secretary's message in his voice mail, reminding him of the time to appear today at the county courthouse, he's heard no human speech save that of the voices on the television, which he keeps on most of the time. Ariel won't return his calls. His friends, plucked from the ranks of people like himself, the self he was for the last twenty years, rich, powerful, well connected, don't return his calls. He is anathema.

It is in the dark of the night when Adam knows the most isolation. In the gray dawn, he shrugs off his self-pity as self-indulgent. But in the night, when the street is silent and the only sound in his apartment is the *tink tink tink* of the leaky bathroom faucet, Adam feels the weight of solitude bearing down on him. He has never cultivated a real friend, someone who knows him well enough to offer the simple support of a shared beer at the local bar. He lacks the quiet comfort of companionship, of sympathy. Strangely enough, the only person who comes to mind in the witching hour of sleepless waiting is Veronica. The only one who might understand his need to move far beyond his upbringing, to forge a new life. Once her existence was reintroduced into his life by accident, she persists in entering his thoughts. He finds himself wondering if she ever thinks of him, the little boy she never even said good-bye to. He could have hated her; instead, he had forgotten her. Denied her.

Adam sorts through the array of newspapers fanned out across the long counter as if he's choosing the right cut of meat. Behind the counter, lottery tickets are on display, the true meat and drink of the small store. There is a coffee service, a double-burner stainless-steel maker offering one glass pot of regular and another of decaf. The regular is fresh—there is profit in being an early riser—and Adam helps himself to a large cup. He picks up a package of peanut butter crackers, which have become his breakfast of choice.

"Four-seventy-five." The proprietor shifts his cigar to the other side of his mouth.

Adam digs out three crumpled bills and makes up the rest in coins—coins he should have saved for his laundry. He's got to make an ATM stop sometime today, see if he can get by on a hundred till next week. Maybe he better do it before the sentencing. The sentencing. A wave of dismay percolates through him; the hand holding the coin trembles slightly, as if Adam is standing on the platform as a train blasts through.

Will the judge send him to jail? It wasn't an outright assault, despite what Sophie kept slipping into the testimony. It was a slap. She wasn't really traumatized; that whole bit about counseling and fear of men is hogwash. He isn't a danger to anyone. He hasn't made it impossible for her to work. Her leave of absence from Dynamic is a sham. The accusations and effect of his, albeit stupid, action had risen in graduated levels of absurdity as the trial went on.

Adam takes in a breath, letting the pain of breathing distract him from his line of thinking. Lately he has experienced pain like that from cracked ribs, as if he'd been the one attacked. "Do you have anything stronger than aspirin?"

The proprietor gestures toward a small display of patent medicines and shrugs. "Tylenol, Advil, the usual stuff. My wife likes Aleve."

Adam studies the boxes, reads the ingredients, thinks back on the various commercial claims each one professes, and then checks the price. "You take credit cards?"

"Ten-dollar limit."

Adam gathers one of each brand into his arms and dumps them on the counter with his paper and the coffee.

"Thanks, pal." The proprietor bags his stuff and hands the plastic bag to him. Outside, Adam shoves his papers under his arm, shifts the plastic bag of drugs. Glancing next door, he sees the tropical fish store woman unlocking her door. She's dressed in low-rise jeans and a tank top that just about touches the waistband. Her hair is still damp from her shower or from the early heat, and it hangs in gentle waves to her shoulders and is the color of molasses. She nods to him, a fellow early bird.

Adam has seen her before, just not this close. He spends a great deal of his day watching the street from his bolt-hole of an apartment. He's watched her perform what seems to be a daily ritual of washing her front window—a willowy undulation side to side, up and down as she squeegees the plate glass with her long-poled blade.

What can he say to her? He feels a little like a voyeur face-to-face with his object. Up close, she's older than he thought, not a girl, despite her youthful clothes, but a woman maybe in her late thirties, early forties.

Adam hesitates too long and she disappears into the shop. Taking a sip of his coffee, Adam waits to take advantage of a lull in the increased morning traffic. A moment later, the woman reappears, her hair bundled back out of the way with an elastic, a bucket of water in hand.

"Morning." There, he's established that he's a human being.

She gives him the wary look of a woman alone on a city sidewalk, and he becomes conscious of his scrappy attire. "Mornin'." Nothing more. She turns to her window washing.

"Hot again." Points for having a conversation, points off for being platitudinal.

"Sure is." Her accent is tipped with some flavor not from here. Southern? Midwestern?

"Keep cool."

"You, too."

Sure, a hot courtroom his destination, an unknown penalty. A life off the rails. He's cool. Absolutely.

Chapter Five

They spotted the dead dog first. The rest of us, Mom, Dad, and two others, were shocked into a momentary silence before coming to our senses and barking invectives at the men, and the woman. She's the one who knelt over the body of my late challenger, running her hand gently down his side as if he might enjoy the feeling. I stopped my noise to watch.

Two uniformed men and one woman stood in our cellar and swore grandly at what they had come to see. It was a little stagy, their response, as if they were pleased to have been proven correct, that they had chosen well. I yarked. Mom and Dad shrank to the back of their cages. One of the others actually growled, catching the attention of the men, who stopped swearing and grimaced with some decision. I yarked some more, a little uncertain and more than curious. What did this visit really mean? The men carried poles with loops of line sticking out of their hollow cores. The woman seemed more confident and unlatched the cage containing my mother and my siblings. Mom shrank back but was silent, which the woman took for a good thing. "Come on, Mommy, I won't hurt you." I stopped my yarking, wanting to hear more of this voice. Fitty, my dad, sat down and did something that was extraordinary in my mind, something I had never seen him do, but I understood immediately the reason for it. He put one paw up against the mesh of his cage front. An imploring "Hey, I'm with you," sort of gesture. The men visibly relaxed. The woman tentatively held out a hand to Mom. Mom wasn't having any of it, and pressed herself even deeper into the cage. In her experience, someone wanting her out of her cage meant only two things, a fight or a fuck. The woman snapped her fingers softly and made a clucking noise with her mouth, a sweet little kissy noise. Mom sighed. Capitulation. Slowly, my mother made her way to the woman's hand, sniffing it with wariness wanting to be trust. Once Mom was out of the cage, a collar around her neck and a man's strong hand hanging on to her leash, the woman gently handed out the six pups into a big box.

I yarked a question to the room: *What's going to happen?* No one answered because no one knew. Mom cast a look in my direction, her tail swinging gently to and fro in a clear message: *Whatever it is has got to be better than this minute.*

Dogs are existentialists. We think of now. But we do have a capacity for learning, which is predicated on our understanding of the past, not as some block of time, but as an action, a pain, a smell. Our idea of the future is limited to hunger pains, I will eat, and anticipation of a walk at a certain time every day. Those of us removed from that cellar that day lacked the imagination to picture a happy place; we knew only that things were going to be different.

Eventually, they came to me. Mom and Dad and the kiddies were all boxed or muzzled, the growling dog had been silenced with a little happy juice, and the other dog was acting all goofy and "happy to see you." I took a hint from him. I didn't want one of those muzzles on me. I suffer a bit from claustrophobia. *Aaah aah aaaah,* I said, cranking the length of my tail into raptures. We gladiator types look amazingly happy when we loll our tongues and split our jaws into grins. The men and the woman bought my act. They slipped a loop around my neck and we all headed up the narrow stairs to the first floor. I'd never been up there. It reeked of boys' sweat and a pungent smoke. Pizza boxes lay on the floor, tantalizingly out of reach from my nose, as I was constrained by the rigid pole one of the men had in his grip. Beer cans were neatly stacked in a pyramid beneath the cracked window in the otherwise-empty room.

I didn't get to look around for very long, as we were quickly hustled out of the place and into the street. A white van with its back doors wide open idled at the sidewalk. One by one, my parents and the other two dogs were hoisted into cages in the back. We were used to cages and didn't protest. Before I was lifted in, another man, one I hadn't seen before, came out bearing the weight of my last competitor, wrapped in a slippery blue tarp. The man's face was grim, as if he was mourning the loss of a friend he'd only just been introduced to, or that he was sad to be right.

There was a moment's inattention as the body of the dead dog wrapped in its slippery shroud slipped out of the man's grasp, thumping to the ground and leaving the empty blue plastic sheet in his arms. The people gasped in unison, and I noticed a lessening of the grip on the pole, a subtle inattention brought on by the clumsy dropping of the dead dog. I bolted.

Chapter Six

Adam sits beside his lawyer on a cold metal folding chair behind a rectangular table in the second-floor courtroom. The veneered surface of the table is lifted here and there, dried out by decades of overheating in winter and summertime humidity. On the floor beside him, faithful to the end, is his old briefcase. His Cartier fountain pen, a parting gift from his coworkers at his last corporation before being lured away to Dynamic, rests fully capped on the untouched lined yellow pad in front of him. Adam wants to cross his legs, to ease the unexplained pain in his ribs, but he knows that he must remain four-square, feet on the floor, forearms gently touching the tabletop, hands reverently clenched. The picture of a martyr.

"All rise."

Adam stands as if a military man. Which is what he might have been had he followed the advice of his guidance counselor in high school, who was impressed enough with his top grades in an underachieving parochial school, but not enough to recommend anything better than a state college, or the military. His last set of foster parents—foster father, really—believed the military was the place to become a man. He'd been to Nam. "Make a man of ya." Whack, then the shoulder jab. "Toughen you up, boy." Jab, jab.

Sophie stands at an identical table with a female lawyer who looks a lot like a college intern. They both wear subdued suits, Sophie's in navy blue and the lawyer's in gray; both have their long blond hair pulled into severe ponytails. They could be sisters.

Sophie. If only she'd added those two critical, essential, defining, unalarming words on that "While You Were Out" slip. *In*. Fucking. *Law*. Sister-in-law. Sterling's sister, who wanted to talk about a surprise party for Sterling's birthday. Then they would be sitting pretty right now, both of them enjoying the fruits of his labors, he as CEO designee of Dynamic, she as the future CEO's PA, which was tantamount to queen bee of the corporate hive.

Instead, they stand side by side in a courtroom after all the words have been said, all the excuses his attorney can make— stress, responsibility, high-powered job—in an attempt to justify the unjustifiable. That the stress of his professional life and the excitement of the anticipated actions of that day had overwhelmed him makes him sound weak, unreliable. The court-ordered shrink has applied the psychobabble of his profession and subpoenaed managers to tout an exemplary work record. Exemplary except for this one egregious mistake. That uncharacteristic moment of loss of control has cost him everything.

And in this corner, Sophie's own militants have presented a compelling story of stress, responsibility, high-powered job, and an equally exemplary work record. Her shrink has rolled out the heavy guns of post-traumatic stress syndrome.

Adam keeps Sophie in his peripheral vision, not turning his head to see her sitting there, her plump mouth pursed in righteousness. Victimhood worn like a mantle. Shoulders back, head held high. Judge Judy, of whom he's seen a lot in the past few months, would send her on her way, telling her to suck it up, saying her inaccuracy was the cause of all this. A seasoned professional staffer, she had made a neophyte's mistake. In-law. All the difference in the world.

The judge enters the courtroom. After him there follows a scent of cooler air coming from an air conditioner placed somewhere a lot more pleasant than this chamber of horrors. He seats himself, and the dozen people in the room are allowed to resume their seats. Behind Sophie are her parents and her boyfriend, a burly fellow with a red-and-green tattoo running up his neck, as if some tropical plant is rooted beneath his black T-shirt. Behind them is a gathering of her friends and supporters. A short line of reporters, press credentials hanging around their necks, sit in the last row of chairs.

Behind Adam, there is no one.

Ted Abramowitz, his lawyer, later shakes his hand and congratulates him. "It could have been worse, lots worse." The pumping hand action of the happy lawyer threatens to turn into a backslap. Worse? Than what, a death sentence? The judge has sentenced Adam to two years probation and one year of community service, plus assigning him court costs, monetary damages, and counseling. Should this end here? Not likely. Sophie's plump lips thin into a dissatisfied line. Her lawyer pats her on the shoulder and a look passes between them; a civil suit will follow.

Abramowitz assures Adam that he should be ecstatic. How so, Adam wonders, with a smear like this on his pristine record? Because he's been unable to defend the takeover plan, the whole thing looks like a colossal mistake. And Wannamaker looks even more godlike, having saved Dynamic's reputation by calling a halt. To say nothing of the fact that he's going to have to fight to get any severance from Dynamic. No golden parachute was offered, just the boot heel of his pension—don't let the door slam on the way out. Seems as though even the most morally suspect of giant corporations have limits. Not only that: Who will hire a top exec with a criminal record, however lightly handled?

To say nothing of his divorce.

His esteemed lawyer licks his lips in anticipation of further business. He's going to be living off the fatted calf for some time at this rate. Although Abramowitz comes from one of the city's better-known legal firms, it is a firm Adam has never used. Quick on the draw, Sterling engaged their personal lawyers, and was rewarded with the services of the best of the best in attorneys, a golfing buddy, a man Adam once thought of as a friend.

"Now we should figure out where you'll do your service. We can get you someplace that won't be too onerous. Maybe tutoring at the community college." Ted Abramowitz stuffs his briefcase with the thick file folders of Adam's case. Adam isn't listening to the second-best lawyer money can buy. He is jobless, convicted of a stupid mistake that wasn't his fault. His wife is poisoning his daughter's mind against him, and his lawyer thinks he's had good news?

Once the verdict has been read, the press clamor for a sound bite. Abramowitz waves them away, fairly easily, as this case isn't that interesting laid against the backdrop of the recent economic woes. Adam's case, and the press's interest in it, has been relegated to an inside page.

"Are you sorry?" One female reporter, a thin, narrow notebook in hand, waits for an answer. She wears jeans, and her dangling credentials identify her as from the local weekly, the giveaway paper. She looks about fifteen years old. Has he gotten so middle-aged that all young women look like teenagers? That they all look like his last memory of Veronica?

Adam's lawyer bleats, "No comment," but the girl catches Adam's eye, holding it with the force of her own question. And for a confused moment, Adam thinks she means about his sister. That's been the strangest thing, this regret that, in the end, it wasn't Veronica after all.

The girl reporter and the disgraced executive stare at each other, she wants an answer to fill out her story; he has no answer. The moment is broken when the bailiff beckons to Adam and his lawyer. The judge wants a word.

As suggested by the breeze that had followed the judge into the courtroom, Judge Frank Johnson's chambers are cool, and after the fuggy warmth of the old courtroom, Adam feels goose bumps rise on his arms. Without his robe, and on a level with them, the judge is whittled down to an ordinary-looking man. A tracery of blond-going-to-white fringe from ear to ear, and a pair of Buddy Holly glasses sliding down his nose. Not as old or as godlike as he had seemed behind the bench.

Adam suppresses a cleansing breath of relief; maybe he's going to be more lenient now that the case is out from under the scrutiny of the public eye, no longer subject to the outrage of Sophie and her lawyer.

"I've asked you in here to talk about your community service." The judge drops into his big swivel chair and points to the visitor chairs opposite his desk, two more cold metal folding chairs. Once again barricaded by his status, the judge lets his momentary benignity evaporate. "I'm placing you myself."

Adam's lawyer bleats a little protest. "We've discussed tutoring."

The judge sits forward, leaning on his desktop and peering at Adam over the top of his big glasses. The effect rucks up the skin of his plain, large forehead, making Adam think of Bozo the clown without whiteface. "March, you may think that you've gotten off lightly, I could have given you jail time. Probably should have. But I think that your biggest issue isn't violence, but arrogance. I've seen the shrink's report, know that you acted out of some sort of emotional self-defense, but the truth is, you're one arrogant son of a bitch and you need to be taken down a peg."

Adam feels the sigh of relief contract into a choke. "I don't know what you mean."

"It's not that you don't have a moral compass; I suppose you do. Despite the opposing lawyer's contention that you're a psychopath, you're not. But your moral compass is way off true north. You're lost, man. You need to eat a little humble pie, and I'm about to serve you a big bite."

Adam looks at Abramowitz, noticing for the first time that the man has a weak chin.

"You will report to Bob Carmondy at the Fort Street Center Monday morning. You will do whatever he requires of you."

Adam nods. He waits for his lawyer to say something, to protest or agree, but the man and his weak chin just sit there.

"Report back to me in six months." The judge pushes himself back, making the giant swivel chair rock. They are dismissed.

Chapter Seven

Ariel Carruthers March greets Adam in the riding school lounge still in tall boots, her helmet still on her head, her scowl reminding Adam of Sterling when she was young enough to permit herself facial expressions. "You don't have to get here so early. You don't have to watch."

The implication is that he never did before, that he always spent the time waiting for her on his laptop or his BlackBerry, so why does he have to stand and watch her now? This is more blatantly expressed by her posture; he is an embarrassment to her. Surely her riding friends know all about him, their parents discussing Adam March and his fall from grace at the dinner table. Adam knows this as certainly as if he were still invited to those dinner tables. Ariel is suffering from acute adolescent mortification. Here stands a father nobody else's parents want to know.

"I like to watch." Neither one of them believes this.

"I have to put Elegance away."

"Okay, hurry up, though." Adam hates the cajoling tone in

his voice, a tone he has only just started using with Ariel, as if he's become afraid of her.

Ariel wrenches open the door that leads to the stalls, letting it slam behind her.

Adam leans against the wall, hesitant to sink down on the tumorous couch or the fur-covered matching chair that serve parents as waiting-area accommodation. The lounge smells of an animal-induced fug, cat pee and wet dog. It doesn't matter how much he spends on Ariel's various training facilities, because to him they always smell bad. Usually, Adam just waits for Ariel in the car, preferring that to sitting in this room with its seventies furniture and stink. But he only gets to see her every other weekend now, and he's taken to watching her interminable lessons simply to be able to see her as much as time permits on these Saturdays foreshortened by scheduled commitments. The riding lesson, the tennis lesson, the important birthday parties. Foreshortened by stalling. Ariel is not happy about spending time with him and she makes sure he knows it.

Adam tries not to think about how, not that long ago, Ariel was Daddy's little girl. She played the part so well. "Take me, Daddy!" When she was little, Ariel wanted to go everywhere with him, cried and tugged at his pant leg as he headed out the door on yet another business trip. He remembers the chirp of her babyish voice on the phone, asking him to remember to bring her something special from Hong Kong or London. When had the pleas for his attention devolved into demands for possessions? At some point, she'd stopped asking him to stay home on weekday mornings until it was time for her to go to school, stopped warbling the kind of endearments to him that some of her friends did with their fathers. He stopped being Daddy and became the Nameless One. And this "situation" hasn't helped. Now they are strangers forced into companionship by the courts. Twenty minutes later, Ariel finally reappears, tiny low-slung breeches pasted to her pipe-stem legs, her T-shirt with its slightly suggestive motto arced over her pubescent breasts, hiked well above her belly button. He says nothing and is still rebuffed when he reaches out to hug her, given the side of her face, her mouth screwed up as far away from his lips as it can get.

Ariel and Adam get into his car without any conversation. His daughter slumps into the passenger seat and plugs herself into her iPod, an effective wall. Do not disturb.

When Ariel was born, Sterling declared that one was enough. And that was okay; he didn't need a big family. Dandling this tiny creature on his knee, Adam was as terrified as he'd ever been. He knew nothing about being a father. Thank God the nanny they hired had been a keeper and so much of his worry vanished as Mrs. Sanchez made sure that Ariel was happy.

"Good lesson?"

Ariel pulls away one ear bud and cocks an eyebrow at him.

"Your lesson? Was it good?" A wisp of something slides across the field of his memory. There is a familiarity he hasn't seen before in Ariel's expression. She is growing up; her facial bones are becoming the structure of the woman she will be. She is adopting expressions that come only with disappointment in men.

"Yeah. It was all right." A flat, expressionless answer. Before his fall from grace, she'd chatter to him about her riding lessons all the way home, often the only conversation they had, and one that he only half-listened to. His shrink, Dr. Stein, tells him to be patient. Ariel's sense of security has been damaged. Everything she ever thought about her father has been compromised by his actions.

Adam tries again. "Oh, come on. What was good about it?" His peripheral view of his daughter's profile reveals a firmly set jaw. She replaces the ear bud. Slowly, her head begins to nod in time with whatever questionable music is pouring into her ear. A sweat-darkened lock of hair falls across her cheek. She loops it back over her ear, and suddenly Adam knows what's familiar to him. She looks like his sister. Ariel is exactly the age Adam remembers his sister best, fifteen, the year she ran away. The year when she was his only ally.

"Hey, little bro, can I help you build your tower?" Adam's sister grabs a handful of red and yellow Legos. He's building a fort, but that's okay. If Veronica wants to build a tower, then that's what they'll build. The idea of ten minutes of her attention warms him, a slight flush of pleasure Adam will never quite experience again in his lifetime. The pleasure of an adored sister spending time with him. Veronica loops a strand of dark blond hair behind her ear. The strand falls back across her cheek as she reaches for another block.

Adam presses his hand against the place over his ribs where he has an inexplicable pain.

Chapter Eight

As usual, Adam is up before dawn. He stands at his one window, staring down onto the quiet street, waiting for the lights to go on in the newsagent's shop. He's in the Harvard sweatpants that he's lived in for the weekend, yesterday's stale T-shirt—an old team-building promotional shirt from his days as division leader for Dynamic's cosmetics division, and is barefoot. He'll slip on his boat shoes to run across the street once the shop opens. The fading streetlights reflect against the jolly little fish dancing across the rainbow of A to Z Tropical Fish, making them luminous in the gray light.

As Adam stares with vacant disinterest at the quiet pre-dawn street scene, his attention is caught by the shadow of something moving rapidly north to south on the sidewalk. It is a dog, its breed and color indistinguishable in the gray light, and it is dragging something behind it—a pole. It would be almost laughable to watch, the way the dog seems to be trying to dodge the object at the same time as move forward, its hind end cantilevering sideways while its front end moves ahead.

The pole is relentless and doesn't give up the chase. From this height, Adam cannot tell if it's a big dog, male or female, black or brown. In a moment, it's gone, vanishing beyond Adam's sight line.

At last, the lights go on in the newsagent's shop. Adam collects the key to his apartment, slides bare feet into Top-Siders, and goes down to get his paper. The businessman walks by, as timely as ever, his eyes resolutely looking anywhere but at Adam. Adam thinks that there should be some sort of gang sign, some arrangement of fingers and fists that would be the sign between men of business, maybe fingers curved into a stylized dollar sign. He'd seen the boys in his former gated community practicing this signing for homies. Outfitted in gargantuan hooded sweatshirts, worn in all weathers, and droopy yet costly jeans, these teens, all boys from Sylvan Fields homes, where the mean income is in the seven figures, get down with their bad selves and do God knows what behind parental backs.

A mere seven blocks from Adam's middle-class bolt-hole, the real deal sailor-walk down the street, greeting one another with complicated hands.

Adam resists the faint urge to call after the guy, throw some business-speak at him and identify himself as a fellow soldier of commerce, lately on the DL. Instead, he goes into the shop and picks up his papers.

"Mornin'." The fat man on the stool shifts his unlit cigar.

And also with you. Adam nods a greeting and helps himself to the coffee.

"How's it goin'?"

"Fine. Nice day."

"Coolin' off."

"Fall's finally here."

This will likely constitute the most pleasant conversation of his day.

Back on the sidewalk Adam sees the tropical fish store lady unlocking her door. Same or similar outfit of jeans and T-shirt, but with a light fleece vest added. Her hair is already pulled back into a workaday ponytail, making her seem plain and unremarkable. She sees him standing there with his papers stuffed under one arm and the paper cup of coffee in the other. "Mornin'."

"Good morning." He raises his plain paper cup to her in a little salute. "Fine day." Adam hears himself repeat the same weatherish small talk he has with the news guy. He would like to say something more interesting.

She smiles at him, erasing the impression that she is either plain or unremarkable. Adam so seldom sees women without the artful application of makeup that it takes him a moment to recognize actual skin, not flawless, but natural. A nice smile. A friendly greeting trumping beauty. The first smile he's received from a woman in a very long time. And just as suddenly as it appears, it disappears.

"Is that a Dynamic Cosmetics T-shirt?"

"Why, yes, it is."

"They test all of their beauty products on rabbits. Did you know that?" Her voice is pitched low, as if she is letting him in on a secret she finds appalling. She presses on the word *beauty* as if it tastes bad. "Where did you get that shirt?"

"I work . . . worked . . . for Dynamic."

"Really." This is a dismissal.

"Awhile ago."

"Did you know that's what they do?"

"Yes. It's so that beautiful women don't suffer damage."

" 'Vanity over humanity.' That's what we called it."

Adam suddenly remembers the campaign against Dynamic that PETA and several other animal rights organizations had lodged six years ago. No Animal Testing Ever—that was the local group who lodged such a successful campaign that Dynamic Industries decided it was important enough to pay lip service to. The one that, as cosmetics division head, *Adam* had paid lip service to. NATE—that was the acronym that had played over the papers for months, along with daily photographs of angry protesters. There were disruptions, editorials, eggs thrown at the offenders.

Adam developed a plan where Dynamic claimed to have ceased all animal testing—well, all rabbit testing. It was a cleverly worded apologia, which satisfied NATE.

"I take it that you are an animal rights person."

"Activist. Yes."

Adam knows when it's a good time to retreat. There is a break in the traffic. "Take care."

"Have a nahss day." A slight southern lilt to her words. Southern for "Fuck you."

Adam drinks his coffee while standing at the window, looking down on the street as it slowly becomes active. It's like watching time-lapse photography, people appearing and disappearing along the sidewalk in clumps of two or three; children skipping alongside adults, doors being pulled open, a steady stream of cars rushing up to stoplights. The door of the tropical fish shop stays propped open, but the NATE woman does not reappear.

Adam thinks of the NATE campaign and how proud he was to have figured out a way to get them off Dynamic's back. Tell 'em what they want to hear. Throw some money at an animal charity. Make "reparations." He doesn't remember this fish store woman from the sea of faces that appeared for almost a month beneath his window at the division headquarters in Westborough, their nonstop chanting becoming like a tune stuck in his head: "What do we want? No animal testing. When do we want it? Now." He and his execs called them "the Free Roger Rabbit mob."

Adam and his team justified what they were doing by promoting a corporate belief that such testing was necessary so that the eyeliner wouldn't damage nerves, so that the mascara wouldn't blind the user. What were a few bunnies compared to that? The bottom line decreed that the products developed by Dynamic for its line called Fraîche Crème, with its inexpensive, oftentimes imported ingredients, be marketed to the high-end users with a 200 percent markup. That didn't allow for lawsuits or unhappy socialites scarred by chemical peels at their luxury spas. The NATE people had to be appeased, but not allowed to be a roadblock to profits.

And Adam March had made that happen and been awarded a rich promotion to corporate headquarters and the penultimate job in the company's hierarchy. His glory days.

As Adam turns away from the window, he sees the stray dog dashing back down the street, the pole still following.

Chapter Nine

I really wasn't panicked. Despite the four feet of aluminum pole dangling like a misplaced tail, I knew I wasn't attached to some demon, but had slipped the grip of the man, who then raced after me, yelling invectives guaranteed to emphasize his mistake rather than my escape. Woo hoo. I was free. Free at last.

Thanks to our boys' relentless training program, which involved a treadmill, I had a lot of stamina. The pole thwacked against immovable objects, ringing hollowly into the sensitive caverns of my ears, but other than that, I was whooping it up. Up the street and down, ducking into narrow alleys with the enticing scent of garbage emanating from Dumpsters soldiered behind restaurants, the ugly backside of sophistication. I knew that freedom was fragile, and that I'd better find a bolt-hole quickly. The men were hot on my trail, and the sight of a fifty-pound dog with a four-foot pole tagging along would certainly catch the attention of even the most oblivious of passersby.

I had to ditch the pole. Unfortunately, my physical limitations being what they are, it was pretty near impossible to get the noose from around my thick neck without opposable thumbs. I tried shaking, ducking, twisting, clawing, and whining. Nothing helped. I needed a friend. Now, this being neither fairy tale nor Disney, no one of my own species was a likely candidate. What's a dog to do?

Being a dog, I sort of forgot about the problem as the amazing scents of the street wafted up to my nose. I began sniffing around, identifying others of my kind and following them on their travels. If females, I quivered. If males with balls, I growled and lifted my leg higher to cover their mark. As I made my way down one narrow alley, I inhaled the scents gathered between the buildings, snuffling in the olfactory stimuli. An experienced street dog would know that it's madness to go down one of these easily blocked passages. But I was, at that time, not well schooled in the lessons of the street. But I was a lucky dog. At the far end of the alley, a form crouched against the wall. At its side, a dog. I meandered along, snuffling and marking, the pole dragging gently behind me on the rough pavement. The form, as I drew closer, smelled human, deliciously unflavored by the foul perfumed scents our boys splashed on themselves.

Here was a human in all his primitive, animal glory. Funky. His true identity was not masked by frequent washing. His dog, a smallish long-haired bitch, growled at me but didn't really mean it. She was just letting me know that he was there and that she wouldn't take kindly to interference. She gave up growling and stood and shook herself, and I saw a flash of metal dangling from a collar. I remembered the leash dog mourning the loss of his disks, but I still couldn't quite wrap my mind around their significance. Our kind don't usually revere totems.

I shook myself in reply. *I mean no harm.* We greeted, and I could scent that she was well fed, despite the appearance of her person.

She sat and scratched behind her drooping ear, then stood and sniffed at my pole. *So, they had you and you got away. I know how to get out of those.*

I sat and waited to hear how.

The bitch nudged her person awake. He started; then his head sank back to his chest. He was as furry as a bearded collie. Matted, too. She yipped. He opened his eyes and saw me.

"What have we got here?" His voice was like a load of kibble spilling onto the floor. Rough, interesting. "You bite?"

I walked away, just out of reach of a sitting man.

"I won't hurt you." He didn't move from his crouched position against the warm brick wall.

His companion stalked over to me and sniffed my nose, her tail addressing my doubts. *Okay.* I moved a little closer.

"You want that thing off?"

I danced a little on my front feet, his voice was so calm and kibbley. *Maybe I do.*

He didn't do any of the things I would have expected of a man. He neither lashed out to grab the pole nor stood up to intimidate me. He just kept crouching against his wall and waited for me to decide. I caught the fumes of alcohol when he spoke, his breath more humanized than his skin. I glanced up at his eyes, hooded and hollow. He had no fire in him; he had no fear and no opinions. I moved closer, close enough that he put out one hand for me to sniff, palm flat, no threat.

I inhaled the smell of the city, all the scents that I had been snuffling down as I made my way clear of the men and their van; as I put distance between myself and the cellar where I had spent my life, all of these beautiful, evocative scents were on his hand, as if he'd scooped up whole handfuls of the air and brick and pavement and garbage that made up the world beyond my eyesight. That, plus the very interesting odor of fish chowder. I knew what the guy had had for lunch. Which made me realize I was inordinately hungry and thirsty.

Okay. Take it off.

The man carefully slid the noose from around my neck. Patted my head and slid the pole under a Dumpster without getting out of his crouch. He put his head down again and instantly went back to whatever state it was he'd been in before his companion woke him.

Thanks. I lolled my tongue in gratitude.

No problem. The bitch snuggled back down beside the man and curled her fluffy tail over her nose.

I sloped off in search of sustenance.

All I had to do was follow my nose. I found pizza crusts and an empty ice-cream cone, the dregs of melted ice cream within the cone adhering to my long tongue as I slid it into the conical wafer. Mmmm. Wandering along neighborhood streets, I came across improperly fitted trash can lids, flipped them off with barely a nudge. Within these cylindrical buffets, a host of treats, including, but not limited to, steak tips, french fries, an actual half chicken. And, best of all, a ham bone the likes of which my kind will commit murder to get.

Needless to say, I chucked it all up an hour later, but then I consumed that. Waste not, want not when you're a dog on the street.

Water was a little harder to come by. There was the fountain in the park, but that meant getting too close to people. It hadn't rained in a long time, so puddles were out of the question. A backyard hose with a drip helped. I lapped at it like a gerbil, then went off to find a safe place to bunk down. I wasn't yet streetwise, but I had pretty good instincts. If my objective was to stay out of the hands of people, then I needed to stay out of sight. On the other paw, as it were, I needed what the people had to offer in the way of food and water. Although strong-jawed, I knew hunting wasn't ever going to be my strong suit and that a life beyond the city, in the less populated hills, was out of the question. I needed a little advice.

That there were others loose on the streets was evident on every street corner and against every brick building. I just needed to track a likely mentor down. It wouldn't be hard. The trace left by one male in particular suggested that he'd been on the streets for some time, which meant he knew the ropes, which meant, if I could catch up to him, he might be susceptible to obsequiousness and help me out.

By this time, and it had been since before dawn, I was wrung out. Instead of taking the time to try to find my hoped-for guide, I found a fairly protected niche in the low-growing bushes of the city park. It bore no sign of previous habitation, no circled-down foliage, no nesting, no scent of any other creature within those underslung branches. Like I say, I was a neophyte. I thought that if I couldn't see out, they couldn't see in. It wasn't more than fifteen minutes, just as I was entering that dream sleep we all need, when the sound of soft yelps startled me awake. There was a moment of confusion, when I thought I was back in my cage and my siblings were begging for lunch. The yelps turned into a low, oddly compelling howling.

Apparently, I'd chosen a bush situated behind a very popular human mating area, and suddenly, I was eye-to-eye with a humping human, both of us openmouthed with surprise. I dashed out of my imperfect hidey-hole; he stood up, genitals dangling, and grabbed his pants. I do believe he thought I was going to attack him, the way he yanked his mate up and fled almost as fast in the opposite direction from that of my own flight. Okay, bushes in the park, no good. Another lesson.

Only slightly refreshed, I trotted a zigzag out of the city park and back onto the streets. I had to keep up a steady quick-step, although the pavement was beginning to wear on my pads. I'd never spent much time on pavement. People were everywhere, and I dodged them like a video-game master. No one was going to get a hand on me. I wasn't going back to that cage.

Mostly, I kept to the alleys, having already figured out that my kind kept to those canyons like wolves in the wild. Miraculously, I found a nook ready-made for sleeping, about the size of my cage, which was oddly comforting, beneath a set of back stairs. Yes, it bore the scent of my kind, but the scent was very old, and I had to take a chance that this place was up for lease. There was even a ragged cloth, which I nosed into shape. It felt like a good place, and I was instantly asleep. I'd rest awhile and then go see what else I could find to eat. Maybe see if there were any females around looking for some company.

Before I fell asleep, I licked my paws and thought, This is

extraordinary. Not twelve hours ago, I was cage-bound, my life as circumspect in its routine as a monk's. My battle of the week accomplished, kibble in my dish. My whole life contained in that cellar. Now here I am, making my own plans, eating like a king, thinking already about mating.

The only problem with this living in paradise was that my wound, the jagged rip my late opponent had sliced into me, had begun to hurt.

Chapter Ten

The Fort Street Center is in the worst part of town and serves homeless men, providing a hot meal, a gathering place, and, for twenty of them, a place to sleep out of the elements. Adam knows about the center only because it's one of the hundreds of charities that solicit him every year. He's maybe thrown a few bucks its way, without really thinking about the mission or the nature of the cause.

Homelessness is not a word that Adam thinks about with any degree of interest. To him, a "homeless man" is a bum, a street person, a schizophrenic off his meds. A panhandler. An annoyance. Someone to dodge as he goes down the street, much like a stray dog. Might be diseased or drunk. Shaking empty paper cups, begging for coffee money. Giuliani got rid of the squeegee men in New York, so why couldn't this city find a way to get the street people off the street? That's what Adam thinks whenever some indigent crosses his path on the sidewalk.

If Adam has given any thought to the why of homelessness, it is to believe that as he is a self-made man, these must be self-undone men. Victims of bad habits and bad decisions. Everyone knew of the guy who chose to live on the street rather than in his home, where his abandoned wife or caring children couldn't keep him. Common knowledge. Or the guy who just fucked his life up so badly, no one wanted to be near him, his own violence and temper putting him on the street. The guy who won't even try to hold on to his family.

Adam has spurned his lawyer's offer to go with him. He will report to the Fort Street Center by himself, a man with free will. No hand-holding, no audience. No billable hour. Not sure what to expect, Adam dresses in his usual business attire. Most likely this Bob Carmondy fellow will be overjoyed to have a man familiar with business at his disposal. Maybe the worst that will happen is that he'll hand Adam the books. These nonprofits are so often run on shoestrings, or, worse, like lemonade stands. Adam looks at his freshly shaven face in the mirror as he knots his Harvard tie. He tries not to see the dark circles of restless nights beneath his eyes or the faint yellow color tinging the whites, like pale echoes of the brown of his irises. Or the hollowness of his cheeks. The new gray in his hair. He's even looking forward to putting in some volunteer time. That'll look just fine, with tweaking, on his curriculum vitae. It is no longer enough to have enjoyed the career path he has been on: promotions and bonuses labeling him a man of substance. The ignominious departure from Dynamic has made him less than attractive; in this day and age, corporations are reluctant to hire people fired for such a violation as his. Only embezzlement would have been a harder crime to overcome. Time will help, counsels his lawyer. Get past the headlines, the blogs, the pillory of public discussion. Sit tight. It'll blow over. In the meantime, his bank account, the only one Sterling didn't get, is dribbling away and he is powerless to stop the constant leak. Sterling resolutely refuses to give up any of the houses, the masseuse, the flower arranger. These aren't luxuries, but necessities; she mustn't give up her standard of living, not for her sake, but for their daughter's. Ariel deserves the best-possible everything. She makes it sound like if she doesn't have access to their timeshare jet, it will be Ariel who will suffer the humiliation of commercial air travel. Her young life will be ruined.

Lying awake in the middle of the night, Adam realizes that Sterling has never wanted for anything. Not once in her gilded existence has any desire been left wanting. Ever. The basic needs so well met that luxury itself became a basic need.

He has known the want of basic human desires: the pangs of hunger, of real hunger, when his foster mother served only what she thought a growing boy should eat and locked up the rest, the desire for affection; the basic human need to be touched gently.

When his thoughts begin to drift in that direction, Adam finds oblivion in cheap blended scotch.

This will help. In a year or two, working with the homeless will look like philanthropy. A break from high-stakes corporate life; not quite the Peace Corps, but, with the right tweaking, enough to gloss over the empty place on his CV.

Oh yes, it certainly will. Cheered, Adam dusts an invisible speck of lint from the lapel of his charcoal-gray Hugo Boss suit. Just where is that solitary businessman now?

Although Adam lives only six blocks away from the center, he drives his Lexus to Fort Street. It's a world away from his current neighborhood, but Adam is hard-pressed to distinguish much of a difference between his street and Fort Street. A similar group of mom-and-pop businesses line the side of the street opposite the faded brownstones that are home to a host of other nonprofits serving mankind. Maybe the difference is in the check-cashing service rather than a paper store, and the pawnshop with a litter of chintzy lamps and questionable statuary in the window instead of jolly fish cavorting across a rainbow of letters.

Remarkably, Adam finds a parking place right across the street from where he thinks the center is located. There is no sign identifying the center, just an American flag with the ubiquitous MIA/POW flag suspended beneath it, both flags barely moving in the midmorning breeze. Before parking, he wonders briefly if he should find a garage instead. The men gathered on the stoops of the brownstones eye him as he idles, but he shrugs off the worry. It's broad daylight. Getting out of his car, he drops a couple of quarters in the meter, locks his car with an over-the-shoulder flourish, and crosses the street with a "Don't fuck with me" stride.

The Fort Street Center is in a building much prettier than his own, a nineteenth-century town house built in a time when this part of the city was the good part. The bow windows and brownstone stoop are black with grime, but the ornate trim and sturdiness of the building is still evident. Adam checks the address written on the index card handed to him by the judge's law clerk against the black-and-gold number in the transom above the big black door. Number 27. This is it. As Adam puts his foot on the first step, a man swings the door open and stumbles out. He's wearing, despite the warm fall day, a greenish snorkel jacket with bulging pockets, its orange lining exposed by tears under the arm. Even from this distance, Adam can smell the odor of him, the punky, slightly uriney smell of old clothes and unwashed body. The man goes down the three wide steps, pausing for a moment to take Adam in, then meanders down the street, kicking aside an empty plastic bag, muttering in an angry grumble punctuated with a single comprehensible word. Fucking. Fucking. Fucking. Adam slides a moist hand down his tie, shrugs his perfectly tailored jacket into place, and jogs up the steps.

If he expects to be greeted as a visiting dignitary, Adam is mistaken. It takes a few minutes to find the man in charge and he is forced to speak to the indigents hanging around the narrow hallway, who point him to the director's office.

Adam knocks at the open door to a room that might once have been a large room but is now split into two smaller ones. A man Adam presumes to be the director is sitting at a desk, facing the open door. His feet, in the largest shoes Adam thinks he has ever seen, are on the desk, which is piled with manila folders. He's on the phone, the curling cord twisted into a contortion of wire. Seeing Adam there, he waves him in with a wide gesture, mouthing "big donor" and pointing to the phone.

Adam is impatient, not appreciating having to wait to introduce himself and get this over with. The director smiles over the mouthpiece, a helpless "What can you do?" smile.

Rocking slightly on his heels, his hands jammed into trouser pockets, Adam examines the various newspaper-reprint photographs on the wall. Each one pictures the director shaking hands with a familiar politician: Ted Kennedy, John Kerry, Mayor Menino, Bill Weld. Deval Patrick. Each one is a study in two smiling faces, below which, hands are locked in a stagy clasp across bodies.

At last, the director drops the phone into the cradle, further tangling its overstretched cord. "Sorry about that. Potential donor. Gotta listen to their ideas."

"Adam March. I'm here to, uh, volunteer." The word *volunteer* sticks a little in his throat, as if he isn't able to recall the proper verb; he's been thinking of this as a sentence.

"Robert Carmondy." Carmondy is a big man. He knows this and puts it to good use. "They call me 'Big Bob.'" He reaches over the breadth of the desk and cheerfully squeezes the life out of Adam's hand. Whack. A manly Big Bob shoulder slap nearly takes Adam off his feet. "Glad to have you here. Siddown."

Big Bob's office is a tiny space filled mostly with a desk, a file cabinet too full to close the drawers all the way, and Big Bob. Adam turns to the only other chair in the room, the seat of which is filled with even more unfiled folders. Bob makes no move to accommodate his well-dressed visitor, so Adam lifts an armload of folders and sits down; finding no surface available to place the folders, he ends up holding them in his lap. Bob looks at him with a slight smile, and Adam wonders if he's going to be asked to start filing.

"Let me tell you about this place." With that, Big Bob is off on his well-rehearsed narrative on the genesis of the Fort Street Center: the evolution from a crack house to a safe house; his own brush with homelessness, getting off the drugs himself; and the constant need for money.

Adam smiles. This is where he can be of service. "I have some ideas."

Bob cuts him off with a teacher's gesture. "We follow a strict protocol of confidentiality. We don't know what happened to these guys; we don't rehab, counsel, or criticize. We just feed 'em; wash 'em, if they'll have it; bunk 'em, if they want; and street 'em. They don't live here. They can come and stay, but this is a way station. Capice?"

"I do."

"Okay, then." Big Bob rocks back against his chair, which protests like a wounded animal.

"What do you need to know about me?"

"Nothing. You're here and you'll do what I need you to do."

"I have some ideas." Maybe Big Bob hasn't heard him the first time. "I've been looking into some grants—"

Big Bob snaps forward, the back of his chair crying out in relief from the released pressure.

"No ideas necessary. You need to suit up and report to Rafe in the kitchen."

Adam straightens himself on the edge of the chair, realigns the slipping folders on his lap. He clears his throat, finding his executive voice. "I can be of much more use looking into finances, grants."

Big Bob stands up, shoving his desk chair back against the wall. "Let me walk you down."

"Mr. Carmondy, I've got an M.B.A. Surely you can use some help."

Big Bob sets one meaty hand on Adam's shoulder, gives him a friendly squeeze that hurts like a Vulcan pinch. "I'm sure we do." Bob lowers his mouth to Adam's ear. "Judge Johnson is pretty clear about assignments. You will do what we need you to do. And what we need is kitchen help. Ideas are fine; actions are better. And, Adam, it's Big Bob."

Adam March stands in his Hugo Boss trousers, his brand-new Calvin Klein T-shirt, purchased out of a sense that it was easier to buy new underwear than to go to the Laundromat once a week, and a white uniform jacket with a faint gravy stain emblazoning the left side. A paper hat completes his ensemble.

He is humiliated. This is his community service, doling out hot lunch to indigents. Doing whatever the "boss" wants. The boss being Rafe, a wiry black man with a shiny shaven head, hands the size of palm fronds, and a drill sergeant's refinement. Rafe points him to the rack of waiter wear and tells him not to wear good pants again. "Jeans'll do, long as they're clean and not ripped."

Ripped jeans. Just who does this guy think he's speaking to?

"We serve hot lunch from eleven to two. Give 'em as much as they want, but don't get fooled by the greedy ones. Everbody gets enough, but not more than enough. We feed about thirty-five men here a day, sometimes more in winter, less in summer. It ain't cordon bleu, but it ain't junk food, neither." Rafe says *cordon bleu* with a perfect French enunciation. Adam is still hung up on the perfectly pronounced *cordon bleu* linked to the grammatically suspect surrounding of the sentence. Rafe might talk street, but Adam suspects another influence.

"An another thing." Rafe places one of his alien hands on Adam's shoulder. "You treat these men wi' respect. You ain't here 'cause you love 'em. You here 'cause you fucked up. So did they, so that's something you all have in common. Got it?"

Adam straightens his shoulder under Rafe's hand and lifts his chin. He is eye-to-eye with his new boss, his brown eye holding the deeper brown eye of the man, taking the measure of an opponent. Rafe narrows his eyes, sure in his authority. Adam has seen eyes like that before in the boardrooms and back halls of business. Kings of their domains. Men certain of their power and their place in the world.

Adam nods, a curt acquiescence.

"Now I need you to go into the back room and bring out a case of niblets."

And thus Adam March begins his penance.

Adam is put to work as runner, carrying steam trays filled with food from the kitchen into the dining room, then taking the empty bins back to wash them in the industrial sink. The old brownstone has suffered from its change in purpose from elegant home to abandoned crack house to its new life as a shelter. The interior walls have been cut away to open half of the first floor into a large room, filled now with long cafeteria tables no doubt donated from some refurbished high school, the benches fixed to them so that the men have to sling a leg over to get seated. The floor-to-ceiling windows are shrouded even on this warm fall day with industrial-strength curtains, pulled closed so that the men served are protected. No one can stand and stare at them, recognize an old friend or neighbor in straitened circumstances. No one can look out.

Adam hasn't bench-pressed this much since high school. The aluminum trays are filled with slices of meat floating in a thick brown gravy with what appear to be shitake mushrooms folded in. The whipped potatoes are stiff and creamy, real potatoes, really whipped. But they weigh a ton, and Adam fears that his back will go out, and then where will he be? What if he gets hurt on this community-service job? What happens then? Can he sue someone? After fetching the canned corn from the massive stockroom, Adam is put to opening the number-ten cans one after another. What is served to the men is mixed with half as many lima beans and sautéed into a mixture that he might have seen on his plate at any benefit dinner Sterling dragged him to. The lovely odor of cooking food is obscured by the rank scent of the men who line up in front of the steam tables. Even though he isn't—yet—assigned to serving, their smell fills the high-ceilinged room like a miasma, and he gets a whiff every time he comes up behind the man who is ladling out portions onto divided plates. With each customer he greets by name, the server, another middle-aged black man, asks the same question: "One piece or two? You wanna a roll wi' that?"

Adam is reminded of high school, St. Joseph's, where the last two sets of foster parents coincidentally sent him. The ancient cafeteria with its warped floorboards was also the gymnasium. The students passed through an alley, where the food was kept behind glass, pointing to their choices—mac and cheese or hot dog, ziti or a thin slice of overcooked ham steak with a floppy ring of pineapple. Because the cafeteria was also the gym, the odor of unwashed bodies pervaded the air, and the food never tasted good. Most of it was tossed in the massive gray barrels on wheels next to the exits as the kids rushed to get outside to sneak cigarettes or make out in the corners.

When he wheels the big blue plastic barrels to the back dock from the dining room after the meal is over, Adam can't help but notice that there is almost no food in them.

Adam is supposed to put in four hours. It's been four and a half. He's exhausted, wrung out by the unaccustomed physical exercise. He is hungry but has lost his appetite. No one has suggested that he eat. No one has dismissed him. He stands in the doorway of the massive industrial kitchen. Rafe is humming, jigging up and down to some tune on his iPod. He's fixing four plates, heaping up leftover beef, potatoes, and the succotash. He sees Adam in the doorway and beckons him in. "Take one."

Adam can't make himself touch the plate until he washes. He feels extraordinarily filthy, as if he's been handling garbage, as if he hasn't been wearing plastic gloves. "Where do I wash?"

Rafe pulls one ear bud out of his ear. "Men's room out to your left."

Adam sees himself in the speckled mirror over the sink, the ridiculous paper hat tipped over his forehead. He looks like he works at McDonald's. He grabs it off and tosses it in the bin. Gall quickly dissipates into despair.

He has no intention of eating here.

The four plates are now on a freshly wiped table. Someone has folded up the other tables and rolled them all to one side of the room. The floor, no doubt to protect the original hardwood, is covered by a cheap linoleum with a fake wood pattern, and it is filthy with dirt and sand, along with dropped paper napkins and food. It is the single most disgusting place Adam has ever been expected to eat. He is about to say that he's out of there, when Rafe, standing up, waves him over not like a gracious host, but like a commander. *You will sit and eat. This is part of your penance.* "Sit down, man, 'fore this stuff gets colder." The man who has been standing for the last few hours serving up food to the continual flow of men pats the space next to him. Another flashback to high school, the flush of pleasure at being included in a group. But this is no group in which Adam would ever want to be included. "We never got properly introduced. You can call me Ishmael." The black man grins at his well-rehearsed line and sticks out a hand for shaking. He's pulled off his toque, revealing a head full of dreadlock coils. Like Medusa's snakes, the coils bounce around, threatening Adam.

Adam takes Ishmael's hand, a little surprised at its soft warmth. After hours of handling hot implements, Ishmael's hand actually feels feverish.

"March." Adam steps over the fixed bench and sits down to his plate of lunch.

Rafe, opposite him, gestures to the other man of the foursome, an overweight white man with psoriasis covering half of his face. He might be fifty or sixty—it's hard to tell with the disfiguring scales crawling up the side of his face. "This here's Mike."

"Hello, Mike." Adam picks up his fork but is pretty sure he won't be able to eat.

"Adam here is our new CSI."

Adam throws Rafe a puzzled look.

"Community service investigator." He throws his head back and laughs. "Get it? You gonna investigate how the other half live." Rafe chuckles himself into control and starts eating.

Adam flushes with embarrassment. He hasn't expected that his enforced volunteerism would be common knowledge. Where were confidentiality laws when you needed them?

Ishmael entertains them as they eat with a constant stream of chat and jokes, as if hours of asking the same question have warmed him up for the main act. Mike shovels the food into his mouth, gets up, and takes his plate into the kitchen without a word. Big Bob joins them from upstairs, sits down at Mike's vacant spot, tipping the table a little under his weight. "How'd it go, first day?"

"I guess you'll have to ask my boss." Adam has moved the beef around on his plate, nibbled a forkful of potato, which has just a hint of garlic, and a mushroom, which, he's surprised to find, actually is a shitake.

"He'll do. Just has to give up his prissy ways." Rafe scrapes the last of the gravy onto his fork and runs a paper napkin across his mouth. "Damn good, if I do say so myself. Adam, you best get it right now that I'm the best there is, was, and will be in the world of industrial-size cookin'."

Adam politely cuts a piece of beef and puts it into his mouth. Although it's cold by this time, the flavor is good and the meat is tender. A note of some unidentifiable seasoning moves it out of ordinary and into quite nice. Adam eats the rest of it.

Big Bob raps a little drumbeat against the tabletop. "Okay, then. Carry on." As soon as he lifts his weight from the bench, the table relaxes and Adam feels like he and Ishmael are about to tip over. Mike has reappeared with a push broom and is tracing a pattern onto the fake wood back and forth, back and forth, working his way from the far end toward their table. The three men get up and Ishmael fetches a cloth to wipe it down again.

"You can go." Rafe places his huge thin-fingered hand once again on Adam's shoulder. "It gets better."

Adam strips off his white jacket, now dotted with new gravy stains, and jams it into the laundry bin.

Outside, there is a parking ticket under his windshield wiper and a pigeon has crapped on the windshield of his Lexus.

Chapter Eleven

Adam awakens sweating, despite the window open to the freshening fall day. His pulse ticks in his ears, the remnant of nightmare fright. Despite every effort to provide himself with a good night's sleep via Messrs. Walker or Dewar, Adam fights every night with an array of dubious images. If he dreamed of Sophie or Sterling or buildings falling down, that would make sense. Instead, he dreams of city streets and being late. Of not being able to hear what's being said to him. Of not knowing where he is. Cryptic dream messages, or dreams with no meaning.

He wishes he could get away from waking before dawn. It's been months since he's had to be at work at seven-thirty; months since he's thought to go for a run. He has plenty of "me time" now, too much to fill the hours. His job at the center occupies him during the easy part of the day. The mornings and the nights are his burden.

His headhunter isn't returning his phone calls. He hasn't scrounged up any interviews and is apparently sick of having to say so. Adam thinks that consulting is an option. Hang out his shingle, get some business cards, and advise companies on strategic planning or how to plan a takeover. His headhunter hasn't been encouraging there, either, but what stops Adam is the work of pulling it together, of putting the *effort* into an action plan; inertia enfolds him in its cottony warmth. He flips on daytime television.

Dr. Stein hasn't much to say about it, either. He wants Adam to keep a journal, record his feelings. Feelings. Shit. What exactly does the good shrink think Adam might be feeling? Abandoned? Under siege? Mistreated?

Adam takes his place at the window. Just past eight-thirty, the early-morning rush has faded into the workaday flow of traffic, both in the street and on the sidewalks. The dry cleaner is busy. No matter what the economy, people still need their "dry clean only" items cared for. The newsagent's place is active twice a day, early morning and at five o'clock.

Adam rarely sees anyone going into the tropical fish shop; those that do tend toward the little old lady or the ten-year-old picking out his first fish. He's avoided the shop owner since their uncomfortable discovery of a common history. He still watches her wash the window, but he's no longer interested in pleasantries.

The Fort Street Center, whether he likes it or not, has become the centerpiece of Adam's day. It is the only thing, five days a week, that gets him out of the house, and most days it provides the only nourishment he gets. He's forgotten all about the made-to-order Norwegian granola he used to require. Cheese crackers and coffee from the newsagent in the morning, scotch at night.

Adam pulls away from the window, his palm print fading

as his sweat evaporates, a smear of fingerprints at eye level. One of his foster mothers had been a bear on the subject of fingerprints. Adam had spent his eighth and ninth years living in dread of making a mark on polished surfaces or glass. Mrs. Markowitz would have whupped his behind to see the fan of prints marring his curtainless picture window.

He'd had seven in all, seven sets of foster parents from the time he was five and a half, an average of thirteen months with each. The last, the Potters, had kept him the longest, all the way through his last two years at St. Joseph's. The day he turned eighteen, he was emancipated, suddenly outside the protection and purview of the state, magically independent. Even though he'd longed for that moment, the sudden reality of it, three days before his high school graduation, had shocked him with its finality. "You can stay, but we'll have to ask for board." Mrs. Potter, a rake-thin woman just beyond middle age, with enough beds to make something of a living taking in foster kids, needed the bed and needed him out. Nothing personal, just practical. Today you are a man.

They were reluctant at first, as they told him over and over, to take on an unadoptable teenage boy, but his social worker had convinced them to take a chance. What that meant was that he ate more than the others, which practically wiped out his state subsidy, and that they were on top of him about his behavior, always suspicious that he was upstairs smoking dope or hanging out with street gangs, plotting mayhem. That he could have been doing those things but wasn't was no consolation to them.

The Potters were too busy with four other kids, always much younger, all cycling through the foster system, and all into adoptions or reclamation by rehabilitated parents, to pay much attention to his education. They lacked the energy or imagination to prod him into doing his homework. They were just happy never to be robbed or caught in the imagined cross fire of their foster boy's shootout with a rival gang. Adam despised them, and once the door was shut, he never contacted them again.

His college essay, a self-indulgent treatise on life in the Commonwealth's foster system, had earned him a ticket out of that system. A partial scholarship to the University of Massachusetts–Amherst had given him a place to go. An unexpected interest and acuity in finance and economics opened up Adam's world from the narrow confines of the blue-collar, conservative, clannish environment he had lived in up until then. Working nearly full-time as a bus driver for the Pioneer Valley Transit system had financed his schooling and stoked his determination never to go back to Dorchester. He had escaped by virtue of his brains, and by those same virtues, Adam would rise to the top. He would forget his past and forge a future that was unlimited. He didn't entertain himself with visions of returning to one or another of his foster parents with a disdainful "I told you so." It never occured to him. He put his past behind him and never looked back.

Adam made it into Harvard Business School. Three-quarters of the way through his M.B.A. program, he'd been recruited by his first major corporation. Done with the M.B.A., already two rungs up the corporate ladder, and enjoying the first fruits of high pay and glorious benefits, he'd met Sterling. Here was a nymph from another world—no, not another world, a creature of the world Adam intended to inhabit. Her father, the blue-blooded economist guru of the decade, Herbert Carruthers, was the guest speaker at a corporate retreat, and Adam had sat at the edge of his seat to soak in everything the great man could offer. When his boss took him over to introduce him to Carruthers, Sterling stood beside her father with a calm detachment. She was used to young sycophants wanting to touch the hem of his garment.

"You must be very proud of your dad," Adam whispered to Sterling as he waited to be introduced. "Such an inspiration."

Sterling had looked at him with the hauteur he would fall in love with. A look that said, Yeah, so what? Tell me something I don't know.

"Going around with him to these retreats must be a great way to meet eligible men like me." He smiled the toothy smile of his peers. At least his genetics had provided good teeth, despite a spotty dental regimen. Her lips slowly slid into a smile, revealing her own perfect teeth. She was so naturally beautiful then. Tall, slim, her blond hair artfully tossed. She could have had any one of a dozen Park Avenue–raised young men as her choice, but she'd chosen Adam. His glossed-over history mattered less to her than the fact of his wunderkind trajectory. Her father approved of him because of that glossed-over history, liked the idea of a self-made son-in-law. If Adam had cut down the number of foster homes, had implied a decent upbringing grounded in hard work, instead of telling the truth, it was only because the truth had no bearing on who he'd become. No one wanted to hear about the loneliness, the rootless existence of a boyhood spent without a home to call his own. A charity case.

Of Veronica, of their father, he said nothing. They did not exist. They had no hand in the making of Adam March.

Adam hadn't thought a lot about those days until the foundation stone of his reinvention had been uncovered. Dr.

Stein keeps picking at him, wanting him to come to some understanding of his feelings. He prods at Adam to admit some insecurities, to admit weakness. To understand why he has "anger issues."

Adam sits forward on the low chair, resting his elbows on his knees, hands folded and beneath his chin. "In business, in life, it's he who has the most arrows in his quiver who gets ahead—by any means. Sometimes that looks like anger."

"Why was it so important to get ahead?" The shrink fashions air quotes around the words *get ahead*.

"It's what people do," says Adam. "It's how the world works. Even you, Doctor, planned at some point in your life to do something to get ahead. To achieve, to make your mark. To end up somewhere better than where you started. It takes a tough man to do that." Adam sits back, his chin tipped a little forward, pugnacious.

"We're talking about you, Adam, not me." The doctor closes his notebook. "And Adam, until you come to grips with the fact that you have anger issues, abandonment issues, you are not going to heal."

"Heal from what? A lousy childhood? Angry about that? I'm way beyond that. I'm no longer that kid, that punk whose father would show up once a year, take me out to McDonald's, and say nothing about why he couldn't raise me himself. But I knew what it was called. Voluntary surrender. Voluntary." Adam stops himself. The phantom pain pulses in his rib cage. He hears his own breath as it sounds when he wakes before dawn from a nightmare. "It was better when he stopped coming at all." Adam laughs, a little burst of air, mirthless. "I used to pack my stuff in a paper bag on the day I knew he was coming. Just in case he was going to keep me. When I was nine or ten, I sat on the stoop, paper bag beside me like some kind of loyal dog, and waited. And waited. And at some point, my foster mother—can't remember which one—made me come in. Never said a word about why he didn't show. Made me put all my stuff back in the drawer. I think that's when I realized I didn't want to go with him anyway. Why should I? I didn't need him; I could make my own way in the world."

"Are you sure that isn't what you tell yourself now?"

The tiny buzzer indicating their hour is up goes off and the psychiatrist slaps his knees with his yellow pad. "See you next week."

Adam blushes a little, having to ask Stein to cut their sessions down by half an hour. He can't afford a full hour anymore. Dynamic took his health benefits when they fired him and he can't afford the COBRA payments now that Sterling has decided that Ariel needs to have intensive SAT tutoring, with a full professor from Lesley College.

"Against my better judgment, but all right. Thirty minutes twice a week."

Adam is too embarrassed to ask if the psychiatrist offers a sliding scale. Who would believe a man in a thousand-dollar suit would qualify for it?

He's seen him a half dozen times before. Standing on the corner, empty paper coffee cup out. "I just needa cuppa coffee, mister. Can you spare some change?" He's dressed in greasy army pants and a faded army jacket with a bold green empty place where a name badge must have been when the jacket first saw service. Regardless of the weather, the panhandler wears a black wool watch cap, pulled low over straggly gray hair leaking out like seaweed. His cheeks are hollowed out, his eyes bleary above pouches of flesh tinged gray. It seems to Adam that any time he's on the downtown streets, people like this one have their grimy hands outstretched, their jagged teeth hidden, their obsequious begging not compelling, but annoying. This one he sees whenever he comes out of his shrink's building, stationed like a sentry at the corner in front of the Dunkin' Donuts. Adam wonders why the authorities don't just throw him in jail. He's one of the pushy ones, probably crazy. "My dog's hungry." That's his particular refrain. There's a big ugly mutt with him. In the summer, the dog sat in the shade of the buildings as if smarter than his owner. When Adam came across the pair in the winter, they huddled on a cement dust-colored quilt, leaning together against the wind that blew through the canyons of the city, the bum's hand with the ubiquitous Starbucks cup out thrust. The dog, a lantern-jawed pit bull type, sat, but its weepy red eyes followed Adam as he walked by.

Sure enough, pushing through the revolving door as he leaves his shrink's building today, Adam sees the panhandler and his dog at his favorite post. But he's no longer the bum with the dog; by now, Adam knows that the men call him "Jupe," short for Jupiter. The last thing he wants is to be forced to drop a coin in the man's outstretched hand just because he drops mashed potatoes on his plate a couple of times a week. They do not know each other. He does not want even the slightest acknowledgment of acquaintance to pass between them. Adam wears his Armani suit, his "I mean business" Cole Haan shoes. His red silk tie beams authority. He is not the man who wears the McDonald's cap and shovels food out from a steam table. Adam spins around the revolving door one more time, launching himself out in the other direction.

Chapter Twelve

By the third day of my release from captivity, I was a hurtin'
puppy. The part of the wound that I couldn't reach with my
tongue was swollen and oozing. I was feverish, off my game,
and not even hungry. I was in deep trouble for a creature on
the street. My reflexes were shot, my nose runny. That's why,
when the men came, I put up very little fight.

As docile as a lamb, I went off in the white van, my street
adventure over. I cast a longing look at my nest under the
back stairs of what turned out to be a tattoo parlor. I suspected
that one of the artists inside, who'd come outside for a ciga-
rette or a toke, had spotted me through the metal stair treads
and dropped a dime. My sort don't evoke the "Oooh, I found
a puppy. Can I keep him?" reaction from people. So the men
showed up in their big white van, blocking off one end of the
short, narrow alley with it and filling the other end with
themselves. It was only prudent to acquiesce.

Maybe I was just a creature of the cage after all. It was cool
and comfortable; the docs fixed up the wound, gently poked

me with antibiotic-filled IVs until I felt like a new dog. They clipped my toenails and gave me a lovely bath. They also castrated me, but I wasn't initially aware of that, as they did it while they were repairing the chest wound, and I was already knocked out. I ate their food and licked their hands. I'm no dope. The friendly dog gets the best deal.

My kind are notoriously hard to place. Our ferocious reputations and notorious applications preclude us from easy adoptions. No little old lady looking for a companion is likely to choose a pit bull, not even a crossbred like myself. First, we look strong. Second, we look fierce. Third, we ain't all that attractive. Leave the fluffies to them. Then there are the young men who wander in, looking for a manly dog. Forget it. The authorities weren't born yesterday. No used fighters for sale here. That leaves the younger couples willing to take on a dog with a bad rep and a PR problem. Not all that many of them out there, and a lot more of us.

The key is, behave like a Labrador. Let them stick that fake hand into your food dish and not react. Bring the stupid ball back and drop it in their laps. Pretend that fake kid is a real child and all you want to do is lick its face, protect it from harm. Drool a little. Give 'em your best play bow. Oh yeah, I was totally socialized.

So I got my first person. A nice middle-aged lady looking for a watchdog. Living on the edge of town, a block or so from the rough part, she thought she needed a big tough-looking dog with a heart of gold. She would have been all right, too, if she just hadn't persisted in being frightened of me herself. Okay, maybe it didn't help when I greeted every passerby as a threat to the homefront, and nearly took her off her feet when I lunged at passing dogs, but I wasn't sure of protocol. I'd been raised in a cellar. I'd been trained to fight. That was what had been expected of me, and this change of direction was confusing.

I left after a week. I just couldn't take her mincing around, talking to me in that infernally soothing baby talk that did nothing to disguise her fear sweat. Made me want to fulfill her prophesy. She accidentally left the gate open and I took that as a not-so-subtle hint to beat it. I wandered by a few weeks later and saw she'd replaced me with a yapping fluffy. Perfect.

It wasn't long after that when I finally met my mentor. He'd been leaving signposts for me, aware of my desire to meet him. A rangy-looking male, mature in years, and uncontested king of the neighborhood, a gladiator like me, the hallmarks of a fighter's life written in his skin. We came upon each other on the corner, where his territory and my tentative claim conjoined. I knew that he'd been around there from his mark; he knew I had, too. I was surprised to see him with one of those tags dangling from a collar around his thick neck; surprised, too, to find out he was a companion, when his scent described a street dog.

We greeted; I offered submission with a lick of his chops. No sense making the king annoyed right from the get-go. I didn't want to look like a challenger, I just wanted a little advice. He was headed east, so I followed. We walked along an overpass, chatting about where I'd been so far. He snuffled along my spine, checked my genitals, and winked. *You'll miss them less than you think. Otherwise, a little incarceration is sometimes a good thing. The next best thing is a street man. They're not unlike us; we both forage and sleep rough. We are both invisible to the general population, and sometimes we're both rounded up. The difference between being alone and in company with a man is that the food is easier to come by. He shares and he can open things we can't.*

Our DNA is full of the original partnership between us and humans, forged for exactly the same reason this old boy had forged his alliance with his companion. Safety, food, a voice in a speechless world.

You should get one.

I shook, cocked my leg against a lamppost. *I'm not so sure. I think I want to keep solo for a while more.*

Caged? Meaning was I new to freedom.

Yes. I bowed, stretched, and left my new friend as he caught up with his person coming out of a building. Even from a distance, I could smell the scent of hot food on him. I watched from a safe distance as the man slipped his hand out of his pocket and offered a slice of meat to the king of the street. I may want to rethink this solo thing. The man and my mentor made their way down the street, he with his head bowed, a soft mutter coming from his mouth, and my mentor with his nose just at the man's heels. A picture of companionship.

Chapter Thirteen

The idea of standing over the ultraheated water in the industrial sink as he sprays plate after disgusting plate makes Adam slightly nauseous. The smell of food combined with warm dishwater has permeated his skin and he cannot seem to shower it off.

The center is busy when Adam arrives for his shift. Already a dozen men are on the stoop, waiting in the cool air for the dining room doors to open. There is an activity room on the first floor, a television set, a small library of paperbacks, even a computer with Internet access available to the guys, with a lock on porn sites, but the room remains empty, as it has the whole time Adam has been here. The men are like nervous bunnies, willing to eat from the hand of charity, but not willing to spend too much time in its lap.

Adam does not speak to the men. He still doesn't know most of their names, or recognize their individual faces; he doesn't look at them, just at their empty plates when he's assigned to the steam tables. They don't converse much, even with one another. There's a quiet about them, as if each one is solitary in his world, the proximity of others in like circumstances not a bond, but a wall.

Adam hates the fact that Big Bob insists that everyone use the front door, not sneak in the back door via the alley. He's had to tell Adam twice. Everyone here is a man and comes in through the front door.

"What's that supposed to mean? I'm a volunteer, a temporary helper. Why do they need to see me come through the door?"

"It has to do with dignity. It's our way of leveling the playing field."

Adam feels the ache start up again in his ribs. Whose dignity exactly is Big Bob talking about? Wouldn't everyone be happier if he could just come in the kitchen door?

Jupe and his dog wait for the dining room door to open, lined up with the others on the steps, a very few passing the time with quiet conversation, often with only themselves. Adam licks his lips, tilts the ball cap that he's begun wearing lately, and soldiers past the group, which becomes as silent at his approach as teenagers when the principal walks by. As Adam mounts the steps, Jupe's dog bows and yawns; his tail wags. Adam feels the flush of embarrassment, as if he's been caught avoiding someone he knows. He nods to the men.

"March, you gonna work the tables today. Mike's down wi' the flu." Rafe keeps bopping to the rhythm projected into his ears, speaking a little too loudly. He's sauteing onions in a massive

frying pan. The scent breaks through the miasma of soapy dishwater and wet industrial-strength mops to tickle Adam's juices.
On a stainless-steel cutting table lies an enormous purple-
brown slab of liver, waiting for Rafe's knife to carve it into thin
slices. Two caldrons the size of oil drums bubble on the range,
potatoes on the boil. Liver and onions and fried potatoes for
lunch. Despite his intellectual revulsion, Adam tastes the saliva
forming. Rafe tosses the mess of onions up and around, up and
around, without losing a single thinly sliced ring.

Working the tables means being near the men. Adam's job is
to carry a bucket and sponge around, wipe each table off between groups, pick up the detritus left behind, make sure the
condiments are full, act, in other words, like a busboy. The
men come in as fast as he can make a place ready for them, so
he's often wiping as new men sit down, their plates heaped
with the luscious-smelling onions and the tender liver. Liver
was a frequent item on the menu during his boyhood, a cheap
piece of meat with touted values. Not everyone can cook liver
without making it tough and indigestible. The idea of it is ab-
horrent to Adam. In his adult life, he has never allowed liver on
the table. Ariel has never even seen liver and onions. The one
housekeeper he and Sterling had early on once suggested it and
had her ass handed to her. Liver and onions are the food of poverty. Yet the tantalizing smell of it neutralizes his associations.
Rafe, he already knows, isn't going to let a lousy piece of liver
out of his kitchen; not only are his cooking skills top notch but
his pride is equal to any top chef Adam has ever met. Looking at
a plate of hand-cut fried potatoes tumbling against the thinly
sliced liver with its garnish of perfectly sautéed onions, Adam is
surprised to find himself looking forward to his own lunch.

But first he has to walk around the room, where the delicious scent of fried onions is countered with a backwash of dirty clothes, unwashed heads. Instantly, he loses his appetite. Adam keeps refilling the wash bucket with hotter water, more Pine-Sol. Anything to get the smell of the men out of the room before he's expected to sit in here and eat.

"Excuse me, sir. Can I bother you for a clean fork? This one has a bit of food stuck between the tines."

Adam stands behind Jupe, wash bucket in his hand. The phrasing coming out of the old bum's mouth is at such odds to his appearance, to his "Buddy, can you spare some change?" street patter, that for a moment Adam thinks that Jupe has some ventriloquist's hand up his back. "Sure." He takes the offensive fork and dumps it in his wash bucket. Like a good waiter, Adam fetches Jupe a new fork.

"Thank you." Jupe goes back to eating, slicing his meat with fork in left hand, knife in right, daintily cutting one piece at a time, keeping his fork, in the British manner, in his left hand as he eats. Every now and then he slips a piece of meat into his jacket pocket, a bum's sleight of hand.

Adam washes down the other half of the table. As he does, he can't help but glance at Jupe, who is surrounded by men wearing their entire wardrobes. The old man wears his watch cap pulled low, the long gray hair spiking out from beneath the tattered edge and lying against the threadbare collar of the army jacket. Like many of them, Jupe is probably old enough to have served in Vietnam. There are one or two who are still fighting the war, as they jump out of their skins whenever Rafe drops something in the kitchen. Big Bob calls them his "Stressies." As Adam moves to the table behind Jupe, he spots him slipping half of his portion of liver into his pocket. Some of the men are known hoarders, as if the center were going to disappear and they'd be left hungry. But Adam knows that Jupe is sharing his free meal with that dog of his, the one stationed at the bottom of the stairs. Big Bob has told Jupe over and over not to leave the pit bull there; it frightens people, he says. Jupe says the dog does whatever he wants to do. He's an independent thinker.

It's late by the time the last of the men leave the dining room. Adam feels contaminated, like he has spent a lifetime with his hands in hot water, running the sour-smelling sponge over tabletops and seats. His earlier anticipation of lunch has long since been squelched. All he can smell is Pine-Sol and sweat and the peculiar rubbery smell of his own hands after hours encased in Playtex Living Gloves. He's folded the tables and tucked them together, run the wide-headed broom around the floor. At the staff table, Rafe and Ishmael are wound up about the baseball play-offs. Big Bob is heading to the table with his plate loaded. "Go get some lunch, Adam."

Leaving the push broom at ease against the serving counter, Adam goes into the kitchen, whose smell is redolent of the liver and onions. He stares for a minute at the slices of meat left in the warmer, brown now, almost the same color as Rafe.

His third foster mother sits him down in front of a plate of her liver and onions and whacks his head every time he puts his fork down. The liver is dry, forming a nasty paste in his mouth; he can't make it go down. Tears begin to ooze out of his eyes, not from crying exactly, but from the release of frustration. He's only been in this house for a few weeks. By now he understands that he is always going to be temporary. He shouldn't get comfortable in any house he is brought to, just try to behave, try to be unobtrusive. But his foster parents are always finding ways to make him do wrong. At night, he can hear this foster mother arguing with the man who isn't her husband, although the social services people think he is. Sometimes Adam can hear crying; other times, he hears only the slap that silences it. They'd fought last night, and today he is being forced to eat something so vile, he can't swallow it.

Shifting the lump of chewed meat in his mouth, Adam whispers, "Veronicaveronicaveronica." A mantra of protection muttered under his breath. Someday, Veronica will come and punish those who have been cruel to him, unloving. In his narrow bed, or, as here, the den couch that serves as his bedroom, Adam rehearses the heroic return of his half-imagined sister. She didn't mean to leave him behind. She can't find him because he's been moved so many times. Veronica's myth is embellished during wakeful nights. "Veronicaveronicaveronica." Talismanic hope.

The lump of masticated liver slowly works itself down his throat—it's like swallowing a rock—and suddenly is cast up.

Foster mother number three slams a fistful of mashed potatoes into his eight-year-old face.

Adam yanks his catering jacket off and tosses it into the laundry bag. He crumples the paper hat, dropping it into the barrel. He goes out the back door. He's not coming back. Fuck the judge. Later, Abramowicz points out that a contempt-of-court citation will lead to worse things than mopping up after street people. Once again, a judge is in charge of Adam. He is, as much as the men he serves daily, in the system.

Adam stares into the empty night street, waiting for the lights at the newsagent's to come on. Waiting for his life to begin again.

Chapter Fourteen

The one thing about being on the street in the nice weather is that you feel smart. Too smart to depend on anyone, too smart to need anything but an open Dumpster and a leaky faucet. Then it gets cold. I and my kind began to scrap over good nests, the sort that have shelter from the biting wind and some sort of accommodation, a blanket or a dry newspaper. Too many nights, I found myself in the fetal position, with my back against the nominal protection of a wall, the dry culvert or the underpass not already occupied by someone unwilling to have a roommate. My beneath-the-stairs bolthole of the summer had been reclaimed by its former owner. My sublet was over.

My mentor showed me some of the better backyards. His man traveled in the early hours through sleeping neighborhoods, rifling through the heavy plastic trash cans with the kind of lids that defied those of us without thumbs. He'd toss my friend delicacies and take for himself objects, which he thrust into the pockets of his coat. I stayed well behind. My

Chapter Fifteen

It has been snowing since before dawn. Wind-whipped flakes so small, they look like needles slashing down in the streetlights. The snow comes sideways, reverses itself, and swirls in the opposite direction. The media have been prophesying this storm for days, and the gleeful look on the weather lady's face this morning is positively the radiance of a woman who has been proven right. She reminds Adam of Sterling.

They are now officially divorced; the final decree was handed down three days before Christmas. Sterling had signed where she needed to an hour before he arrived. He'd stared at her showy signature, Sterling Madeleine Carruthers. Unwilling to stay married to him, she had abnegated his place in her life by reverting to her powerful maiden name. He no longer existed for her. Just his money. The power and reputation of her father, Herbert Carruthers, had made it easy for the courts to assign Sterling the majority of their joint assets: the houses, the cars, the portfolio. The court has also entailed a percentage of his future earnings in alimony and child support. His fledg-

mentor positively forbid me contact with his person, who v
a one-dog man, and I wasn't going to screw that up. Inste
he'd point me in the direction of a dryer vent or an
conditioning unit sequestered behind sheltering bushe
very comfortable and weather-tight nest.

Except for the remnants my mentor might leave me,
was getting harder to come by as people spent less time
doors, and my loss of condition made it feel twice as co
me. The restaurants offered fewer leftovers, as if the hu
population was bulking up for the cold weather and wa
less food. My water sources were turned off, and that wa
hardest challenge, save for the occasional heated bird
The park's little lake was sometimes the only water avai
and that was frequently under a sheet of ice. My cage-b
upbringing had not educated me in the skill set necessa
carrying out ice breaking. I waited until the geese wore
in the ice with their foot action and then ventured out.
I know, but thirst is a powerful motivator.

Cold, hungry, and mostly thirsty, I was still happier
the street than in that cage in that cellar, waiting for a fi
for my hour on the treadmill, or that blessed ten m
of backyard relief. Here I defecated and pissed wherev
whenever I wanted to. I'd even begun building up a lit
ritory for myself. Despite my involuntary neutering,
liked the girls and introduced myself to a number of
Sweet. No one was in heat yet, so it was just dating.

All in all, it was okay. That is, until the blizzard.

ling consulting business hasn't taken off—or, to be honest, is nonexistent—and he takes a certain satisfaction in the fact that he has so little income to offer them.

Sterling and her parents took Ariel to Greece for the holidays, citing her distress as a reason to take her out of reach of Adam for even his court-agreed-upon holiday visitation. Somehow the court didn't mind, his rights clearly of a lesser importance than hers. Immediately after they returned, Ariel was kept out of his reach by other obligations. Adam wonders if Sterling lies awake at night making up reasons for him not to see his only daughter. Even when he does manage his Saturday-afternoon visits, Ariel is sullen and uncommunicative, as if he is a stranger to her, someone she's forced to share space with. He excuses her behavior as symptomatic of adolescence, but he's hurt. Like all divorced fathers, he knows that he is trying too hard, making her visits to his small apartment all about fun and nothing about reality, sushi instead of dining in, video games instead of conversation. Ariel stoically resists having fun with him. She comes to visit but refuses to stay overnight; she doesn't want to sleep on the futon and won't swap with him.

It is like hosting a foreign exchange student who speaks no English. The pantomime of good father, devoted child is lost in translation.

Adam stares out, hoping that the newsagent will open despite the weather. Hoping, childishly, that Big Bob will call and tell him to stay home—yippee, a snow day. Ever since the first below-freezing day, the center has hosted twice as many homeless as Adam had seen in the warm weather. Men flock in to grab a little food and a lot of warmth. Many won't stay, but a group of ten or so use the bunks in the dormitory upstairs, mainly guys fairly new to the street, who haven't toughened up yet. Big Bob welcomes them, hands them bedding and a pillow, and points out the rec and dining rooms. He takes their names, offers to receive mail for them, their monthly Social Security checks, their army pension checks. A place to call home.

The light goes on across the street. Adam shrugs on his parka, finds his ski hat tucked into the pocket of his coat and puts it on. He shoves his feet into his boots, laces them loosely, grabs a clean travel mug from the collection he has acquired. The carless street is filled with unsullied snow; the stoplight waves in the wind like a demented flag, threatening to rip loose from its wires and plunge into the intersection. Adam pushes against the wind, the blinding snow making it a dreamlike quest, his objective coming no closer. When he finally makes it across the street, his cheeks are tingling, his eyes watering, and he's breathing like a long-distance runner. Adam has to fight to get the door open, the wind pressing it closed against his pull, a zephyr's game of tug-of-war. As the wind takes a breath, Adam gets the door open. "Mornin', Artie." Adam scoops up his crackers and drains fresh coffee into the travel mug with CUMBERLAND FARMS printed on it. He looks for the papers, but they haven't been delivered.

"Hell of a day." The newsagent shifts the unlit cigar to the other side of his mouth. "Fit for neither man nor beast."

"Or papers, evidently." Adam digs into his pocket for change.

"They'll get here. Don't you worry. Come on back in an hour."

"If I can. Getting worse out there."

"You be careful out there, Adam."

"You, too."

Now it's hard to push the door open, but once he does, Adam stands in the shelter of the doorway, pulling up the hood of his parka, taking what might be the last hot slug of coffee out of his plastic mug. As he's about to step into the storm, a figure appears, another soul out in the storm.

It's the businessman. He trudges along, head down, full-length dress coat buttoned to his throat. Tears are streaming down his cheeks from the wind and cold. Adam feels like he should grab the guy and send him home. Why is he walking? Why is he even trying to go to work? Even Adam would have called it off today. Either this guy is an idiot or his boss is.

"Hey, Buddy . . ." Adam sticks out a hand, the one holding the plastic travel mug, to stop the guy.

"Get away from me, you freak." He thrusts an arm out to fend Adam off, knocking the Cumberland Farms cup out of Adam's hand. "Go get a job."

"Well, fuck you, too." Adam darts to pick up the mug before too much leaks out of the drinking hole. What the fuck? Pulling the strings of his hood tighter, Adam catches sight of his own grainy reflection in the newsagent's plate glass. He starts to laugh. He looks like a Fort Street Center client in this getup. No wonder the guy freaked. *Buddy?* Did he really call the guy "buddy"? He must have picked it up from the men. They all use it, a generic "buddy" directed toward the people they solicit— "Buddy, can you spare some change?" They use it with one another, a dining room filled with buddies.

If the center is closed, where will they go?

. . .

Unbelievably, another figure struggles out of the storm. The aquarium woman. She's bundled in a gigantic parka that makes her look like she's been swallowed by a polar bear. The wind is forcing her back, so that every step taken is a battle won. Adam feels the wind beat against his back as he runs to her. With his ballast, she is finally able to get to her storefront. Adam takes the keys from her hand and unlocks the door, then stands back to let her in.

"Come in. Come in." Inside, she disarms the alarm, stamps her feet to rid them of the snow. Her cheeks are bright pink; a lock of dark hair not captured by her scrunchy is dripping with fast-melting snow. "Thanks for the help. It's windier than I realized."

She shrugs off her parka, revealing a thick fisherman's sweater, corduroys tucked into Uggs. "I'm Gina DeMarco." *Ah'm*. There it is again, that faint coloration of accent. "Welcome to A to Z Tropical Fish and Pet Supply."

Adam pushes his own hood off. "I'm Adam March."

Gina stops smiling. "Adam March. You didn't just work for Dynamic Cosmetics; you were the boss." She says *boss* like it tastes bad.

"Yeah, I was." He's not going to deny it. He ran that division well, even if NATE disagreed with some of its policies.

Adam steps away from the door, looks around at the rows of glowing aquariums full of colorful fish, racks with collars and leashes, shelves with squeaky toys and treats, baskets with tartan pillows, displays with all manner of canine and feline likenesses on coasters, mugs, figurines, place mats. There is a freestanding cage containing the brilliant colors and racket of a pair of parrots, which are happy to see her arrive. A hand-printed sign says NOT FOR SALE.

A gust of supercharged wind bangs against the shop door, rattling the pane of plate glass. "Gina, you can't think that anyone is going to come out on a day like this and buy a fish? This is a 'stay at home, where it's safe' storm. The National Guard is posting warnings against driving. The state—"

She cuts him off. "Electricity goes out and I'm out of business. I've got to be here to get the generator working. Besides, big fish have to eat, or some of them will eat each other."

The center won't be closed. Adam pulls his hood up over his watch cap. "I've got to go."

Gina runs the back of her hand along her forehead to wipe away the moisture from that lock of wet hair and picks up her dripping coat. "Have a nice day." *Nahss*. He is dismissed.

Adam lets go of the door handle, turns back to her. "How will you get home?"

"I won't. Not till the storm ends. I can't take a chance."

Adam debates for a moment whether he should offer to stay, but he can't come up with a reason for doing so. She is obviously capable, and, after all, they are strangers, nodding acquaintances, onetime adversaries, maybe still adversaries in her mind, and not responsible for each other. "Okay. Good luck, then." He pushes hard against the door, putting the force of his shoulder against it, against the wind.

Adam March goes back into the storm, trudging toward Fort Street, hoping he's made the right decision.

Chapter Sixteen

It was a bitch of a storm. I huddled under the culvert with several others, a nominal truce in place. My mentor was there, alone. A little wiry-haired bitch went up to him in submission, obsequiously licking at his muzzle, begging for kindness. I'd scented her before in the neighborhood, a tough little cookie with an underbite.

Two fat Labradors made up the rest of our party. They'd gotten out of their yard; surprised to find the electric fencing neutralized and unable to handle the temptation, they had fled down the street and immediately gotten lost. Nice pets, kinda naïve. We all knew that their people were going to be frantic. Because of that, we knew they posed a real threat. Being leash dogs, not street dogs, the pair of them had left a trail a mile wide and a fathom deep. It would only be a matter of the storm ending before the authorities and a host of volunteers would be rushed out to seek the lost. Signs would be posted. Cunning photos plastered on every telephone pole, smiling, panting yellow Labs, Buffy and Muffy, or whatever their human-given appellations were. Reward!

But for now, the storm kept us squeezed into the tunnel, our body heat protecting us all from the cold, which made the fat Labs a welcome addition for a while. A bite of snow, a quick pee, and we rearranged ourselves to snooze the day away.

My mentor lay back-to-back with me. Out of mild curiosity, I asked him where his man was.

I don't know.

So he just wandered off?

I think he might have been captured.

By the men?

He went into a building and never came out.

The food building?

No, one he's never gone into before. We're not welcome in any building; that's why we stay outside. Buildings aren't for us. Besides, we might be captured if we go into a building. You should remember that, stay out of buildings unless they are empty.

I was surprised then to hear my mentor whine, a plaintive, lonely sound evocative of worry.

I don't know where he is.

You'll find him. After the storm.

He's gone.

As I said, dogs are existentialists. We don't understand the concepts of past or future. My mentor's man might have been gone six days or three hours. In any event, my mentor was uncharacteristically mournful. I rolled over, aligning my back with his for his warmth. But all through the storm, I could feel him shuddering with anxiety.

Chapter Seventeen

By the time Adam makes it to the stoop of the center, he feels as though he is Shackleton reaching his destination. He half-expects seal stew on the menu today. Mike is outside, flailing impotently with a broom against the rising drifts on the steps. He looks at Adam, the angry psoriasis on his face rubbed red in the cold, but he's smiling, the first time Adam has ever warranted a greeting from the notoriously silent man. "Welcome to Fort Street."

"Thanks, Mike. How'd you get here?"

"I never left."

"Wish I'd thought of that." Adam claps a hand on Mike's thickly padded shoulder and goes in.

There are more men in here than Adam has ever seen. Although lunch is an hour off, the dining room is open to accommodate the crowd and they sit at the cafeteria tables, still wearing their soaked jackets, unbuttoned or unzipped. It's something that has long since stopped puzzling Adam. These men take no chances with personal items. The worst fight he's seen, and he's witnessed quite a few, was when a Vietnam vet accused another vet of stealing his pocketknife. Claiming that the object in question was his own similar weapon, the accused hauled off and bashed his accuser in the face, drawing blood and inciting the group into cheering them on. Rafe and Big Bob had pulled the pair apart before the knife became part of the fight.

Knives, Adam has learned, are one of the most highly valued objects a homeless man can have. Protection, threat, a tool, a memento of childhood or war. They are also forbidden inside the center. Everyone knows that a blind eye is turned on pocketknives, like army-surplus store Swiss Army knives, but anything with a blade more than six inches long is immediately confiscated. The knives the men use in the dining room are stainless-steel table knives. This isn't prison, but it is a safe house. Big Bob has rules.

Adam kicks the snow off his boots and pushes his way through the crowd to get to the kitchen. Rafe is there, bebopping to his iPod, skillet in hand, his toque jaunty on his shaven head and his jacket still clean. He glances up and sees Adam in the doorway. "Hey, bro, good of you to come early."

"It's a bitch out there."

"We half-figured you'd bag it today. You a volunteer, man. No cause for life-threatenin' action."

Adam sags against the doorjamb. The effort of walking through the storm has tapped him out. His legs are quivering with the exertion. He's still got his cheese crackers in his pocket, but somewhere along the route he lost his mug. Or maybe he left it at Gina's A to Z Tropical Fish, where she braved the storm for goldfish and parrots. And here's Rafe, telling him that he didn't have to come. For a split second, Adam thinks that he should be mad, that Big Bob should have called him to tell him that. Should have called and said to stay put. Told him to sit there and watch the storm on the television, keep warm, keep dry. A good manager makes sure his people are informed.

Then he thinks, Maybe he did call. He's been walking to work since seven-thirty. The feeling of incipient anger passes. He hasn't seen Ishmael, and the noise from the dining room is unusually loud. "No. I'm here. But I wouldn't mind a cup of coffee before I get started." Rafe adjusts the heat under the skillet and walks to the cupboard. He takes down a mug for Adam and fills it from the Bunn coffeemaker. Adam slides onto a stool; the snow adhering to his jacket trickles onto Rafe's clean floor.

"Here you go, man."

Adam pulls off his wet hat and stuffs it into his pocket before taking the mug from Rafe. "Thanks." Two sets of brown eyes meet, and Adam sees a flash of respect in the other man's eyes. Adam quickly takes a sip of the strong coffee, the flush in his cheek partly the heat and partly wonder. He's never seen respect without fear before.

Today there are women in the center. Fort Street has a sister center two blocks over, but the ferocity of the storm has blurred the divisions. No one cares which center they're in, just happy they're out of the storm. An unofficial attendance is taken by Big Bob as he wanders through the groups, greeting individuals, mentally tallying who is here and who isn't. He'll make a phone call soon to see if some of his people are seeking safety at the Alice Crandall Center. AC, as they call it, is named for its benefactress, the woman who had donated her Victorian brownstone to the city for a shelter for battered, homeless, displaced women. AC is more radical than the Fort Street Center, but an amiable relationship exists between the two managers.

Adam is relieved to see Ishmael come in out of the storm; he's been worried that he might have to serve all these guys alone and run steam trays, too. Like a dog, Ishmael shakes his head with its mass of dreadlocks, spraying the walls of the back hall with droplets. He tucks his dreads up under his toque and sits to change his boots for the shoes he's brought in a plastic bag. Ishmael, too, looks at him with a smile. "You made it, man."

What the fuck? Did everyone expect that he'd shirk his duty? Adam finds himself growing a little annoyed at the suggestion that he's a wuss, a coward, a fair-weather volunteer. He's fucking *walked* all the way here. Six blocks that might as well have been six miles, it took him so long.

He's about to tell Ishmael to stuff it, when he feels Big Bob's hand on his shoulder. "I tried to reach you."

"I got an early start." Adam shrugs. "I'm here."

Big Bob squeezes Adam's shoulder. Like that of a good teacher or a respected scoutmaster, this small manly sign of approval is clear and touches Adam in a place he'd long ago buried. It has been so long since anyone approved of him. He'd been compensated, rewarded for performance with bonuses. He'd enjoyed the claps on the back from upper management for achieving goals. Even once the applause of a roomful of executives for a PowerPoint presentation outlining an acquisition. They had cheered like pirates coming across a gold-laden barque.

The only approval Adam has lusted after for more than two decades is that of his father-in-law. Adam has grieved as much for the withdrawal of Herb Carruthers's esteem as for any other loss. Herb Carruthers had approved of Adam, had, as a sonless man, treated him like an heir. Sterling, Papa's darling, had absorbed the lessons of her socially connected mother and, when Adam asked her to marry him, insisted that he get her father's blessing.

Adam invited Herb to meet him at the Harvard Club. Both were greeted as members, one freshly made, the other a generation ago. Adam loved the club, loved that he was a welcome member, that he had earned the right to sit in this room, an equal among giants even at the age of twenty-six. Over a meal of grilled salmon, Adam carefully laid out his ambitious plans, constructing a vision of the future that his potential father-in-law would approve of. A highly attainable future, particularly with Carruthers's influences, but Adam carefully avoided any presumption of expectation that, as a father-in-law, Carruthers would be of help. Instead, Adam affirmed that he envisioned a good life, one in which Sterling would enjoy all the rights and privileges of her class. The older man never raised his eyes off his plate, shoveling in the food like a longshoreman while Adam laid out his game plan. Finally, Adam paused, waiting for Carruthers to say something.

Plate cleaned, Carruthers sat back, wiped his mouth with his linen napkin, and belched. "That it?" Now his blue marble eyes met Adam's, his pupils tiny pinpricks even in the soft light of the room. Predator's eyes.

"I won't disappoint you, sir." Adam fretted that he'd come across as too pompous, or that Carruthers would detect in his speech the Dorchester of his adolescence, despite his carefully cultivated Harvard accent.

"One question."

"Yes, sir." Adam felt a little pull of anxiety, a shadow of fear that Carruthers might approve of him as a wunderkind but not as a prospective son-in-law. That Carruthers wouldn't approve of him after all.

"Do you sail?"

Adam's little pull of anxiety faded into warm relief. "No, sir." An honest answer.

"You join my family, you'll have to." Herb Carruthers stood up and offered his hand to Adam. Done deal.

Big Bob's hand on his shoulder squeezes a rough emotion out of Adam, a sense of what he has lacked most of his life: someone who genuinely approves of him.

"I should get to work."

An hour later, Big Bob joins the men behind the steam tables. "I'm missing Jupe." Ishmael ladles out a bowl of butternut squash soup, sprinkles a garnish of parsley on top, and slides it on a tray. "He's weird about that dog. Maybe he won't come in if his dog can't."

"I'm not stopping anybody today. Slicker is here with his dog. Course, she's in his pocket, but he knows I know she's here." Big Bob drums his fingers on the metal counter. "No, he's been acting a little off the meds lately. In fact, I don't recall seeing him yesterday, either."

Adam hefts a new tray of potatoes into the steam table. "Check the hospitals?"

"I usually start with the police. Okay, then. If anybody sees him . . ."

"We'll give you a shout." Ishmael fills another bowl.

Adam takes the soup bowl and places it on the ledge. "So, Jupe's mentally ill?"

"We ain't allowed to say, but if I was to make a guess, I'd say that he's one of those brilliant guys whose mind kinda lets loose on 'im. Used to be some kinda professor at MIT or one of them colleges. Rocket science. That's why they call him 'Jupiter.'"

"I figured him for a vet."

"Nah. Got those clothes outta the Army Navy Store. Lotsa guys wear 'em so they don't get hassled. No, he's a professor. You get him talkin' about the stars and you get an earful."

"You think he's out there?"

"I hope not. Freezin' to death ain't pretty."

"You think he's not coming in because of his dog?"

"Could be."

"Why would anyone sacrifice warmth and food for a dog?"

"Like them Katrina people refusin' to get rescued 'cause they wouldn't let 'em take their pets. That's devotion, man."

"That's madness."

"Maybe." Ishmael ladles out the last of today's soup and nods to Adam to remove the pot.

"I hope he gets in."

"Me, too."

Outside, the wind has picked up speed, making a steady high-pitched whistle against the corner of the building. Zephyrs spin down the deserted street. The lights blink, fade, regain strength, and Adam wonders about Gina and her tropical fish.

Chapter Eighteen

The snowstorm had lapsed into stillness by the wee hours of the next day. At full light, I awakened from a running dream and found men standing in front of our culvert. I don't know why none of us heard or scented them. However, the snow packed all around the entrance to our makeshift den announced our presence in the space beneath the road loud and clear to them; they didn't need noses or ears to find us. Those happy Labs had come and gone and come back, all the time leaving big sloppy footprints that just screamed, In here! I should have told them to beat it when I had the chance.

My first instinct, as with the others, was to book it. We turned to the other open end, but these were professionals, and we were trapped, men at both ends, standing in their big boots, poles and lines in their hands, even a dart gun.

The Labs came out, goofy and relieved to see men in charge. I hoped that maybe having recovered the missing pair, the authorities might cut the rest of us a little slack. Not so.

The wiry bitch made a run for it, feinting and ducking between long legs up to the knees in snow. The snow was her undoing; she couldn't run on top of it, and she sank, yapping her disgruntlement. A hand scooped her up and boxed her effortlessly, the yapping muted but not over.

I looked at my mentor. His boxy head was lowered, his grinning mouth open and his teeth showing. He didn't growl, but his lips quivered with warning. I suddenly realized that he was making a mistake. My single incarceration had taught me to play nice. He'd been inside before. He was legal; his tag said so. But for him, incarceration now, with his person missing, was unthinkable. His bold attachment to one man, a man more like us than like his own species, had prejudiced my mentor.

How will I find him? He won't know where I am. My mentor let out a thin whine, a plaintive, weak sound. Aware suddenly of his unseemly show of weakness, my mentor looped the whine into a full-bore growl. Hackles up, teeth bared. Take no prisoners.

They took us instead.

It was okay for me. It was the same shelter where I'd been for my rehab. The food was good, the inside warm and dry. Not exactly a spa, but not a bad place to spend a couple of days out of the weather. I didn't plan to stay long.

I tried to tell my mentor this, but he didn't get it. He was panicked, and nothing I said seemed to make him any more at ease. He just kept growling.

It was his undoing.

Chapter Nineteen

Adam pushes past some of the men squatting in the narrow first-floor hallway of the center; they're full, warm, and reluctant to leave, even though the storm is long over. The snowplows have leveled the ruts in the street, and the sunlight is blinding as it reflects off the pristine drifts. Mike is shoveling the sidewalk in front of the center.

Most of the men had bunked in the dormitory-style bedrooms upstairs; some did not, sleeping crouched against the walls instead, always on the half alert, as if not in the sanctuary of the Fort Street Center, but still out in the mean streets of the city. Adam has been at the center all night, partly because there was no way he was going to fight his way back over that same treacherous six blocks in the bitter, if now snowless, wind, and no way he could get a cab to come fetch him. Even though Rafe and Ishmael happily bedded down in the small office space designated STAFF Adam could not bring himself to flop puppylike among his coworkers on sleeping bags of debatable cleanliness. Big Bob, too, stayed up all night, he and Adam dozing in the chairs in Big Bob's office, their catnaps punctuated by Bob's hourly phone calls to police and other shelters in search of Jupiter.

It's been nearly twenty-four hours since Adam arrived at the center, windblown and frozen. By nine o'clock, he's served morning coffee and doughnuts, courtesy of the local doughnut shop, and he hopes that Big Bob will give him the nod to make his way home now that the streets are plowed and the sidewalks are slowly being shoveled. He's a god-dammed volunteer; he is required to put in only twenty hours a week, and he's put in twenty in one day.

"Do me a favor?" Big Bob covers the mouthpiece of the phone.

"Sure." Adam feels a sinking in his belly. A favor. Two words that, no matter what his position in life, have always had the power to make his mind race with quick reasons to decline. "Shoot."

"Go down to Memorial and see if Jupiter's there." Big Bob's thinning yellow hair sticks straight up, his meaty hands dragging it back and forth like greasy wheat sheaves in a breeze. His pale blue eyes are bloodshot.

"I'd really like to head home." The last thing Adam wants is to go to the local hospital and look for an indigent who's probably frozen to death in an alley due to bad judgment.

"It's on your way." Big Bob's voice isn't unlike his own voice in a previous life—assertive, attention-getting, and brooking no argument.

"How will I know he's there? They aren't going to let me wander the halls. There are rules."

"You talk to Pam Stone; she's the head nurse on six. That's where he'll be if he ended up there. She'll help."

"Can't you just call her and ask her if he's there?"

Big Bob pushes up out of his chair, resting the flat of his hands on his desk. Adam thinks of the Incredible Hulk. "She can't say. HIPAA."

"So I waltz in, asking for a crazy guy in a watch cap who's possibly raving about voices from outer space, and they point me in the right direction?"

"March, we don't use that word here. And he might be unconscious, unable to be identified. A John Doe."

"Or dead."

Big Bob sits heavily in his much-abused chair, reverting back to pre-Hulk condition. "Or dead. Check the morgue."

After the garish cheerfulness of the lobby, the sixth-floor medical ward is an abrupt plunge back into the fifties. Lodged in the oldest wing of the city hospital, it is also the only floor untouched by renovation. It smells precisely like a hospital—a hospital caring for indigents and the poor. It's an odor similar to that of the center: Lysol and unwashed clothing stuffed in plastic bags. The overhead lighting casts a greenish glow on the cracked linoleum. A handrail is mounted at hip level on a beige wall, with not so much as a single fake watercolor to break up the monotony. A lone wheelchair is the only traffic in the hallway, and Adam slips by its occupant without looking at him.

"I'm looking for Nurse Stone." Adam finds the only upright person on the floor to ask, a young volunteer with a resolutely cheerful smile on her stricken face, her braces glinting in the greenish light.

"She's in with a patient."

"I'll wait." There are no chairs nearby, so Adam rests an elbow on the counter of the nurses' station, his cheek against his fist. The slight hum coming from the overhead fixtures seems to have a Doppler effect as he feels himself drifting off. Loud and soft, loud and soft. Drifting on the open ocean of exhaustion, Adam struggles to keep his eyes open.

"Can I help you?"

Startled awake, Adam is embarrassed to feel a slight moistness at the corner of his mouth. A tall middle-aged woman stands in front of him, her hot-pink scrubs a flash of color in the beige hallway. "I'm looking for a man. One of our . . ." Adam hesitates. What's the word Big Bob uses to refer to their people? "One of our guests at the Fort Street Center. He didn't show up during the storm. He's got some mental problems, and Bob Carmondy thought he might be here."

"What's his name?"

Damn Big Bob. He never said what the guy's real name was.

"I'm not sure. They call him Jupiter."

Pamela Stone tightens her crossed arms across her hot-pink midsection. Adam looks down, unable to meet her disapproving glare. She wears soft rubber Crocs on her feet, also hot-pink. "You know that I can't tell you who is a patient here?"

"Yes, of course I do. But Bob suggested that you still might be able to help. We just want to know that he's okay."

"If you were to wander down the hall and notice that a friend is here, there's nothing I can do about that. And you happened to be next of kin . . ."

"But I'm—"

Pam Stone holds up a staying finger, nearly touching

Adam's lips with it. "I never heard you say that you weren't. I have to assume that you are."

Adam leans close to her ear. "I don't even know the guy's real name." Then he's embarrassed, thinking of his unbrushed teeth, his own unwashed state.

"Abernathy. Charles Abernathy." Pam Stone walks away from Adam in a rush of furious pink.

Okay, job done. He's here. I can go home. Adam pulls his cell phone out of his pocket, thinking he'll call Big Bob, and then a taxi.

"No cell phone use here? Interferes with the machines?" The teenage candy striper with the big braces waggles a finger at him, then frowns. "I hate that rule."

Shoving the phone back into his jacket, Adam heads down the hallway toward the elevator bank; a big window at the end of the corridor filters the winter light through a wire-mesh guard, the bright spoke of light making Adam squint. He goes past four wheelchair-wide doorways, each of which opens into occupied patient rooms. The light in his eyes causes him to look away and into the rooms, but the arrangement of beds prevents him from seeing their occupants. The fourth door opens into a larger room, arranged with three beds. Propped at a thirty-five-degree angle in the hospital bed closest to the window, and therefore more visible to the hallway, is the thin form of Jupiter. At least Adam thinks it's Jupiter. This guy is clean-shaven and his hat is gone. The hair against the pillow is yellowish and streaked with gray; it's long, but combed back, as if someone had groomed him. A rush of panic leavens Adam's belly and he can't decide whether to make a run for it or go in to pay a call on a man he doesn't know except from across the steam-table divide.

Jupiter—Charles Abernathy—spots him.

There is an exquisite moment when Adam might be able to keep moving, to pretend that he hasn't seen the man. He can keep going, squinting into the sun at the end of the hall, blinded. He can call Big Bob and go home. Favor fulfilled.

But Jupiter smiles—a reflexive grin on seeing a familiar face. Even from the distance of a room's width, he knows Adam, and, as if panhandling in the street, he calls to him, "Hey, buddy!" Fuck.

Suddenly, his parka weighs a ton. Adam unzips it and shrugs it off, then walks into the room, where he stands at the foot of the bed. "How are you doing?" He smiles like a Welcome Wagon lady, all teeth, no substance.

"A little embarrassed. Sometimes I think I can go without my medications, but each and every time I'm proven wrong. They're going to send me back to the mental hospital to get adjusted." Jupiter fingers air quotes around the word *adjusted*. "But I need to ask you a big favor." It's almost as if Jupiter has been expecting him.

Two favors in one day. Adam grits his teeth and smiles. "I'll see if I can help."

"My dog." Jupiter's pale blue eyes begin to leak tears. "I don't know where he is."

"He'll be fine."

"No, I need to know he's fine. I need to know where he is. He's probably in the pound."

"You've got tags on him; they'll keep him."

"They're old. And they came off another dog. I just have them so that I don't get hassled."

"Well, even so, don't worry about him. You need to worry only about yourself."

Jupiter begins to cry in earnest. "I can't stop worrying, and if I worry, I can't pay attention to my doctors." Suddenly, Jupiter throws himself into a sitting position. "I'm getting out of here. Hand me my pants."

"No. No. Stay put." Shit, now he's going to be responsible for the guy going AWOL, or AMA, or whatever it is when you leave a hospital before you're discharged.

"I can't. Benny is my life." Jupiter is weeping loudly, inconsolable. He swings skinny legs over the edge of the bed. The leads that snake beneath the thin fabric of his johnny pull tight against the monitor that records his vitals. A buzzer goes off down the hall.

"Okay, okay. Simmer down. I'll go. I'll go." Adam wants him back in the bed. The sight of those skinny legs with the topography of lumpy veins and knobby knees is too much intimacy. It's easier to say he'll go than to fight with the guy and get that pink nurse down on him. "Hush, just relax. I'll go to the pound."

"You will? Promise?" The tears stop and a snaggletoothed smile erupts.

"You get back in bed and I'll check."

Jupe does what's asked and Adam makes a run for the elevator.

"Just hang on to him till I get out. It won't be long. I promise. Thank you. Thank you. Thank you."

The elevator door closes off the sound of Jupiter's happy, grateful shouting.

Chapter Twenty

I'm telling you. Shut up. What was that song? When the student becomes the master? I'd had it with my mentor. How had I ever thought this whining, yapping, cowering, fear-aggressive punk was worthy of my adulation, God knows. I kept telling him to play it straight. Not to snap every time one of the people came along to feed him. How dumb animal is that? But he kept it up. His separation from his man was more than he could take. Frankly, I just didn't get it. I know that many of our kind pair-bond with humans, but the slavish devotion beyond the unknown days of their separation seemed a bit much. We're dogs; we aren't supposed to remember much beyond regimented training. Move on.

I, on the other paw, played it like Olivier on the boards. I loooove people. Smooochie smoochie. Yes, kiss my ugly chewed-up nose. Give me a home where the kibble pours free and squeaky toys abound. I fully expected that a reprise of my past performance would win me another easily escapable home. Of course, I'd wait until spring. No more winters on the street. What I hadn't counted on was the lack of interested adopters in February. Seems like everyone wants a spring puppy or isn't considering the daily walk while the temperature is in the thirties and the wind chill makes it feel like an arctic blast. People really only want dogs in the summer. I languished.

The staff were kind, and my prestreet life had enured me to a caged existence, but I was bored. By now I was used to coming and going as I pleased, tooling around my staked-out territory, greeting the neighbors, checking out the Dumpsters. Outside of the daily leash walk up and down the block and being fed twice a day, I didn't have much to keep me occupied. I slept. Which is good fun, but really I wanted to see some old friends, and once my mentor vanished into the door at the end of the hall, from whence no one returns, I had no one around who knew me from my street days.

It was enough to make a grown dog yawn.

Chapter Twenty-one

If Adam thought the hospital reeked, the animal shelter trumps that revulsion with the additional pungency of animal pee. Even in the sparkling clean and bright reception room of the city's animal shelter—the term *pound,* he has learned, is politically incorrect—Adam can smell the lingering odor of overexcited parolees.

"I'm here to find a guy's dog. He's in the hospital." Adam has waited three days before beginning to hunt for Jupiter's dog. Leaving the hospital, Adam had headed straight home and slept the rest of the day. Waking only long enough to eat a bowl of cereal, he'd gone right back to sleep, the first night in months he neither medicated himself with scotch nor dreamed. When the cab pulled up in front of his building, Adam had paid the man off and trotted across the street to the A to Z Tropical Fish and Pet Supply. The door was locked, but he could see the bluish green glow of the aquarium lights. Gina must have weathered the storm and gone home, he thought.

The next two days, Adam had been too busy with appointments, lawyers, psychiatrist, and laundry even to look up the location of the city animal shelter.

"When did he lose his dog?" Yet another in-charge woman in pastel scrubs.

"I don't know, during the storm maybe." He tells this to the youngish woman with yanked-back hair, purple scrubs, and matching Crocs. Does everyone in the quasi-medical profession wear these weird shoes? How can anyone tell the nurses from the aides or the vets from the receptionists these days?

"What kind of dog is it?"

Adam thinks back on encountering Jupe and the dog on the street, or Jupe and the dog waiting on the stoop. "Shorthaired, dark-colored." Adam has paid so little attention to Jupe's dog that it's like trying to remember a detail from someone else's life. "I think he has white on him. About yea high." Adam sketches a line at his knees. "Its name is Benny."

"Terrier?"

"No. More like a boxer, but with a tail." Adam is growing confident, sure of his description now.

"Pit bull?

He shrugs. "I don't know. Maybe. Why?"

The girl pinches her bottom lip with two fingers. "I'll have to talk to the vet in charge about this. Just fill out what you can." She slides a form onto a clipboard that has a pen dangling from a piece of twine. She pushes it across the high counter to Adam. "We have the welfare of the dog first and foremost as our responsibility."

"So, returning a lost dog to his owner is counterintuitive to that?"

The girl looks pained. "Please wait over there." She points to a pair of orange plastic chairs.

Adam's mouth is dry. Dr. Stein says that he can begin to recognize the symptoms of his anger by thinking of his posture and the taste in his mouth. Are his hands shaking? He's supposed to take deep breaths and mentally flick away the disturbance before it grows too big. In the reception area, there is a Poland Spring water dispenser but no cups. Adam is half-tempted to stick his mouth under the spigot and get a mouthful of water that way. He deliberately slumps his shoulders, then rolls them back and down, shaking off the tension. He rotates his head around, then tilts it from side to side. There. Now smile. He prides himself on handling frustration a little better than in the past. Now delays at the post office or being stuck in traffic don't rile him in quite the same way. Adam doesn't attribute this to the slow pace of his days, or the loss of meaningful work; he thinks he's simply making progress toward what Dr. Stein calls "centeredness."

"Mr. . . ." A big man in a ponytail bangs through the swinging door separating the reception area from the rest of the facility. He's wearing blue scrubs and, predictably, blue Crocs.

"March. Adam March."

"Dr. Gil."

The name on his badge says something else, Gilbert Dufrense. *Dr. Gil.* How user-friendly. How he must charm the little old cat ladies.

Adam hands him the clipboard and waits in silence as the vet studies the form Adam has filled out. "This isn't your dog?" For the first time, the vet looks up at him.

"I expect that your staffer has informed you of the situation. I have a sick friend, whose only concern is getting his dog back."

Dr. Gil sets the clipboard down on the high counter and gestures toward the hard plastic chairs. Adam makes no move to sit down. Already this errand has wasted half his morning. "Mr. March. We have a policy."

"You don't have the dog, do you?"

"We did. I think."

"Two things come to mind here. One, how do you know you have or don't have this guy's dog when neither one of us has taken a look? Two, a sick man's civil rights are in jeopardy here." Adam is wishing that he'd shaved before coming, worn something besides his usual jeans and faded Red Sox sweatshirt.

The blue-scrubbed vet fingers his chin contemplatively. Adam notices that his hands are encased in latex gloves, as if he's forgotten the purpose of the gloves is to keep him safe from contamination. "Two pit bull types were brought in. One is familiar to us; we know him. The other was . . . hostile."

Adam shrugs. "Benny is probably not hostile." Adam is trying to think if he's ever seen Jupe's dog being either hostile or, conversely, friendly. He has no recollection, but logic tells him that a street man's dog is probably going to be one way or the other. It's probably significant that he can't recall any of the other men petting the dog. "Why don't we just make this easy and go see if his dog is in there."

Dr. Gil suddenly snaps off the latex gloves, folds them together, and shoots them over the high counter and into a wastebasket as if that's the highlight of his day. "Okay."

They walk down a short corridor past doors labeled SURGERY, EXAM ROOM 1, EXAM ROOM 2.

At the end of the corridor is an unlabeled door, and Dr. Gil pushes the swinging door open to the cacophony of barks, yelps, whines, growls, ululations, and howls. The noise is like being on a Wall Street trading floor. The vocalizations are accompanied by the sound of wire doors being rattled, metal water bowls tipped, nails tap-dancing on cement and on the metal shelves of the upper cages. Prison movies come to mind.

"Are these dogs up for adoption?"

"Some might be. Some are fostered."

"Meaning?" He knows what it means to kids. It just sounds more humane in reference to animals. Kinder.

"Put in temporary homes, see if they can make it as pets."

"And the others? Adoptable?"

"Not always."

Like him. He remembers his social worker sitting him down and explaining that he had no hope of a real home. "You're a big boy now, Adam"—as if it was good news she offered—"Before you know it, you'll be all grown up, and on your own."

Adam looks around at the faces pressed up against the bars of the cages. Ears are pointed toward him, and he imagines they have no concept of their hopelessness. He is repulsed by the smell, an amalgam of wet newspaper, cleaning fluid, and dog. The vet walks ahead of Adam, pointing into each cage, left, then right, and calling out the closest breed match to the occupant's description.

"German shepard?"

"No." The smallish tan-and-black dog with one upright ear lifts a lip in a halfhearted sneer.

"Beagle?"

A definite hound-dog look. Weepy eyes and a guilty expression. "No."

"Border collie?"

"Look, I said he's a black-and-white shorthaired dog." The fluffy Border collie stares at Adam with one blue eye and one brown eye.

"Describing dogs is more art than science. One man's shorthair is another man's retriever."

They have come to the end of the line. One dog remains, but Adam has already come to the conclusion that Jupe's dog is long gone. He's about to ask if there is another shelter in the city, when he sees the last dog. This one is in a short run instead of a cage. There is nothing in it but the dog and a water bowl, as if he's just in there for a change of scenery. As if he might be leaving shortly. As if he's at the end of the line.

He's a brindle dog, one lop ear, the other a ragged half of an ear; a splash of white on his chest, on which is a long, narrow, still angry-looking scar that glows pinkish in the fluorescent light of the kennel. He sits with a quiet dignity among all these raucous others. Adam stands at the locked cage door, his fingers gripping the diamonds of wire, staring at the dog, willing it to be Jupe's dog. The dog raises its eyes to meet his. His mouth opens; a long, wide tongue lolls out. He stands up and his tail swings mildly from side to side. He has the look of someone with just one last hope in the world.

"This one."

"Are you sure?"

Sure is exactly what Adam isn't. "That's him."

"You can't adopt for someone else."

"So I'll 'foster' him till Charles gets home."

"Look. I know. You're trying to do a favor for a friend. But this is not our policy." Dr. Gil puts his hand on the latch. The dog in question cocks his head, eager to see what comes next. "Especially with these dogs. Pit bulls."

"But you, a vet, would rather destroy him without benefit of judge and jury?"

"He's got the scars. He's been fought. That kind generally don't make it as pets."

"But he's already a pet." Adam feels a surge of anger. He isn't someone who is told no; he is someone who says no. "I'll post bail."

There is a long, uncomfortable moment as the two men eye each other. Finally, Dr. Gil shakes his head. "You need to fill out adoption papers, show us that you either own your own home or that your landlord will allow you to have a dog."

"I have a better idea." There is rack filled with choke chains and leashes. "I'll take him and give you a big donation." Adam pulls down a leash from the rack.

"You'll pay the regular adoption fee of two hundred dollars and sign a paper that says you won't give this dog away."

"Except to his rightful owner."

"That you'll return him to us if you choose not to keep him." The vet folds his arms across a meaty midriff. "That is our policy."

Adam doesn't know why he's arguing with this Dr. Gil, except that he is unwilling to cave in to this pompous guy who probably couldn't make it as a real doctor and so is treating animals instead. Adam is determined to walk out of the shelter with the goddamned dog. He's not going to be told by this Big Bluie that he can't take a stupid dog that's likely going to be destroyed anyway. Adam's not in it for the money; no one will compensate him for taking this dog out of this place. He won't be receiving any state paycheck. No one will hold him up as a humanitarian. No foster father of the year title while all the time he's making life miserable for some innocent kid. Threatening the strap if a towel gets left on the floor.

Adam pulls himself up. What the fuck is he doing? Suddenly, the clipboard is in his hands and he's walking out of the shelter, two hundred dollars deeper in Visa debt, which he has no hope of recovering, and holding the leash of a dog he is fairly certain isn't the right one.

They stand on the sidewalk, waiting to cross the street to his car. Adam glances down at the dog. The mutt is looking up at him, tongue lolling for all the world like he's happy.

"You goddamned better be Benny." Adam jerks the leash and the pair cross the street.

Chapter Twenty-two

"I got his dog." Adam ducks his head into Big Bob's office. "Just what am I supposed to do with him?"

"Jupe's here."

A slight scrim of sweat breaks out on Adam's forehead. Thank God. Despite his assurances to the vet, Adam has no intention of taking the dog home. Right now it sits in the back of his Lexus, the back window cracked open, a towel on the cream-colored leather. He has no idea if the dog will sit quietly or wreck his car. "Is he all right?"

"He's better. More himself. But he'll be happy to see that dog. It's all he's talked about since he walked in, how you're going to find it. Sorry to have put that on you, man, but it's a good-deed merit badge." A euphemism for points earned on his community service. Every hour he works is documented; every hour Adam spends in the center becomes one less he has to serve. A "merit badge," in Big Bob's lexicon, earns him another hour of service. Of course, Adam has just spent several hours and two hundred dollars performing this service, but he decides to let that go. "I'll go get the dog."

The inside of his car smells like a mix of medicated shampoo and dog breath. The blunt-headed animal greets him like a lost friend, tag wagging, tongue drooping out of his split-grin face. "Come on. Your master wants a word with you." Adam hauls the dog up the back stairs of the center.

Jupe is waiting in the empty dining room. It's long after lunch and most of the men are either gone or settled in the activity room. The tables are folded and garaged against the far wall. Jupe has a new watch cap, and his army-surplus jacket is buttoned up to his neck. Adam can see that his eyes are clouded with the comfort of legal drugs. He has the look of a man standing on solid ground for the first time after a long sea voyage.

Adam half-expects that Jupe's drug-induced calmness will abate at the sight of his missing dog, and he is going to hand the leash over and make a run for it before Jupe can give him a grateful hug. The last thing he wants is an embrace. It's late and he just wants to go back to his place, crack open the JW, and relax in front of the television. It's all he wants. The solitude of slow numbness.

"That's not Benny."

"Of course it is." Adam thrusts the leash at Jupe's hand. "Take him."

The dog sits down. He looks from Adam to Jupe and back again.

"I know my own dog. This isn't him. This is some stray."

"Sir. He was the only . . ."

Jupe's tears start down his gunneled cheeks. He doesn't sob, or make a move to wipe them away. "Benny? What's happened to him? Did you look everywhere?"

Adam pokes the leash end against Jupe's fisted hand. "He's a nice dog. Take him."

Suddenly, Jupe's face changes; some older part of himself shows, the professor or the father or the good husband. "Do you think that affection is so easily transferred? Do you think that you could love a stranger child who is given to you as a replacement for your own? Do you have the slightest idea what it means to love someone or something? My dog is my friend, my companion, my protection on the street. I failed to love my family enough, or myself. But I love Benny." And just as suddenly, Jupe reverts to the craggy, hollow-cheeked man of a moment before; then he shrugs back his shoulders and walks away from Adam and the dog.

The dog stands up, shakes, and yawns.

Adam swallows hard. His chest feels as hollow as the Tin Man's. He can hear his pulse in his ears; he knows that he's got to take charge of the moment, but he's stuck, feckless. He feels the dog nudge his leg as if to say, Let's get out of here.

Big Bob has watched the whole scene, as has Rafe, standing in the doorway of the kitchen, his palm-frond hands stroking his cheeks. Adam thinks he hears laughter, faint ripples of amusement at his expense. The familiar knot of frustration twists in his belly, this being thwarted that provokes his just-below-the-surface anger. He has put himself on the line here for some indigent and now he's stuck.

"Hey man, that's a nice dog." Rafe's voice is just one degree to the left of teasing. "Lemme get him somethin' to eat."

Adam is slow to turn around, slow to decide if Rafe is taunting him or sincere.

"Well, you tried." Big Bob doesn't come close enough to slap Adam on the back; in fact, he stays at a distance. "I guess you'll have to take him back."

"Yeah. Great." Adam has an appointment with a potential client in half an hour on the other side of town. "Can you keep him here till I get back?"

"No. Don't think that would be a good idea."

"I can't keep him."

"Take him back on your way across town."

"I don't have time. Come on. I found the goddamn dog, or at least found one like him; the least you can do is keep him here for a couple of hours."

"No. Sorry. It's cold out, he can wait in your car."

Adam yanks the leash attached to the choke chain and hauls the dog out of the dining room and into the back hallway. Rafe is there with a plate of leftovers and a bowl of water. The dog makes noisy, fast work of the mess on the plate and laps water to the bottom of the bowl. Rafe watches with the same self-satisfaction on his face as when he takes a moment to observe the men enjoying his food. "He's a hungry one."

"You want him?"

Rafe makes a little piffle noise. "Can't. No pets allowed where I live."

"Lucky you."

" 'Sides, my wife'd kill me, I bring one of them home."

Adam is nonplussed. Rafe has never mentioned a wife before. Then again, neither has he. It's like their lives begin and end in this old Victorian building. Their conversations revolve around sports or politics, the differences between them offering very little common ground; neither he nor Rafe ever speak of a personal life, or only in a glancing way. "Well, maybe she can change her mind."

Rafe strokes his cheek with his fingertips, as if contemplating the idea. "No."

Adam tightens his grip on the leash and yanks the dog away from the plate he is still licking.

Adam opens the back door of his Lexus. During the hour and a half the big mutt has spent lolling on his backseat while Adam has been doing his dog and pony show for a group of entrepreneurs who don't look a day over twelve, he has managed to stink up the car with his farts and glaze both the door and the back windows with nose prints. His face splits into a grin as he lolls his tongue out at Adam's arrival. His tail wags, slapping the white leather with a tympanic rhythm.

Adam hauls the dog out by the collar and marches to the door of the animal shelter. A strategic retreat is more honorable than a complete defeat. He'll turn the dog over, try to get his money back, and forget the whole debacle.

Closed.

Fuck. It's only four o'clock. What kind of weird hours does this place keep?

Briefly, Adam looks around for a place to tie the dog. Maybe he can just leave him and then put a message on the answering machine why he did; surely someone comes in on weekends to feed the inmates. As quickly as the suggestion occurs to him, Adam shrugs it off. He'd probably get sent up on cruelty charges for doing that. The last thing Adam

March needs is more trouble. He has a date with Judge Johnson next week, and he is harboring a self-indulgent hope that the judge will cut him some slack, maybe even give him a reprieve. "Well, stupid, I guess you're with me." He loads the dog back into his sullied Lexus and heads home.

Chapter Twenty-three

Adam has only a vague notion how to take care of a dog. He's never had one, never allowed one in his house. Although Ariel had clamored for a puppy time and again, a fat black Labrador retriever like the ones that all the other kids whose parents had houses on Martha's Vineyard dragged along from home. "Why not? Why can't we? Why can't we?" Adam's answer was an unequivocal no, with the blame tossed, from time to time, on Sterling's shoulders. "It wouldn't be fair to your mother; she has enough to do." Which, even as a small child, Ariel saw right through. Adam got smarter. "It wouldn't be fair to"— and he'd name the incumbent housekeeper—"she has enough to do." Ariel had to be satisfied with her horses, which at least lived somewhere else.

So to find himself in his small one-bedroom apartment, in a building with no yard, face-to-face with one of the least attractive dogs ever made, Adam thinks he must be out of his mind.

The dog, a rusty brindle with white markings and that weird hacked-off ear, sits staring back at him. Every now and then his mouth opens and that banner of a tongue lolls out. He makes a gasping noise, slips the tongue over his nose, right, then left, and retracts it into his mouth, all the while keeping his eyes on Adam, as if he's waiting for a speech, or a tap dance. Or a fight.

"Don't get too comfortable; you're going back tomorrow." Adam wags a finger at the dog. Swallowing the last of the scotch in his glass, Adam heads into the bedroom, shutting the door behind him. He drops his clothes on the floor, refills the scotch glass with the bottle he keeps on his nightstand, and climbs into bed, exhaustion waving through him and making it impossible even to read to the end of the article in his *Business Week* magazine. He finishes off the scotch and turns out the light.

Instantly, he hears the scratch of claws against the wood. "Go to bed." *Scritch. Scritch.* Like some Stephen King predator. "Knock it off." The scratching becomes rhythmic, persistent. "Stop that." His landlord won't give him back his security deposit on that happy day he moves out of this dump if this mutt has damaged the woodwork. Adam leaps out of bed and wrenches open the door.

The dog is sitting, his tail swishing back and forth on the floor, his mouth gaping. *Aowr. Aowr.* It almost sounds like a syllable. He stands up, all happiness to see Adam back in the room.

Adam slams the door shut, gets back into bed, and pulls the spare pillow over his head.

. . . .

For once, he's slept late. Groggy from unaccustomed deep sleep, Adam comes out of his bedroom, and nearly steps in the pile of dog shit laid carefully in front of his door. The dog is sound asleep on the futon.

The screech and cackle of the two parrots inside Gina De-Marco's store grows even more excited as Adam, attached to the dog, walks in. Gina is bent over an aquarium of tropical fish set on a low shelf. Her low-slung jeans gap at the tantalizing space just below the last bump on her spine. She stands up, her mouth crooked in a little surprised smile, which quickly fades. "What have we here?" She stands aside to assess the dog, then looks at Adam. "Would never have pegged you for the pit bull type."

"I'm not." The dog leans against the choke chain, trying to get close to the decorative cage with the parrots.

"Okay. So that's not a pit bull on the end of a leash?"

"It's a long story." Adam snugs the animal back to his side.

"Where did you get him?"

"Shelter."

Gina's disdain suddenly disappears. It is replaced with a grudging approval. "Wow. Good for you. Rescue dogs are the best; it's like they know they've been saved. I've got three greyhounds—"

"It's temporary." Adam isn't interested in rehearsing the whole sorry tale. He just wants some dog food. "I'm not keeping him."

"Fostering is good, too."

Fostering. The word has no heroic connotations for Adam. "No. Not fostering."

Gina ignores his assertion, as if he's a little boy refusing to eat his peas. "What's his name?"

"Doesn't have one. Doesn't need one. I'm taking him back to the shelter as soon as the doors open."

"Why did you get him if you're not keeping him? These are living creatures; you can't decide that they don't fit and then return them like a damned shirt."

"Like I said, it's a long story. I was trying to find a guy's dog, and this isn't it. He goes back."

The dog is leaning against his collar again, his pale brown nose working hard.

"Give him a chance."

Yanked back to Adam's side, the dog sits.

Gina leans over the counter, exposing that crescent of skin above her jeans. She reaches into a jar and pulls out a dog biscuit. She cautiously approaches the dog, whose eyes are fixed on the biscuit in her hand. He lowers his head, swipes his tongue over his lips. "Here, fella." Gina offers the biscuit and the dog shows good manners in taking it gently from her hand. She stands up and smiles. "He seems like a good boy. You should keep him."

The idea is ludicrous, adding an ugly dog to his list of worries. Adam doesn't even know what the pet policy is in his building, but he's willing to guess it's not in favor of dogs like this. "I can't keep him."

Gina reaches out and touches Adam's arm, as if consoling him. "Sure you can." He hears that subtle southern drawl. "He likes you." He likes the feel of her hand on his arm, the persuasive touch of someone who thinks she can change his mind.

"Well, I don't like him."

"You will. He's a beauty."

Adam laughs. "Not really. And he drools. And smells."

"That's normal." Gina runs the same hand that's touched his arm over the dog's head. The dog wriggles beneath her hand. She makes baby-talk noises at him, then looks up at Adam and sighs. "It can be very rewarding, bringing an animal back from a rough beginning to a satisfying life. I've done it with greyhounds, and several friends of mine have adopted pits."

"Doesn't matter. I told you: I'm not keeping him."

"Then why did you bring him in here?"

"I have nothing to feed him."

Now she looks at Adam with a tight-jawed disappointment. "Give him a chance. Haven't you ever needed someone to give you a chance?"

Adam almost laughs at her sincerity, at the storybook ending she's shilling. "I have always made my own chances."

"And see where that's gotten you."

"What do you mean?"

"I see you standing there, staring out your window all day. Too many hours for a guy with something better to do."

Adam feels the flush build, the hum of annoyance vibrating through his skin, the urge to snap.

Gina turns away from Adam, leaving him alone in the shop while she goes into a back room. She comes out with a small bag of dry dog food, two cans of wet food, and a tennis ball. "This'll take care of him for a couple of days. Just remember to give him fresh water, too." She gingerly offers the mutt another biscuit. "I think you're making a mistake."

"You think he's got so much potential, I'll be happy to give him to you."

"I would if I could, but I've got those three greyhounds. They take up a lot of space."

"What do I owe you?" Adam fishes his wallet out of his back pocket.

"It's a gift. For the dog. Throw the ball for him a few times. You both could use the exercise."

"No, no gifts. I'll pay."

"Forget it." Gina's full mouth is drawn into a thin line. She folds her arms across her middle, her hands resolutely not taking any money from him.

He doesn't know exactly what he's done wrong, but he's done something. All women have that ineffable power to transmit disappointment without words, and he's getting a full dose from this woman he barely knows. She bags the food and hands it to him.

"Thank you."

"I guess he's better off dead than unloved."

"Dead? He'll get adopted."

"Not very likely."

"You just told me you have friends who adopt pit bulls. What makes it less likely for this one?"

"Where was he?"

"End cage."

"Nuff said. That's death row. They've given him his last chance with you."

The dog, who has given up pulling on the leash and trying to sniff at every nose-level object in the pet shop, suddenly relaxes the tension on the leash and sits. He looks up at the two humans, his muzzle following the conversation like a line judge. Adam turns away from the counter and nearly trips over the dog. The touch of his knee against the dog's ribs is enough to get a yowl out of the animal. "Hey, that's enough out of you." Adam jerks the leash.

"Who, me or the dog?"

Adam doesn't answer, yanks the dog to his side, and walks out. Really, the woman is too much.

As they wait for the light to change, Adam hears the dog growl, a low, throaty rumble that is aimed up the street. A middle-aged man in a track suit is walking a Labrador retriever. The dog's growl elevates to something more like a roar and Adam is nearly taken off his feet as the dog lunges fiercely at the oncoming dog. The bag of dog food hits the pavement and the tennis ball rolls out. The dog is powerful enough that it takes both hands to keep him from reaching the yellow Lab.

"That dog is dangerous, mister. Put a fucking muzzle on it, will ya?" The Lab's owner pulls his own dog to one side and hurries by, fuming about city ordinances. The pit bull is barking at the top of his lungs, as if the very existence of that Labrador is an insult to him. The Lab glances back at the raging dog and then looks longingly at the rolling tennis ball.

"Knock it off!" Adam pulls on the leash, but the dog is oblivious to the pressure. As soon as the guy and his dog disappear around a corner, the dog sits, licks its lips, and scratches at his half of an ear, then looks up at Adam as if expecting praise.

The dog has to go. Now.

Chapter Twenty-four

I was embarrassed at having to do my business in the house, but then again, I have never been house-trained. I wouldn't have even considered soiling the area—it was, after all, not a lot bigger than my cage back in the cellar—but he didn't give me a clue as to what was appropriate behavior. His language was familiar. I understood the "Shut up" and "Knock it off" bit, but my own attempt at communication was ineffectual; he didn't speak my language. So I crapped where he'd get the message. No furtive behind the furniture for me. Uh-uh. Right there where he'd step in it. I got the reaction I half-expected. Again, familiar words were tossed at me, but he didn't touch me. He also, after a few minutes of diatribe, had the good grace to be embarrassed himself. "You needed to go out? I should have known. Not your fault." Well, he didn't exactly say that, but I understood by his seated posture, his head in his hands, that he had figured it out.

He leashed me and we banged down the three flights of stairs to the outside. The sidewalk was clear, but the grassy divide between sidewalk and street was filled with snow. I hiked my leg up to mark my new territory against a dug-out fireplug but got dragged along before I could finish the job. This guy had no leash manners at all.

Then—oh boy, what fun—we went into that place where the scents of treats and rubber toys was almost narcotic. The female actually touched me with kind fingers. Something I'd never known before, and something I had a sudden and uncharacteristic craving for. The mommy noises from her mouth were enough to make me long for puppyhood. Ah, if only the lug on the other end of my leash had had the brains to leave me here.

And then, would you believe it? One of those Labs from the night of the storm came sauntering down the street, all up in my face, bragging on being somebody's spoiled pet. I guess I showed him. The cur squealed with fear aggression, and I'd have made mincemeat out of him if he'd had the *cojones* to pull away from his man. The guy at the other end of my leash was surprised, but he had a pretty firm grip. Lucky for that Lab.

He yanked on my leash and off we went back to his crib. If I had hoped for a reprise of my first adopted home, with a nice escapable fenced-in yard, this sure wasn't it. Before he could get his entry door unlocked, I squatted. If I wasn't going to be able to enjoy the leisure of a backyard bowel movement, I was going to have to get busy before he dragged me back into the building. I have my standards.

There is a certain comfort in recognizing human male behavior, and this guy's language was completely familiar. He spoke as my boys had spoken. Muttered, yes, not shouted. And no violence, true. I wasn't confined to a cage, but he kept his distance, as if I was. I just knew that my fighting career was going to be revived. Why else bail me out of the shelter? He was tough—nothing namby-pamby about him—and I just knew that he was looking for someone as tough as he was. Right from the get-go, I knew I liked his looks. Hey, I knew that I was out of condition, but I was certain we'd rectify that soon enough. I was even looking forward to the road work and the weights. We'd be a pair. Yes we would.

Inside, he dumped some kibble into a plastic bowl. Good start. I wolfed it, looked for more. He paid no attention, just sat talking to himself with that little toy they all rub on their ears. Suddenly, he stood up and swore. I ducked. I'm not proud of my cringe reflex; I don't speak of it often, but it's there. I ducked and scurried out of reach. The little table afforded me a place to call my own. Chair legs, table legs, like a veritable "cave" of protection. I could look out and see the man's legs pacing back and forth, but he couldn't reach me.

"What's your problem?" He growled like an alpha dog.

Aowr. I acknowledged his position in this pack of two. He had the hands to open cans; I had to be subservient.

"You lucky bastard. You've got a reprieve. Goddamned shelter doesn't do intakes on the weekend. Goddamn it. They need a better business plan."

I laughed. I had no idea what all those words meant, but I do know when things are looking up. *Aowr.* Hunh-hunh.

"Maybe there's another one I can take you to." He scratched at his chin, then said, "Maybe there's a pit bull rescue. Yeah, that's it." He entertained himself for a long time, but at the end, he slammed his toy down. "Fuck it."

More words, but I knew that they were just sounds. I bent to lick my nethers. I was full, and, for the moment, safe.

Chapter Twenty-five

Today is his kid day. His court-approved, Sterling-approved visitation. He's given up trying to get Ariel here; instead, he will meet her at Sylvan Fields, where he will be forced to wait outside in the car until she drags herself down to join him. He'll take her to lunch at a restaurant he can no longer afford, while she texts her friends, no doubt complaining about her wasted afternoon. Then a negotiated trip to the mall, where she will test his patience by going from store to store, leaving him to cool his jets on a bench like some abandoned luggage, then home to Sylvan Fields, where Sterling will berate him for giving in to Ariel's questionable taste in clothing—this after he's bought her something he cannot afford to buy. Any hope of a consulting job, or employment in his field, has so far proven futile

Adam remembers to take the dog downstairs before leaving. The midmorning air is crystal cold, and he's come down with his bare feet tucked into his beat-up L.L. Bean slippers, and his parka is unzipped. "Hurry up."

The dog is happy to comply. Adam bends over with a plastic bag in his hand. He doesn't know if any neighbors are checking out his dog-owner manners, but he doesn't want to take the chance that someone will complain to the super that he has this dog. Even if it is only until the shelter reopens on Monday. No other shelter will take him. In bailing the dog out, Adam has signed a contract agreeing to return him to the same shelter. No bending of rules.

The dog nudges Adam with his nose, letting him know it's time to go in. If he had balls, they'd be frozen off.

"No more crapping in the house."

Aowr.

"Okay."

Adam dumps kibble in the bowl, fills a pot with cold water, and points at the futon. "You stay off."

The dog's mouth breaks open and the tongue lolls out in a gentleman's agreement.

"Yeah, right. Not till my back is turned." Adam locks the door behind him. He has no idea how long a dog can go without getting into trouble, but he figures he can hold on for the six hours or so that Ariel will tolerate Adam's company. Six at the most. He's just been out, he's been fed and watered, and Adam has thoughtfully left the television on so that the dog thinks he's got company. He shrugs back the fact that he has no idea if this dog has the self-control to behave. Then he consoles himself, thinking that, so far, he's crapped on the floor only once. Hasn't chewed anything, and hasn't barked at noises. If he's been hard to handle on the street, lunging at every passing dog, at least he's been good in the apartment.

. . .

Ariel saunters out of the house barely dressed. Her skinny rider's legs are encased in tights, which end midway down her shin, a skimpy floral skirt is wrapped around her waist, and her coat is wide open. In a nod to the season, she wears short Uggs on her feet, like Gina wears. Ariel's two thumbs are busy communicating with luckier friends. She gets into his car without a word, ignoring his "hi, honey." As Adam moves down the long shrub-lined driveway, Ariel finishes her texting and looks at him. "This car stinks!"

"You noticed?" He aims at droll, but it comes out weak.

"Whew. Smells like wet dog."

"Interesting that you should mention that. It is wet dog."

Suddenly, Ariel takes notice. Her eyes widen. "You have a dog?" Emphasis on the *you*. As if he had suddenly taken up bungee jumping.

"Temporarily."

"Can I see him?"

Adam recognizes a dilemma when it faces him. If he introduces Ariel to the dog, then gets rid of him, she's going to be as mad at him as ever. If he doesn't show her the dog, she'll be as mad at him as ever. The old "rock and hard place" situation where Adam feels so at home. "I've got him only for a day. No sense getting to know him."

Ariel shoves her hands into the sleeves of her coat, her slump eloquent of his failings. "Fine."

"I've booked us lunch at Trois Chevaliers." He knows this is Ariel's favorite high-end restaurant. He lets her have a little champagne when he takes her there. His pocketbook cries

McDonald's, but his pride and his credit card call for Trois Chevaliers.

"Fine."

"School going okay?"

"Fine."

"Any concerts or plays this year?"

"Not yet."

"How's your old pal Kiki?"

Her eye roll is not charming. "We're at different schools."

"Gran and Granny doing well?

"Guess so."

"Your mom okay?"

"Why do you keep asking me these questions? They're always the same and the answers are always the same. Ask Mom yourself."

Adam swallows back his reply: Unless Sterling wants something, she never answers his calls. Anything of a substantial nature between him and his ex-wife is carried out through intermediaries. Ariel, for good or ill, has become his only connection to his past life. His message board. Poor kid. No wonder she hates these forced dates.

Since he first noticed the shadow of her aunt's gestures in her gestures, Adam has seen more and more of Veronica in Ariel. It's as if the foreshortened memories of his sister overlay the reality of his sullen daughter. Ariel's preferred tone of voice echoes the distant memory of Veronica's angry words. *"I'm outta here, old man."* Not screamed, but enunciated clearly and with a layer of contempt that was nearly physical. Long-dormant thoughts of Veronica leap all too often to mind since his breakdown. He's being haunted by the specter of his sister in the expression on his daughter's face.

He tries again. "How's the horse?"

Ariel doesn't take the opportunity to wax on about her horse's abilities, cute moments, and funny habits as she used to with him. "Fine." She plugs an ear bud in and keeps her gaze on the scenery.

This is more painful to Adam than he thinks he can take. It's been going on so long that he wonders if Ariel will ever mellow toward him. What he's done, by having this meltdown, has forever corrupted him in her eyes. And Sterling is keeping it that way.

Ariel treats him like Veronica treated their father—with disdain. Which the old man deserved. She was right to flee the man who would give up his only son to DSS rather than be a single parent. Who left his five-and-a-half-year-old in the hands of strangers. Adam hasn't committed any sin as egregious as that, and yet he might as well have. Ariel treats him like a man in disgrace, barely concealing her contempt. Is it really a contempt more profound than the usual contempt of an adolescent for her parents, or is he becoming paranoid? It's not as if he'd chosen to leave the family home. He's been asked to leave it by a wife who would not stand by her man.

Veronica may have run away, but his father gave up on Veronica. Adam will not give up trying to stay in Ariel's life. He studies his daughter as they sit at a red light. "Why are you so mad at me?"

Ariel doesn't answer; her iPod blocks out the sound of his voice. He is nothing to her.

Chapter Twenty-six

Adam is startled awake. The dog is facing the door, standing close to where Adam has fallen asleep on the futon. There it is again, a soft knock. Wiping the sleep grizzle from his mouth, Adam drags himself off the futon. The dog barks, one sharp, meaningful yap. "Shut up."

The dog returns to his table cave, his job done.

It has been another week. The shelter is still closed, a water-main break having shut it down indefinitely. The animals have been dispersed to shelters across the state, stretching limited resources, and, no, Dr. Gil says, he can't take the dog to one of them. He'd pushed the rules by letting Adam have the dog in the first place. Adam has to return him to Animal Advocates.

Like a bad houseguest, the dog seems to have extended his stay indefinitely.

"I found this on my book rack and thought you might want it." Gina DeMarco stands outside of Adam's door. Her polar bear parka frames her oval face, the white of the faux fur contrasting with the olive tone of her skin. She's a little breathless, and her cheeks are pinked with the cold.

"Come in. Come in." Adam is embarrassed to be found like some old man in the middle of the day. He's in his undershirt and jeans, his sockless feet in old slippers. He fingers the remote control to shut off Judge Judy. No one has ever come to see him here. His erstwhile adversary in the animal rights wars is the first person to cross his threshold since his landlord handed him the keys. A latent civility awakens in him. "I was just going to make a cup of tea. Would you like one?" He hopes that his breath isn't offensive. Rafe served garlic mashed potatoes at lunch.

"I can't. I've left the store. I just wanted to give this to you." She hands him a thin book: *Your Pit Bull, What to Expect and What to Do.*

"You know that—"

"I know you're not keeping him, but you've got him till that shelter gets back in operation, so you might as well have it." She doesn't sound like a person bearing gifts. "No one who comes into my store is ever looking for a book like that. It was stuck in an order for books on tropical fish. Distributor said to keep it, that it was a mistake. You're welcome to it."

To be polite, Adam opens the thin book, which is filled with color photographs of dogs that sort of look like his dog. Like *this* dog. Except that these are posed and have equal ears. Chapters offer history, breed standards, and training— housebreaking, commands like *sit, stay, heel*. Adam glances down at the dog, who is happily taking Gina's petting; he's rolled over to expose his belly to her fingertips.

"Thanks."

"Read it." Gina flips her hood back up. "You should know

something about the dog if you're going to just foist him off on someone."

"Once the shelter is open—"

"Yeah. I know. And you know that's death row."

Adam sets the book down on the coffee table. "Okay. Thank you for bringing it over."

"No problem." She pulls the front door open, and Adam feels a wash of disappointment.

"Wait, I'll bring you a cup of tea if you want."

Gina folds back the hood. She studies him with eyes the color of olive oil, eyes that suggest she hasn't forgotten his association with the cosmetics industry. Then she softens. "That would be nice." *Nahss.* That soft clue to a previous life. "It's been a slow day."

"Okay, then."

"Bring him."

"Why?"

"Just bring him."

Clutching two travel mugs filled with hot water in one hand and the dog's leash in the other, Adam dashes across the street between cars waiting at the red light. The dog lopes beside him, his satchel mouth open as if this is some kind of game, looking for all the world like a pet out for a romp with its person. Adam doesn't look at the dog, just hopes no other dog appears while he's carrying two cups of hot water.

Inside the pet shop, the air is fuggy with warmth and the scent of aquarium water. Adam is greeted by the squawks of the parrots, his eye caught by the tropical flash of color in a winter world. He sets the travel mugs down on the counter and fishes out two tea bags he's thoughtfully put in a plastic bag. "I couldn't manage the sugar and milk, not with both hands busy, so I'll just go next door and see what he's got."

Gina leans her elbows down on the counter, a posture that elongates her neck. Her molasses-colored hair is loose, and a layer curves against her cheek, framing it. "I've got both here. Don't bother yourself." She chooses a travel mug, one he's picked up at Dunkin' Donuts, and levers the cap off.

"I only have Tetley." Adam proffers the plastic bag, lets Gina choose which sachet of tea she wants. He is still in his coat, still gripping the end of the leash.

"Adam, why don't you let go of him? He can't get into trouble here; there's nothing much he can reach."

Adam drops the end of the leash, but the dog stays put, unaware that he's free to move around.

"How's he doing?"

"Except for taking over the futon, and trying to attack any dog he meets on the street, I guess you can say he's being good."

"Being on a leash does that to some dogs. They feel threatened."

"Seems more like he's the threat."

Gina bobs her tea bag, then scuttles it with a spoon she has produced along with the milk and sugar. "I think he's going to be a good dog. He's quiet."

"I haven't heard any complaints about barking."

"No, I mean his demeanor. Some dogs are all movement. This guy likes to take it all in." Gina looks over the edge of the counter at the dog, who looks up at her with adoration. "He's a good boy." This is addressed to the dog, whose tail ticks left and right.

"Are you sure you don't want him?"

"I would, if I didn't already—"

"Have three greyhounds." Adam takes the spoon from Gina and retrieves his tea bag from the bottom of his Starbucks mug.

The object of the conversation suddenly finds it too hard to remain sitting and flops to the floor, stretching out on his side, releasing a contented grunt.

Gina and Adam pay close attention to their travel mugs. There is nothing else obvious to talk about. This is suddenly like a bad first date. A bad first blind date. There's only one thing they have in common—not the workplace, nor a school, nor a mutual friend, but a dog. The awkwardness of being imperfect strangers. Neither wants to resort to the weather, but no topic presents itself for a prolonged moment. Adam is unaccountably tongue-tied and wonders how fast he can drink his tea and get out of there.

Gina DeMarco sips her tea, grimaces at the scorch of hot water through the small aperture, and asks Adam a question. "If I can find any in the back room, would you like a cookie?"

"Sure, but don't go to any trouble."

Gina disappears and Adam breathes a sigh. What an imbecile he is. Why did he think she'd want his company? When Gina comes back with an opened package of Fig Newtons, he takes one and quickly asks her a question to fill in the silence. "How long have you owned the shop?"

Gina nips a corner off of her cookie and shrugs. "It seems like all my life, but I've only owned it per se since my grandfather passed. About twelve years. Before that, I just worked here. Once he started getting a little confused, he stopped waiting on the customers and just tended the tanks. Then one day, he turned the water temperature up on the angelfish and essentially cooked them. I came in and found him scooping them up in the net and then putting it back in the water and wondering why they were belly-up." Gina shrugs, a delicate gesture. "I couldn't leave him alone in here. But we spent a lot of time together even as he declined, so, in the end, I never had to put him in a nursing home. That's all that I wanted; he'd been so good to me."

"You were responsible for him, not your parents?"

"No. A long time ago, my mother and stepfather sent me up north to live with Grandpa; we haven't been much in touch since." Gina's remark has the worn spots of an old story.

Adam tastes the fig on his tongue, rough and sweet. "Where'd you come from originally?"

"I was born in Louisville, but we lived all around, North and South Carolina, Texas. Any place with an army base, any place hot." Gina leans her elbows on the counter. A barricade of donation jars leaves her a loophole through which to conduct business: greyhound rescue, miniature horse rescue, food bank, breast cancer awareness, therapy dogs, Thoroughbred rescue. Rescue this one; rescue that one; rescue me.

She rearranges the jars, soldiering them. "I have another stool back here if you want."

The space behind the service counter is narrow, an alley between the shelves on the wall behind them and the countertop with its displays of flea and tick remedies, pamphlets on how to feed your gerbil, your Betta fish, how to take care of your saltwater aquarium. Adam sits on the wooden stool he finds tucked under the overhang of the desk and sets down his tea. He pulls another cookie out of the package. "Your dad was in the army?"

"Dad and stepdad. My father was killed in Nam. My stepdad was his buddy."

"A lot of our guys are vets who served in Vietnam."

"Your guys?"

Adam realizes the trap he's set for himself. How to explain his "job" to Gina? Stein would have something to say about this, something along the lines of "Here's your chance. Start with the truth and see where it gets you." Stein is determined that Adam give up his sense that he has any control over history.

"I volunteer at the Fort Street Center."

"Good for you." Gina is looking at him with approval, ratcheting up her estimation.

A fan of dismay colors his cheeks. "Actually, it's not exactly volunteering. It's community service." Adam sees the approval meter slide back down. He hasn't practiced how to tell this story; he doesn't know whether to blurt out the salient facts, or just hope she doesn't want to hear more. Gina is intent on her tea, adding more sugar, a dollop more of the milk from the quart she's found in the back of the store. Intent on not asking the question he can see forming itself as she deliberately pays careful attention to doctoring her tea.

The dog, which has been meandering all around the store, dragging the four-foot leash behind him, suddenly notices that he's on the wrong side of the counter from the people. He figures out how to get back there and comes up to Adam, pressing his blunt nose on Adam's leg.

"Look who's here." Gina reaches across Adam's knees to pet the dog. "You want a cookie, too?" Gina produces a dog biscuit, which the dog gently takes out of her hand. "He's a sweetie, although I'm sure he's been fought." She reaches farther over to scratch the dog on the scar on his chest. Her elbow touches Adam's leg. He thinks he feels the touch of her hair beneath his chin, but he keeps his eye on the dog. "They say once they've done that, there's no saving them. But that's not always true."

Adam sips his tea, doesn't look at the dog or at Gina.

"You could call him Cassius. Or how about George? You know, Clay and Foreman? Good fighters who were good men."

"I don't think it's a good idea to name him."

"Because you're not keeping him?"

"Because I'm not keeping him."

Gina pulls on her bottom lip, crosses her legs. "Let's shoot the gorilla."

"I'm sorry?"

"We've got unfinished business, and I think that if we can just have the conversation, we'll feel better."

Adam is stymied. Is she talking about his community service? Then it hits him. "We sold the division; the Fraîche Crème product was discontinued."

"Yeah, but did you really stop animal testing?"

Adam is wholly unprepared for this. "Experiments were under way. Those were finished. No new experiments were begun. And no more rabbits were used." It's close enough to the truth. "I left the division shortly after your protest."

"I know. You didn't leave the division; you were promoted. I remember reading about it in the *Globe*. Best thing we ever did for you." After all these years, there is still an obvious and righteous anger at Dynamic's policies. The hand not holding the travel mug is shaking slightly, as if adrenaline is pouring through Gina.

Adam feels his own righteous anger simmering. He may have been promoted, which would have happened eventually anyway, but for six weeks Gina and her group made his life a living hell. Eggs thrown at his brand-new Lexus, the predecessor to the one he is still driving; damning signs held by NATE volunteers who lined the public thoroughfare leading to Dynamic's access road; shouts and accusations broadcast every night like clockwork on the local television channels; interviews with talking heads, who condemned him personally. Holed up in his division headquarters eighteen hours a day, consulting with public-relations people and attorneys, he barely got home in time to change for the latest dinner party or benefit; never had time to see Ariel before she was put to bed by the nanny.

A jangle as the pet shop door opens breaks the moment. Gina greets her customer by name. She takes a little while to wait on her customer, a middle-aged man fussing about pH balances in his tank. She discusses this problem with him, her elegant brows arced in concern for his trouble, but once she glances back at Adam, who's still behind the counter, her cold glance tells him the topic isn't finished. The customer pays for his purchases and jangles out the door. Once again they are alone.

"He's a regular. Can't seem to keep his fish alive, but he keeps trying. One of these days, he'll either give up or get it right."

"Sounds like the rest of us." Adam swallows the last of his tea, which is still hot and which burns his throat as it goes down. "You can't dwell on the past. You have to move forward."

Gina nods and turns her attention back to her fast-cooling tea. "I understand. Sometimes there are things you just want to put behind you."

"That's right." Adam sets his empty travel mug beside Gina's on the counter. His is a little taller, a little narrower. The handles touch. "Although I'm learning that even if you put things behind you, they aren't gone. They follow along like a phantom." Unaccountably, the image of the dog running down the street with the pole trailing along behind pops into Adam's mind and he realizes that very possibly this is that dog.

For his part, the dog makes a little *rrrooor rrooor* noise and his tail thumps against the old wooden floor.

Gina remains at the register, fiddling with the arrangement of bills in the drawer, quiet.

"I should go."

"Thanks for the tea." Gina hands him the two empty mugs. Slips the cookies back into their package, busies herself with small tasks.

Adam comes out from behind the counter, the dog behind him, the leash trailing. He feels deflated, disappointed, as if he's failed at something, some attempt.

Adam stops at the doorway. "It's history, Gina. Over and done with."

"Yeah. Ancient history. We were both a lot younger then." A hint of sarcasm.

"We didn't understand what we were doing." He hates that he's defensive.

"Doesn't excuse it."

"Maybe not, but a whole lot more has gone on in the world since then."

"Yeah, Enron, nine-eleven, Iraq, recession. Makes the eyes of a bunny seem somehow frivolous."

"What do you want me to do?"

"I don't know." She sounds just a little defeated. "I guess you could make up for it." She looks at the dog meaningfully. "A little payback?"

Adam tugs on the leash, bringing the dog to heel. The sound of the bells against the plate-glass door hurts his ears.

Chapter Twenty-seven

My man and I have taken to long walks now that the weather is a bit better. Sometimes we even run, although I don't like that quite as much. I prefer an olfactory perambulation to a training-level exercise, but, hey, when in Rome. He's developing some stamina. We go as far now as the outer edges of my old territory. Once in a while, when he slows down enough, I catch a whiff of an old friend still haunting the area. Sometimes, I pick up the scent of one of the boys. I tug on the leash when that happens. I don't want to go back into that cellar.

He still hasn't put me in a pit, nor given me any bouts with sparring partners.

Life here is pretty good. I do spend a fair amount of time alone, but I'm free to wander this crib, stretch, lap water, and sleep the untrammeled sleep of the secure. We go for rides. I am not one of those dogs who hang their heads out the window. I sit with dignity in the backseat, casting my glance right and left, surveying with the utmost authority the cityscape rolling out before me. Sometimes we go to places where I can smell my own kind, places like where we met. I can hear the vocalizations of the lost even from the quiet seclusion of the car, where I jump into the front seat the minute he leaves.

Each time, he comes back out and gets into the car without speaking. Each time, I know enough to scarper over the seat into the back.

After one of these visits, he pulled up to a stretch of sidewalk and left me there, the window rolled down just enough to let the enticing scents of the scene filter down to me, but not far enough for me to get my head out. I glowered at a man in a cap who stuck a bit of paper under the wiper, but I kept my mouth shut. I was bored, so I leapt into the front seat for a change of view. That's when I saw my mentor's man crouched against the wall of the place with the warm foodish smells. His street scent wafted my way, so I was certain of his identity, and I got a little excited, hoping that maybe my mentor was reunited with him. But no. He was alone, unaccompanied on his bundle of blanket, shivering in the cold air, desultorily thrusting out his bare hand with a cup in it at passing humans. "Got any change?" His whimper of submission rarely noted by those other people.

I saw my man come out of the building into which he'd disappeared, watched him coming to the car, walking past my mentor's man without stopping, without acknowledging him. He yanked the piece of paper that the man in the cap had stuck under the wiper, then climbed into his seat. Then he dropped his head like a puppy being scolded. "You should have been his dog."

Suddenly, he pushed open his door and grabbed me by the

leash, pulling me out faster than I could comply. We marched over to the squatting man, and my man started barking at him. The othe guy barked back, and I hunched my shoulders, lowered my head, waited for some clue as to what my man expected me to do.

"Take him," my man barked.

"Fuck you," my mentor's man snarled.

"He needs you," my man snapped.

"I don't need him. He ain't Benny," my mentor's man howled.

The guy on the end of my leash yanked me back off my feet and wrenched open the car door. I jumped in quickly and pressed myself against the opposite door. I might have growled then. A little growl of protest: *What the fuck is the matter with you?* I was a little carried away with the moment. It was as close to a fight as I'd been in a while. Yes, I definitely growled, low and in concert with his vocalizations.

He looked at me with these big human eyes of alarm. We were two alpha males faced off over authority. "Don't you ever do that again." I understood his meaning, if not the exact words. I waited, expecting the strike. It's what my boys would have done. It's what I expected. Maybe I even relished the idea—we'd finally get our cards on the table. But he didn't. He slammed the door shut and climbed into his own seat. I was thrown against the back of the seat as he pulled away from the curb.

Chapter Twenty-eight

Adam is ushered into the judge's chambers. The judge is waiting, standing with his back to the room, his forefinger running along the green spines of the law books soldiered on several shelves. He is intent on his search, says nothing to Adam, who is left standing in the middle of the small room. It's an old technique, one Adam used to employ himself with underlings who had inflated ideas of their worth. Keep them standing just until the silence becomes painful, a reminder that your time is way more important than theirs. A little nonverbal, nonphysical bullying. Even so, Adam is beginning to think the judge is overacting.

The timing of this meeting is not good, squeezed in between sessions in a very full docket, and Adam knows that he won't have a lot of time to impress the judge with his progress. He offered to postpone the meeting, but the judge said no, that if Adam could wait until lunch recess, they could get this over with. Adam doesn't know whether to take that as good news or bad. He wonders now if the judge has had his lunch, or if he's hungry and impatient.

It's been six months. Adam has half a year to go at Fort Street; he's worked his way up to ladling soup. He knows most of the regulars by name. Big Bob likes him. He likes his co-workers. What else can the judge want from him? Delaying his conversation with Adam, the judge is weighting it with more purpose than a simple "checking in" requires. He fully expects the man to spin around, point a finger, and . . . And what, Adam doesn't allow himself to imagine.

"Have you learned any humility yet?" The judge has indeed spun around; although he isn't pointing a finger, he does hold a massive law tome out as if it were a Bible and Adam was expected to swear on it.

Adam flushes with anger. He hears the singing in his ears; he feels the sway of rising blood pressure rock him. He breathes deeply. He breathes again. He tastes the iron on his tongue and swallows. "I believe that Carmondy's report will tell you that I'm performing my duties well and with a good attitude." Big Bob has shared his report with Adam, at least his one-paragraph evaluation. He cites Adam's willingness to help in ways that go beyond his job description, and they both know that's spin on his grumbling obedience to Bob in finding Jupe and at least trying to locate Jupe's dog.

"Hmm." Judge Johnson motions to the folding chair opposite his desk.

Adam lowers himself.

"I suppose you think that I should commute your sentence? That six months of good behavior is enough?"

Adam clears his throat. "No. I don't."

This clearly surprises the judge. "Why?"

"I mean that I don't believe you will." Adam pinches the crease in his trousers, crosses one leg over the other in a deliberately casual manner. He understands this man. He knows that the judge would prefer him to be more of a supplicant, that he kowtow in the manner of a man who has seen the light. As he probably should. There is nothing more Adam wants than to be released from his community service. It's taking up far too much of his time, time he should be spending focusing on the consulting business he believes will lead to a good living. He just has to get his first client, who will then recommend him to more clients. An infinite chain of clients all leading to a new brand of success.

Ishmael and Rafe joked with him yesterday. "Won't see you here again; you'll be outta here faster than Big Brown out the gate on Derby day."

"I'll send you a postcard." He was surprised at the fleeting moment of nostalgia that stung his throat. Adam assuaged his momentary self-indulgence with a mental promise to make sure his charitable giving included the Fort Street Center from now on, or at least once he began to recover from his personal recession. "Besides, it's not even on the table that I get off. Don't take my name off the locker just yet." But, even as he said it, Adam knew that he was whistling through the graveyard.

Which is the same reason he's shown up in the judge's chambers in his best suit, with his Cole Haan oxfords spit-polished and, just for effect, his battered briefcase with the mileage scuffed into its leather. Men like Judge Johnson belong to the same golf club Adam does, or did. Sterling got the membership. Men like Judge Johnson attend the same dinner parties and charity galas as Adam, eat the same hors d'oeuvres and drink the same overpriced wines. Except that Adam hasn't seen an hors d'oeuvre in nearly a year, and his solitary drink of choice remains scotch.

It's why he's challenging the judge, calling his bluff. In any other arena, Adam would be Judge Johnson's peer. They'd laugh over drinks and debate economic strategy. Adam wonders if the judge understands this.

The judge sits heavily into his high-backed black chair. He leans forward, his elbows on the blotter in front of him, studying Adam over the frame of his Buddy Holly glasses. His rheumy eyes are unreadable.

Adam picks a dog hair from his knee. A news brief in the local paper announced that the shelter has reopened. Maybe later today he'll make another attempt at getting rid of the dog. He's tried other shelters, but they don't want what he has. At the only one he got to that would, the staffer was blunt. These dogs don't get adopted out; the ones who have fought, they get a one-way ticket. "The pit bulls who are voluntarily surrendered are humanely euthanized." Voluntarily surrendered. Adam had dragged the dog back to his car, frustrated but not cruel. He doesn't want the dog, but he isn't going to be responsible for its death. Adam thinks about Gina. He saw her walking down the street this morning, a trio of deerlike greyhounds gliding beside her. He got his latest bag of dog food from Stop & Shop; if there's any left over, he'll donate it to the shelter when he takes the dog back.

Adam thinks, or maybe prays, that the judge will free him.

"You're right. You've made an improvement, but you're going to finish out your sentence. I'll see you in September. Make an appointment with my secretary on your way out."

The judge cracks open the massive law book, pushes his glasses up into place, and forgets that Adam was ever in the room.

The foyer door sticks a little and Adam kicks it open with the toe of his three-hundred-dollar shoes. He mounts the stairs, his pace slowing to a trudge by the time he reaches the third-floor landing. The weight of his sentence bears down on him. The seemingly endless months of servile punishment, the complication of trying to get his self-employment up and running, and the grip that the Fort Street Center has on his life bear down on Adam step by step, until he thinks he cannot move. He didn't know how much he was counting on release from his community service until it was denied him. He's been picturing himself a free man, ready to take his rightful place in society. He's learned a lesson; he's working on his humility. He'll be back in the saddle, his powers restored to him fully within the next six months. Except that he'll still be serving swill to the homeless. Well, not swill exactly; Rafe would take great exception to that term. Rafe. Ishmael. Mike and Big Bob. Christ, they all but gave him a going-away party. Even they thought he was rehabilitated.

The dog waits, as always, sitting in the dead center of the room, as if he hasn't spent the intervening hours on the futon. The rearranged throw pillows with the deep depressions in them are enough of a clue, but he always pretends innocence, bowing and yawning like some sort of slave to his potentate. Every day, Adam asks, "Have you been on the couch?" And every day, the dog just wags his spiky tail and grins in a "Who me?" masquerade.

Today, Adam doesn't even look at the dog. He drops his briefcase on the floor, pulls off his fine wool topcoat and drops it on the dog hair–strewn futon, yanks at the tie at his throat, and goes into the galley kitchen. The Dewar's liter is half-empty. There is a dirty glass on the side of the sink and Adam takes it. Without even rinsing out the dregs of last night's drink, he is about to pour two inches of scotch into the glass, when his cell phone rings. Adam sees that it's Ariel and he sets the empty glass down. "Hi, honey."

"Can I skip out on you Saturday? Taylor's having a big birthday party at the Copley and we're all going early to shop. I really want—"

"Okay. Go. Have fun, and tell Taylor happy birthday for me." Adam presses the end key even before his daughter can say thank you. She's adept at finding reasons not to spend Saturdays with him, and this is just one more he won't ever get back.

Then Sterling calls. At some point in the last year, their lawyers have stepped out of the middle and she has found it possible to call and badger him with regularity. Perhaps she is even finding pleasure in it.

There is no preamble, no easing into a conversation with Sterling these days. She simply jumps into the topic, like a missile, allowing him no moment of transition from "Hello" to "I want." It is almost like she doesn't want to allow him to speak, that something in his voice might remind her of their life together. Once upon a time, when they spoke on the phone, they listened to each other. They signed off from every conversation with some affectionate postscript: "Love you," or "I'll be home soon," or "Miss you." Now it's the sound of a dial tone. Dismissed.

Worse, once she's gotten the demands out of the way, Adam knows that she'll start reciting his flaws to him: his temper, his untrustworthiness, his destroying her life. Meaning her social standing, which, as far as he can see, hasn't dipped on the sociometer one bit. She's taken their friends with her. She still has the houses. She still chairs the charity events that make the evening news.

Sterling calls only to arrange things to her own advantage, to demand something of him, to treat him as if he were an underling. He has so disappointed her that she is taking it out on him one phone call at a time.

So it is with great reluctance that Adam presses the answer button. Instead of the woman with whom Adam expected to spend the rest of his life, Sterling has become a sledgehammer, beating him over the head with his sins at every chance.

This time, she belabors Ariel's sudden need for her own car. She's taking her driver's test in a month, and Sterling believes that every sixteen-year-old should be given a car for her birthday, a Miata or a Volvo. Something safe, something prestigious. Something that will be the envy of everyone else's sixteen-year-old daughters.

Somewhere along the line, Adam has tuned Sterling's voice out. She is like a buzzing bee, or the chime of someone else's cell phone. Annoying, but hard to swat away. He holds the cell phone away from his ear and wanders around the small apartment. He straightens up one of the throw pillows the dog has flattened out. He rinses the dirty jelly glass, fills it with water. Little words, miniaturized by the phone held at a distance, like some tiny Sterling trapped in the flat oblong of his phone, keeps *zzzzing* through the instrument. He hears individual words; a phrase here and there comes out of the phone with unexpected clarity. They should consider something that might haul the horse trailer that they should invest in if Ariel is going to attend the major shows.

Adam dumps the glass of water into the dog's bowl and unscrews the cap from the bottle of scotch.

Little Sterling's little buzzing voice is farther and farther away. The cell phone is on the countertop. His glass is filled with scotch. There is a moment of silence. Then he hears her miniature voice calling out from the instrument, wondering if he is still there. He doesn't know. Is he? Still there? The Adam that he once was? He can't afford to buy a full tank of gas, much less a high-priced vehicle for a kid who treats him with as much contempt as Ariel does. She doesn't need the latest status symbol, the latest keeping-up-with-the-Joneses item on the list. The idea that their little princess might be deprived is ludicrous. Adam knows about deprived. Deprived is not getting new sneakers when your toes are coming through the old ones.

Adam presses the end button hard enough to shut the phone off completely. Gently he puts it on the counter, pours another finger of scotch into his almost full jelly glass, and goes into the living room.

The truth is, if things had remained the same, if he hadn't scuttled his own life with the auger of fear and temper, he would have loved shopping for a car for Ariel. He would have relished the delight on her face at the sight of a brand-new Volvo or Miata, or whatever was the coolest ride these days, in the driveway with a big bow on it. He wouldn't have deprived Ariel for all the world.

A bubble of anxiety juxtaposes itself against the lead weight of despair; he's not free of Fort Street. How is he ever going to get beyond this descent into poverty? Not since he was an undergraduate driving buses far into the night in order to pay for his education has Adam debated the cost of national brand cornflakes against the store brand. Not since he was in his first year of graduate school has Adam let a bill sit unopened, or paid the minimum due.

The table, under which the dog has ducked, only the tip of his tail exposed, is covered with unopened bills, along with a laptop he is too tired to open, too tired to use to troll the online job searches. Too tired to think.

Adam sips his jelly glass of scotch. The burn diminishes with each swallow.

Chapter Twenty-nine

It was a little awkward to witness, his whimpering like that. Then the full-blown crying. I'd never witnessed something like that in a human. Plenty of my own kind howl, but this was painful to hear. He'd stopped playing with his toy, after which he began shouting so that I hid myself beneath the table. If he started making sounds like that, I wasn't going to hang around. I knew what an angry human could do. I wasn't committed to being here. First chance, I was going to book it. Frankly, I had no idea why I was here in the first place. We weren't training. He wasn't putting me into the pit. He barely acknowledged my presence. I kept to my side of the room; he kept to his. There was none of that pair-bond stuff going on like I'd seen with my mentor and his man, or the guy and the little bitch that helped me get free of that pole, or even the Labrador and his person.

He got quiet. Very quiet. He sat on the futon with his drink in his hand and stared out at the empty room until I put myself into his view just to give him something to look at. Long tears ran from his open eyes to the edges of his face. He sipped and wept. Sipped and wept. I lay on the rug but kept my eyes on him.

When his glass was empty, he lay down, but the sounds didn't cease. Finally I got up, stretched east and west, shook myself, and then sat. If he'd stopped making the sounds, I might have just wandered off. But the sounds went on, a primal sound of despair, of great anguish. Not like a rabbit in a cat's jaws, or even like the losers in the pit. This was more like the howls of those who ended up in the shelter with me, the ones who were lost, separated from their humans, unable to fend for themselves. The sound of abandonment. Not unlike the sad moan of my mentor when he realized he wasn't going to be reunited with his man. Or even a little like the sound I made myself when he was taken beyond the door at the end of the hall.

What else could I have done? I'm only canine, I had to help. I pushed myself up beside him, nosing his hand until it reached for my ears, until I felt his fingers slide along the edges of my good ear, and then I did it. I nuzzled him. I stuck the tip of my nose against his cheek and touched his face with my tongue. He tasted salty. Not a bad flavor. He didn't push me away, so I pressed myself closer, edging against him until we shared the futon. He draped an arm over my back and pressed his face against mine. And then we slept.

Chapter Thirty

Adam dreams that he is walking through a busy hallway. There is something he has to do, but he can't remember what it is. His arms are heavy with the weight of something he cannot see. He is bumped right and left by the crowd of people walking in the opposite direction. He wakes with a start.

The dog has managed to press him against the back of the futon, his whole body stretched out alongside Adam's, his boxy muzzle tucked into Adam's neck, the moist dog breath tickling him. Adam struggles against the weight of the dog to sit up. Abruptly, the dog dismounts from the futon, stretches, and yawns. "At least one of us has had a decent sleep." The dog, clearly pleased at his piracy, shakes vigorously and sits in front of Adam.

Adam strokes the dog's head, noticing just how soft it is. The bone of his skull is rock-hard beneath his hand, but his short brindled coat is as soft and smooth as silk. Adam does it again. The dog opens his mouth and grins, makes a little chuffing noise; his tail ticks back and forth on the floor. "You are one ugly dog." Adam's tone soothes the dog into raptures. "I should call you Uggie, boy." The dog stands up, whipping his tail in excitement at Adam's compliments.

"The shelter is open again, you know? Dr. Gil left me a message."

The dog begins to dance on his forefeet. Excited at this unusual conversation.

"You ready to go back?"

Hunnha hunnha.

"Maybe tomorrow."

Adam gets to his feet. The sky beyond his window is dark, and Adam is uncertain of the time. It could be evening or the dark of predawn. He feels as if he's been run over. The jelly glass is upended beside the futon. Adam checks the microwave clock. Three in the morning. He hasn't let the dog out. He hasn't fed him.

The last of the February nights is cold, clear, and astoundingly silent. Adam takes the dog for a complete walk around the block, letting the piercingly cold air clear out his own lungs and fuzzy brain. It is so quiet, so still, Adam lets the dog off the leash to sniff around an empty lot. The only traffic is a slow police car; the only other soul, the lone cop. He looks directly at Adam, rolls down the window, appearing almost glad of an interruption in his rounds.

"Just walking the dog." Adam holds up the leash.

"Leash laws here."

"I know. Thought I'd flaunt them a little."

The cop smiles and drives off.

The dog is gone a long time, and suddenly Adam wonders if he'll come back. What if he bolts? What if, having been a street dog, he thinks Adam has just set him free? Adam has never let him off the leash before, and he has no way of knowing if the animal will come even if he calls. Adam strains to listen, to see if he can pinpoint where the dog is in the half-acre empty lot. He's disappeared. Run off. Adam pictures the empty bowls on his kitchen floor.

Adam gathers the leash into a coil. He can't even call the dog; he's nameless. He's had the animal for almost three weeks and has refused to call him anything but "boy" or "buddy" or "you." Refused to consider him anything more than an annoying houseguest. "Come, boy. Here, buddy."

The feel of his soft coat was like satin beneath Adam's fingers. The softest thing he's touched since Ariel's baby skin.

In the distance, the sound of snuffling.

"Hey, boy!"

From out of the darkness comes the dog, tail wagging.

An unaccountable sense of relief flows through Adam, and his hand is shaking a little as he clips the leash to the collar. "Good boy." He pats the dog on the head.

Adam goes into the bathroom and pees, brushes his teeth quickly, and pulls off his sweatshirt and jeans, which he drops into a basket he's stuck in the bathroom for dirty laundry. He climbs into his unmade bed. He lies still, then calls the dog. "You coming?"

His last thought before falling into a deep sleep is that he can't imagine what Gina will say if he tells her he's keeping the dog. The dog that is snoring at the foot of his bed. But, somehow, it comforts him to think that she might approve.

Chapter Thirty-one

I almost didn't come to his call. I was loose for the first time in a long time and I honestly thought that's what he intended when he took off the leash. We'd communicated, him through touching me with his hands, me with touching him with my nose. A piece of the barrier that we both respected lowered a little bit. Like unrelated puppies, we slumbered on, tangled up, one with the other. So when he let me go, I thought that was his way of acknowledging that I should strike out on my own once again. Our time together—for what purpose, I still didn't get—was done.

We went outside in the night, the neighborhood around us quiet as only city neighborhoods can be when the people are inside and the cars are furtive. The night animals, the mouse and rat, the city raccoon and skunk, lurked around every corner, but I ignored them, attached as I was on the end of the leash. Not much point in it.

There were no other dogs around; no scent more recent than that afternoon collided with my searching nose. I marked fresh territory. When we got to the empty place and the man unsnapped the leash, I took it that he was releasing me. Well and good, I thought. Fair enough. He's served me fairly well, and I've behaved myself. Now is the time to scoot. Go find that warm shelter beneath a bush, tuck my nose under my tail, and let go of this soft life of bed and kibble. We're done. Shake hands all around and cheerio.

I headed out into the dark, quartering the empty place, checking for the signs of other dogs, the warm smell of vole, of future meals. I became intoxicated with the odors of free creatures. Feces told me of scavengers and gourmets, of those who fed themselves, and those who enjoyed the servitude of humans, the easy dependability of scheduled meals.

Like I'd been enjoying for this little while. I knew that un-likely show of submission on his part wasn't to be mistaken for subservience. I wasn't going to fall for a pathetic belly-up as total submission. No sirree. We'd kept it simple: He fed me; I was pleasant enough. I didn't owe him anything. Con-versely, he didn't owe me anything, either. I felt sorry for him in that moment, that's all. He was grieving, and I offered a momentary solace. That didn't mean we were ever going to be partners.

I heard his voice, understood the meaning, if not the words. A pat on the leg, a low whistle. I continued quartering, but I was torn between freedom and a warm place to sleep. Images of old pals and trash cans insinuated themselves into my thoughts as I found traces of both beneath the hard-packed snow.

He called again, a little louder, a little more concerned. Had I misunderstood? Had he been only allowing me a little pri-vacy, a little decision-making latitude? I raised my head, stood as still as a pointer on mark. A sharpish breeze caught at the scraps of paper nestled among the ragged hills of iced-over snow, lifting them into eddies. I shivered. I really didn't have to sleep rough tonight. I could just go with him. Take the leash.

Come, boy. Here, buddy.

There was nothing in my experience that led me to believe that human beings were ever trustworthy. When I lived in the cellar, the boys who handled us could be pleasant enough, especially when I was winning. Or, with no warning, they could also kick us across the room. Why should I deem a comfortable moment between us a harbinger of a better life and not some anomaly? What did he mean by letting me go and then making those petulant noises? An assertion of pack leadership? No, I'd keep myself to myself. Pick the pack I wanted to belong to.

It was when he went quiet that I heard what he meant. In the absolute stillness of the winter night, I heard him sigh, a sound of capitulation, of disappointment.

I went back to him. Greeted him in the spirit of compromise. Attach your leash to my collar for now. I'll wait till spring to book it.

Good boy.

Chapter Thirty-two

Adam feels a surge of jitters as he snaps the leash to the dog's collar. The hand-painted parrot is turned over to the WELCOME side and the lights are on in Gina's store. It feels as though those little fish that swim across the rainbow of her storefront are in his belly. He's only recently gotten it: the A to Z tropical fish on her window are angelfish and zebra fish. He's tried not to stand in his own window as much, still smarting from Gina's remark about his life. Well, he's about to show her that he can make changes if he wants. He's talked to Stein about this, about this irrational need to explain himself to a woman he has no relationship with, or, worse, who is an antagonistic acquaintance. Stein wants him to examine his motivations.

Gina didn't talk him into keeping the dog. It was his decision, and one he's going to have to live with, or live to regret, for a long time. He wants to make it clear to Gina that while he is committed to keeping the dog, she hasn't shamed him into it; and to get some advice on training. This business of lurching at every passing dog on the street has got to stop. Maybe she can recommend another book.

"Come on." He still hasn't named the animal. Each time a name comes to him, he auditions it to see if the dog will respond. At this point, Boy is the most likely one. The dog neither comes to nor obeys any softly spoken word. Adam has gone through the little book on pit bulls, but it hasn't provided much guidance. So, for now, it's all intuitive. When he picks up the empty bowl, the dog comes. When he rattles the leash, the dog goes to the door. Any sudden movement, like when he cracked his shin on the coffee table and let out a yelp, startles the dog back into his hiding place beneath the table. This is not Rin Tin Tin. This is not Lassie. This isn't even Marmaduke.

"Let's go see Gina."

The year has tripped over into March, but the air is still pure winter. It is just the time of year when warmer weather is impossible to imagine. The men at the Fort Street Center are hardened by this weather, cheeks and lips chapped and noses blue-veined and reddened along the edges. They take the plastic trays hot from the Hobart out of the rack and hold them close. They wear layers of clothing, castoffs donated to the Salvation Army or directly to the center. A big cardboard box sits in the foyer, where donors can drop off unwanted clothing. These days, it's pretty much empty; anything wearable is on someone's body.

Gina is standing framed in the doorway as they cross the street, and for an instant Adam thinks that she's been waiting for him. She turns away; whoever she's been watching for hasn't come. Of course she's not waiting for him.

. . .

The parrots squawk a reasonable imitation of a greeting as Adam and the dog enter the shop. Gina is standing with a fishnet in one hand. Despite the cold outside, the shop is warm and she is wearing a short sleeved, button-front white blouse that fits her shape and leaves a lovely triangle at the base of her throat. Her hair is down, softly grazing her shoulders. She doesn't look like a shopgirl; she looks like she may have a date after work. There is a drop of water clinging to her wrist.

When she sees that it is Adam and the dog standing in the middle of her small shop, she hangs the dripping fishnet on a hook and folds her arms across her middle. She doesn't smile, but her expressive brows arc into question marks. "Thought that shelter was open again."

Adam leans over and runs his hand down the length of the dog's body. The dog's tail swings gently side to side, but his eyes are on Gina. "I'm going to keep him." He waits, his own eyes on Gina's face, his lips parted in expectation of her reaction. He waits to see if the hostility with which she usually looks at him will, even for an instant, abate.

"What made you change your mind?" Suspicious, not approving.

Adam shrugs, a gesture nearly lost in the bulk of his jacket. "I don't know. Things." He is disappointed, feels like a kid with an underappreciated crayon drawing. "Got used to him."

Very slowly, reluctantly, a smile comes to Gina's lips. "If you want my opinion, I think you're doing the right thing."

The disappointment lifts; he has no idea why he wants Gina to be nice to him, but he just does, and even this mild approval feels nice. "I was hoping you'd say that. I still think I'm a little crazy." The dog sits, drops his jaw into a cavernous yawn.

"Have you called Dr. Gil? To let him know?"

"No. Why should I?"

"He's going to want to know. Given your"—she hesitates—"peculiar circumstances, you may want to make sure he understands that you're committed to keeping him."

"All right."

Gina reaches for a dog biscuit. "What are you going to call him?" She holds out the biscuit; the dog takes it out of her fingers like a gentleman.

"For the moment, the default name seems to be Boy."

"No. No good. Every male dog on the planet gets called Boy at least half the time. You want something that will distinguish him from the pack."

"Like being a pit bull isn't enough?"

"No. You're giving him a chance at a new life, a new identity."

"Witness protection program for dogs?"

"Something like that. It's not going to be easy, I hope that you're planning on working hard with him."

Adam has not planned any such thing, fairly satisfied with things as they are. Except for the aggression on the street. "I need to get him so he doesn't pull my arms off every time we meet another dog."

"He's been taught that. He can be taught something else."

"I sure hope so."

"I've got a few business cards from dog whisperers. Let me see if I can find them." Gina disappears behind the counter.

"When did trainers become whisperers? This guy is pretty tough; I may need to shout at him."

Gina stands up. "That's something you can't do. Really. He's got to be convinced that gentle is better."

Adam recalls the dog's quick bolt under the kitchen table

every time he raises his voice on the phone, or at the opposing team's interceptions on Sunday afternoon. "Yeah, he's evidently the strong, sensitive type."

"Don't kid. He probably is. These dogs are made, not born, that way."

"I'm not so sure about that, but time will tell." Adam takes the business cards from Gina, flips through the little collection. He knows that he can't afford a dog trainer, but he plays along. "Which one would you recommend?"

"They're all good. But you should start with K-Nine Etiquette. He's very good with problem animals." She sets her olive eyes on Adam. For the first time, there is something besides disdain in them. "I really think that there's hope for him."

Adam can discern a willingness to be nice, or maybe just a willingness to see that he isn't all bad. That maybe there is hope for him.

"Maybe you should call him Chance. You're giving him one. And I think he's maybe giving you a chance, too." Gina blushes a little, a slow pinking of the little exposed triangle at the base of her throat

"Chance of what?"

Gina turns away, picks up the fishnet, and goes back to moving fish. Whatever she is thinking, she's not saying, and Adam wonders if maybe she's embarrassed herself with her presumption.

"Chance. Yeah. Maybe. You like that one? Hey, Chance."

The dog, who has been poking his nose into the fish-food display, cocks his head at Adam and his satchel mouth breaks open in a doggy smile.

"I think he likes it."

Gina hangs up the little net again and comes close enough

to Adam that he can smell the light floral scent of her shampoo. She bends over the dog. "Looks like we have a winner." She strokes the dog on his bulky head and then touches Adam's forearm. "You're doing a good thing."

Now it is his turn to blush. He likes that touch, so simple, so human. It exposes a loneliness that is the central theme of his life.

Chapter Thirty-three

The fur between my shoulder blades rose even before I could thoroughly identify the scent. In a completely instinctive response, I growled. Low and warning. Not my usual style. It wasn't another dog trespassing into the restricted territory defined by the length of my leash; it was them. The boys. The ones who had kept me and my parents in that cellar, dragging us out only to compete, or breed, or train. I could feel the pulse of hostility stir my heart. Was this deliberate, this crossing of paths? Was this when my sojourn living in daylight would end?

Lately, my man had been talking to me, repeating words over and over until I twigged to their meaning. It was quite fun, and the reward of a Milk-Bone was enough to keep me engaged in the process for whole minutes at a time. None of it bore any resemblance to the training of the boys, which required sticks and chains. We did run a bit now that the streets were finally bare of snow. Nothing terribly challenging, a little quarter-mile jog through the park, around the little lake. He huffed and puffed at the end of it, while I had barely begun to pant. Either my stamina was as good as ever or his was poop.

Once in a while I came out from under the table to sit with him while he played with his toys. He'd even become somewhat generous with his own food, a bite of meat here, a lick of the plate there. Just enough to keep me off balance in my estimation of him.

He spoke one of those words to me now. *Chance.* Then *Quiet.* Two words that had been repeated enough I knew that the first identified me to him, or maybe the second one. They were often linked together: *Chancequiet.* I could feel a little tremor in the leash, telegraphing itself down to me. A firmer vibration of concern, of quickening steps.

I didn't want to stop long enough to get reacquainted, so I started to pull on the leash. He didn't pull me back, tighten that collar around my neck with a jerk like he did when I spoke to others on the street. Looked like my man didn't want to stop, either. We both knew that no good could come of it. The scent of the boys, the sound of their feet on the pavement made me nervous. I didn't want to fight their battles anymore.

Then he stopped in his tracks. The boys were in front of us now, their voices and their postures speaking challenge.

Was this guy going to fight me, when he'd done such a poor job of conditioning me? Or hand me over to these boys and let them put me back in the cellar? I'd be hardly better than a bait dog, which made me think of all the bait dogs I'd trained with—okay, savaged. These boys wouldn't be pleased with me when they found out it would only be self-defense in the pit for me, not physical superiority. They'd tape my jaws shut and let the others have me for lunch.

I realized then that I had fallen into the trap of household pets. I was comfortable, and these old caretakers represented a return to a very uncomfortable life. I pressed myself against his legs, imploring—I'm not proud of it—imploring him to keep the leash in his hand. Don't give me back. Maybe I don't want to be a pet, but I sure didn't want to go back to that cellar. I still planned on making a strike for independence, but not till it suited me. Not yet. Not to my old life, but to the life of a free dog.

Chapter Thirty-four

"Hey, man. Where you get that dog?" Two young men come out of a doorway. They are dressed in loose clothing, dwarfed by their massive black sweatshirts, which bear a famous footwear logo. Their hats, also black, are cocked at a jaunty angle, hoods pulled up over those against the chill air. On their feet are dazzlingly white athletic shoes. One boy is wearing sunglasses that give him an Adam Ant look. The other has a chain draped from his belt to his back pocket. It clinks a little as he saunters in Adam's direction, the volume of his pants forcing him to swagger to keep them from falling down.

"Breeder." It's the first thing that comes to mind.

"Look like my dog. My dog was stolen. You know anything about that?"

"No." Adam wonders what the fuck he's doing in this end of town. He's been walking the dog for an hour, mindful of the training book's admonition to keep dogs exercised. He's actually been enjoying the enforced activity, and with his thoughts keeping time to their walking pace, he's ended up six blocks past the demilitarized zone of the center. He's forgotten to turn around. Adam believes that he is not a prejudiced man, but this is beyond his comfort zone. A white man walking a pit bull sticks out in this neighborhood.

"You maybe lookin' for something?" This is spoken sotto voce by the young man not wearing the blocky sunglasses. His face, framed in the giant hood, is tilted. His eyes are almost friendly. "For some action?"

"No. Just taking my dog for a walk."

"Could maybe get you into somethin' if you want."

"I don't want anything." Adam is flanked. The dog is standing with his head lowered, his yellow-brown eyes raised, his hackles raised. His tail stands straight out like the magnetic needle on a compass; his feet are planted on the soiled sidewalk. He makes an intermittent vocalization that might be a growl, or a protest. A chuffing sound of anxiety.

"Hey, fella, how you doin'?" The kid with the sunglasses reaches down toward the dog, fingers snapping. The dog growls, shrinks behind Adam's legs.

"He look like a fighter to me. You sure you doan want a little action?"

"He's a pet."

"Doan look like no pet. Got that scar there."

"He's a pet." Adam squeezes out from between the tall youths. They step closer to the dog.

The dog lowers his head, his eyes on their faces; the soft skin around his muzzle quivers and then curls, exposing his teeth. Both boys back up.

Terrified suddenly that his dog will actually bite, Adam turns on his heel, yanks the dog around to follow.

One Good Dog • 193

"Sure look like my dog. Dawg." The boys laugh and enter the convenience store.

"Who were you defending back there?" Adam has covered six blocks in six minutes. A Starbucks is on this block, one with outdoor seating even in the winter. They'll stop there, catch their breath, and calm down with a splurge. Double mocha latte in the largest investment-quality size available. "Me or you? Did you know those kids?"

The dog shakes himself and settles down on the sidewalk. Inscrutable.

It is conceivable that they were telling the truth. Gina has said this dog looks like he'd been fought, but then why did he act nervous in front of them if he knew them? The reason suddenly seems obvious. "Did they hurt you?" Adam kneels down on one knee, draws the dog's face to his own. "Did they make you fight?" The sound of laughter as two people walk out of Starbucks brings Adam back to his feet, embarrassed to be seen talking to a dog. Inside, he buys a biscotti, which he will share with Chance.

As they sit there, Adam's pulse slowly returning to normal, the sweet latte improving his mood, a woman passes by on the street. She looks at Chance. The look on her face is one of nerves, as if the dog might leap out at her. Fear blunts her middle-aged face, fear of a breed's reputation, and her path swings wide of where they sit.

Adam recognizes an expression he has seen before, one that once gave him a secret satisfaction. There is a twinge of the pain in his ribs; he takes in a sharp breath. Was he really so bad, so intimidating? Had he mistaken fear for respect? He had often boasted that he didn't need his people to like him, only to do what he required. When he required it. There wasn't one employee, not peer, but underling, who called him anything but Mr. March. There wasn't one worker who shared baby pictures with him even if he walked by as the new dad was showing them to coworkers. There wasn't one person whose job was owed to Adam's proficiency at his own job who sent him a Christmas card.

The end of the biscotti disappears into the maw of the dog, who crunches it with loud abandon. Adam is chilled, sitting on the metal chair as the temperature falls. He has no doubt that the look on his own face when confronted by those gangstas had shown the same wash of fear, fear of those who have control of the moment, of those who will decide the next action.

The phantom pain twinges again and he takes another shallow breath. The dog looks up at him, his yellow-brown eyes hopeful of another chunk of biscotti, the encounter on the sidewalk forgotten. "Time to go home."

Chapter Thirty-five

Rafe is singing along to Tracy Chapman on his iPod, his voice seriously under pitch. "Talkin' about a revolution, yah yah yah." Today he's concocted a meat loaf with brown gravy, his signature garlic mashed potatoes, and a salad tossed in a bowl the size of a try-pot on a whaling ship. This has become one of Adam's favorite meals, which surprises him, as meat loaf, like liver, was a dish forbidden in the March home. Too many meals in his youth featured meat loaf, extended with fillers of bread or cereal, doctored with ketchup. But Rafe's version of the dish could be served in any of the upscale restaurants Adam once patronized, and he tells Rafe this.

"You say so, man? Go on. This recipe belonged to my granny, who got it from hers and so on, back to when our people brought it over on the slave ship."

"Rafe, your hyperbole is matched only by your skill with a spatula." Adam unties the long white apron from around his waist, tosses it into the laundry bin.

The center's chef plugs his ear bud back into his ear, but he is smiling.

Adam is in a good mood. Two things have cheered him up immensely. The first, a client—his first step toward breaking out from under the crushing debt he has incurred since losing his job and his assets. The second, the fact that Ariel actually initiated a telephone call to him. She wants to come spend the weekend with him, unprompted. This is a first, and Adam is fighting a rising suspicion that it isn't about spending time with him, but about annoying her mother. Lately, Sterling has complained that Ariel is acting out. Her usual friends are absent and the new kids she hangs out with Sterling has deemed quite unsuitable. Adam has defended Ariel, chalking it up to adolescent rebellion, but Sterling, in a rare moment of unguardedness with him, wouldn't shrug it off, fretting that there's something going on, something beyond normal growing pains. Sterling tells Adam that Ariel wants to give up riding all of a sudden. Her grades are falling; she didn't try out for the lacrosse team. And yesterday, she came back from town with a stud through her nose.

Adam thinks about Ariel's form of defiance and Veronica's sixties version. Nose rings versus miniskirts. Normal adolescent disrespect versus complete disappearance.

With everything in the center's kitchen all shipshape, Adam shrugs into his coat, pockets the package of meat loaf Rafe is sending home to Chance, and bids his coworkers to have a good weekend. He's in a hurry; the rest of his day will be spent honing the client's business plan. A start-up company, three baby-faced entrepreneurs who have managed to raise a million dollars from friends and family to start a business designing skateboard parks. They hope to be the Rees Jones of skateboarders, and Adam plans to leave the suit coat and tie at home when he makes this presentation Monday afternoon. Then he has to plan some meals for Ariel's visit. This time, he will resist the temptation to take her to a place he can't afford; he'll cook instead. He's learning a lot from Rafe, although proportions have been a little challenging and he's overdosed more than once on a lasagna that lasted for a week. And Chance needs his daily constitutional.

It's been awhile since Adam watched Judge Judy.

At half-past five, the park is beginning to empty out, and Adam finds this is the best time to take his dog out for some exercise. They run around the man-made lake at the center, then cool out walking along the path that loops gently through the gardens. It is still too early for flowers, but there is a certain tinge of pinky green, a hint of reanimation in the bare branches above their heads. The brindled dog lopes along beside Adam, his lolling tongue giving him a cheerful look. As they slow to a walk, Adam plays out more of the leash and lets Chance do his doggy thing along the freshly edged, if empty, gardens.

As Adam and Chance come up over a short rise, Gina appears with her three greyhounds. They both stop at a distance, uncertain about the dogs, about Chance.

"Let me get them leashed." Gina calls her dogs, who all look like antlerless deer to Adam. He glances down at Chance and is relieved to see the dog's tail wagging ever so slightly. Is he happy to see Gina, or is he okay with the three tall dogs? Very slowly, everyone comes together on the narrow path. Noses are working, tails begin to wag, no hostility. The greyhounds move like dignitaries, circling Chance, winding their leashes into a braid, until Gina has to spin to free herself from the maypole dance of the four dogs, a graceful movement, accompanied by her laughter.

Chance tolerates the inquisition. No lurching. No growling. No lifted lips. "Good boy, Chance." Adam thumps him on the ribs. The tail continues to wag.

"He's coming along, isn't he?"

"Yeah. He's definitely getting better about other dogs."

An awkward moment passes between them. What they have is a lack of definition. They have exchanged harsh words, and shared a cup of tea. She's observed him; he's watched her. But what did that make them: the kind of acquaintances who turn around on a walk to join each other, or the ones who keep going? Passing acquaintances? If circumstances were different, if she hadn't been on the egg-throwing side of a long-ago controversy, would she like him? Adam is flummoxed by the thoughts darting around his head as he looks for something neutral to say.

"Well, nice to see you." Gina gathers the three leashes into her left hand. She looks like a chariot driver, the tall, pale dogs fanned in front of her. "Bye, bye, Chance."

"I'm heading out. Is it okay if I walk with you?" Adam twitches the leash and Chance moves closer to his side. "It's good for him to be around other dogs."

Gina nods. "Sure." Not hostile, not warm. If he was to attribute any adjective to her response, it might be *cautious*. He is disheartened. By this time, she shouldn't be so grudging with her friendship—willing to give him a good reference for Dr. Gil, unwilling to forget about his connection to Dynamic Industries.

They walk in the direction of the entrance to the park with its wrought-iron gates. The silence is not exactly comfortable; neither is it intolerable. They both keep their attention on the dogs. Keep the dogs between them. But it is the lingering memory of her touch on his arm that emboldens him to keep pace with her, not to say "Nice to see you, too" and speed on his way.

Gina is first to break the silence. "Who did you finally decide on as a trainer?"

"No one. The truth is, I can't afford a trainer. At least not at the moment." Adam considers that Gina might think it strange that a man like himself can't afford something like dog training, and he almost adds that his daughter's horse trainer is enough trainer for him. But he doesn't. He waits to hear what Gina might say.

"There are training tapes. You can get them out of the library." If she is curious, Gina doesn't betray it.

"Good idea. Although he's got 'Sit' pretty well learned. And 'Come.' We're definitely doing better on 'Come.' 'Stay off the futon' is not so good."

"But not attacking other dogs is. I see some improvement there."

"Sort of. Today is a good day."

"Lucky for my guys."

"Lucky for me."

They have reached the gates. Gina stops at a Prius parked nearby. "Why don't you come by and pick out a dog bed for him? That may help with the futon issues."

"I will."

"I have some that aren't very expensive."

"I'm sure I can swing a dog bed."

Gina unlocks her car door and the three greyhounds jump in, only to collapse around one another on the backseat. She doesn't offer Adam a lift. Nonetheless, Adam smiles as he picks up the pace for home.

Chapter Thirty-six

If Ariel is disappointed that they are not going out for one of their fancy meals, she has the good grace to hide it. In fact, she's quite agreeable, and there is no sign of her iPod or her cell phone. Adam feels like he should be either suspicious or ecstatic. Maybe she's just growing up, he thinks. Maybe the anger is starting to wear off. She is sixteen, tall and willowy. Her physical resemblance to Veronica is heightened by the way she's wearing her hair, not pulled back into a messy knot, nor in those slightly suggestive little-girl ponytails sported by some of the girls he sees walking to school in his neighborhood. Today her blond hair is loose; ripples of natural wave keep it from being plain. A thick cream-colored scarf is around her neck, and she wears a black lambskin jacket over her designer jeans. He can see the tiny faceted stone in the side of her nose, twinkling in the sunlight like a ruby red mole. It's not as bad as he imagined. Surely the hole will close up once she outgrows this need to mutilate herself in the name of fashion. In the meantime, he's learning how to look at her face without looking at the stud. The effect of all of this is that she doesn't look sixteen. She looks older, and he knows that is precisely what she hopes.

Sterling wants him to talk to Ariel about her friends, behavior, attitude, and blowing off schoolwork and reminded him of that when he picked Ariel up. Adam decides to be the good cop. Why spoil this "so far, so good" afternoon? Maybe when he takes her back to Sylvan Fields tomorrow, he'll say something. But for now, he'll enjoy this air of cooperation, this rare unsullied proximity.

As they pull into the parking lot behind his building, Adam pats Ariel's knee. "I've got someone I want you to meet."

Instantly, Ariel's demeanor tenses. "Who?" She unbuckles her seat belt but doesn't open the door.

"Not going to tell you; it's a surprise." He's a little surprised at her reaction. Adam hasn't told Ariel that he ended up keeping the dog he said was temporary. "You'll like him."

Ariel visibly relaxes, smiles, and twirls a lock of hair behind her ear. Three studs frame the delicate edging of pink ear that he once marveled over while watching her sleep. "Okay. Him. All right." She elides those two words into one odd sound. A'ite.

Clearly, Ariel isn't up to accepting another woman in her father's life. He smiles, then thinks of Gina. If he was ready to date, would she be a likely candidate? He's bought a nice dog bed from her, and she was pleasant enough as he got Chance to try the fit on several of them. They both knew that he could find an equally nice bed at the local pet supply warehouse for a lot less, but he handed over his abused Visa and smiled even as he chided himself for caring if she liked him or not. But there is something about her that lingers like an afterimage every time he encounters her.

Adam and Ariel climb the back stairs to his floor. He tries not to see the place as she must. Despite a perfectly serviceable hallway, no terrible food odors from neighbors, even a few door decorations cheering it up, it still has that worn industrial look about it. Gray carpet, beige walls. Uninspired sconces light the hallway, dim even in broad daylight. The only apartment building she has ever spent time in is on Park Avenue in New York. There is no hallway in that building; the elevator opens into the foyer of her grandparents' floor. They own the entire floor.

Adam hurries to unlock his door.

Chance sits in the middle of the living room, the squashed throw pillows on the futon clear evidence that the new dog bed is a waste of money. At the sight of Ariel, the dog's tail ticks back and forth, his jaw drops open, and his banner tongue rolls out. His eyes squint; he stands and shakes. Then sits again. As with every stranger, the dog is cautious.

"Jesus, Dad. What the f . . . hell is that?"

"My dog."

"A pit bull? You have a pit bull?" She is laughing, though, laughing and patting her knees to beckon the dog to her. "Is this the same dog you had before?"

"The same."

"How come you still have him?"

"It's a long story."

"That's what you always say."

Chance lumbers over to Ariel, tail still swinging. Ariel reaches out a tentative hand, allowing the dog to sniff the back of it before reaching under his chin to scratch. Adam wonders where she's learned this approach to strange dogs. He certainly never taught her that. Never knew it himself. There is so much he doesn't know about this young woman. He wasn't there for the first time the tooth fairy made an appearance. He was in Hong Kong the evening of her first junior high orchestra performance. Even long after she was a toddler, she was asleep most nights before he made it home. He, like the rest of his cohorts, brayed about the quality time they had with their children. The family ski vacations in Aspen; the once-a-year tennis lessons together. Surely that made up for the absences. The preoccupations.

"What's his name?"

"Chance."

"Interesting." Ariel moves her scratching fingers up and over the dog's head, down his spine, which gets him to wriggling. "Whose idea was that?"

"Gina."

Once again, the tension shows in the tightening of her jaw muscles.

"She owns the shop across the street, fancy pet supplies and tropical fish. I bought the dog bed from her." His voice sounds dismissive even to his own ears.

Ariel visibly relaxes again, as if a shop owner isn't someone she imagines her father being interested in. She stands up to remove her coat, looks around the apartment, drops the coat on the futon, and goes to find refreshment in the mostly-empty fridge.

Adam doesn't know how he'll entertain his daughter for the next twenty-four hours.

Adam's meat loaf isn't quite as tasty as Rafe's, although he's followed the recipe exactly. His mashed potatoes are acceptable, and he's cheated with a can of gravy. The salad, however, is very good. Ariel not only hasn't turned her nose up at the plebeian menu; she's helped herself to a second, albeit thin, slice of meat loaf.

"So, Dad?"

"Ariel?" Here it comes, some request he is going to have to deny. A new pair of shoes, a better school. Diamond earrings. He'll let her down with an airy promise of some future acquisition.

"I got invited to a party for tonight."

"Are you saying you want to go back home tonight?" He is disappointed; this is probably a request he can't deny, but why didn't she say something earlier?

"No. It's at MIT. A guy I know—"

"No. Absolutely not. Whatever put that idea in your head?" Adam picks up their plates and drops them into the sink. He bought ice cream for dessert. He sprang for sprinkles, remembering that Ariel always asked for sprinkles on her cones. "I've got Ben and Jerry's. Chunky Monkey or Cherry Garcia?"

"Dad, I promised that I'd go. It's all right. I know the people—"

"No. So, Chunky or Cherry?" Maybe if he talks loudly enough, this ridiculous fantasy of his sixteen-year-old daughter attending an MIT frat party will dissipate like a puff of smoke. He tries not to think that the entire day of good behavior, of cheerful conversation, of her even doing her math homework at this table was all smoke and mirrors, a buttering up of the old man.

"But Dad, everyone will be there, all my friends. If I don't show up, they'll be on my case for a week. I got them invitations to this party and they're all gonna meet me. It's totally safe."

The dog sequesters himself beneath the table. Not even the tip of his tail extends beyond the perimeter. He rests his nose on his paws, but his eyes are darting beneath mobile eyebrows.

Ariel is banging around the small room, her voice petulant, then wheedling. Adam's voice moves from rock-solid to cracking with anger. "No girl of sixteen who's invited to a frat party can expect it's safe. Besides, what kind of college man invites jailbait—"

"Mom said I could go."

Ariel must take him for an idiot. "Yeah. And I'm about to be crowned king of England. Try something more believable."

"I can't believe that you're not letting me go. You always said connections are important."

"No. Now that *is* something your mother would say." Adam yanks the faucet on full and is hit in the face with a backwash of hot water. He drops the pans in, squirts in some dishwashing liquid, and starts scrubbing furiously. The sound of the running water drowns out Ariel's voice. He shuts off the tap. Ariel hasn't taken a breath.

"Courtney's going to be there. It's her cousin's friend's party."

Courtney Bevins. Daughter of the man who took Adam's place at Dynamic. His former protégé. The one who convinced Wannamaker that the takeover shouldn't be launched. Oh yeah, Adam's figured that out.

"Courtney and her parents are no friends of mine."

"Mom likes them."

"Even at your tender age, I'm sure you can see how that loyalty is offensive to me." Adam is quiet now. Ariel is quiet. His pulse is starting to normalize. Episode over; let's move on.

"Dad?"

He turns away from the sink to look at his daughter. She is in her coat, her ruinously expensive handbag—not a knock-off, the real deal which her mother insisted she should have, slung over her shoulder. She's changed out of her jeans and is wearing a tight little skirt, knee-high boots with heels he can't imagine anyone walking in. The little lambskin jacket is open, revealing a low turquoise top that fits like a leotard and accents a cleavage he is shocked to see.

She looks at him with a defiance he might find admirable were it not aimed at him. The set of her jaw, the way she tosses her hair out of her eyes with a shake, the way her lips are parted, all serve to remind Adam of what lies in wait for her at a house full of inebriated postadolescent, horny young men.

"I'm going, Dad, and you can't stop me."

"Ariel, don't you dare."

"You don't have custody of me. I'm going. I hate you."

"Don't you talk back to me, young lady."

Ariel wrenches the doorknob, loses control of the door, which bangs hard into the wall.

"Don't you walk away from me."

"Fuck you."

Has she actually said that, or is he hearing an echo from the past? The phantom pain that has tormented Adam less in the past few months bears down now on his chest like a vise.

The door slams.

From beneath the kitchen table, Chance peeks out, but he stays under its cagelike protection.

Adam is frozen in midstep. Dishwater trickles down his wrists under his sleeves. He must stop her, but at the same time he thinks that if she has a few minutes to stand out in the street, where very few cabs travel and where it's a mile to the nearest T stop, she'll be back.

His father did nothing to stop his sister. He stayed in the kitchen. Muttering epithets to himself. He sat back down at the table, opened his paper.

Then he thinks of how she's dressed and imagines who else might stop to pick her up. The dog comes out from under the table, gives Adam a wide berth but keeps his eyes on him. Adam bends over, pressing his wet hands into his sides. Stein has told him to remember to breathe, remember to swallow when the anger comes upon him. One deep breath. Another. Then he can go follow her. The dog sniffs at the overnight case Ariel has brought with her, looks at Adam. "It's okay, boy. It's okay." He is still bent over, eyes closed, gasping for breath like he does when he and Chance circumnavigate the pond at speed.

Chance's nose meets Adam's nose. Startled, Adam stands upright.

And then it strikes him. Maybe his father couldn't pursue Veronica because Adam would have been left alone in the apartment. It isn't epithets he's recalling; it's prayer. He was the reason Veronica got away. There was no one else there to watch over a little boy. His father didn't let her go; maybe he was simply helpless to stop her.

Adam isn't helpless and Ariel's not getting away. Adam grabs his keys and cell phone and slams out the door. He hears Chance bark once as he runs down the front stairs.

Chapter Thirty-seven

Except that they didn't bite each other, this confrontation between my man and his pup was as vicious as any fight in the pit I'd ever seen. Whew. I stayed beneath the cage of the table, my head down low, my ears flat against my head, my eyes on the combatants. Snap and snarl. Woohee.

I watched their legs as they danced around the room, using their voices as weapons. Then the young one banged out the door. He panted, not like victor or vanquished, but like a dog pulled to the sidelines to catch his breath before going in for the kill. I was proud of him and touched his face to let him know he had a partner in the ring.

After he left, I stood for a long time, inhaling the scent of their heated bodies. The room was very quiet, so quiet that I could hear him calling way down on the street. I scratched at the door. Eventually I discerned the sound of a car, its voice as familiar to me as the sound of the man's voice. Then I was left to the ordinary silence of the place. I wandered over to my water bowl, lapped a little, nosed my empty dinner bowl, tried to upend the garbage can with its lovely promise of leftovers, but it was wedged in tight between the counter and the wall and had a diabolically clever top on it, which, so far, had resisted my attempts to open it.

Then I jumped onto the futon, pushed the pillows into a more snug nest, and curled up to await their return. Which turned out to be a very long time, even by dog standards.

Chapter Thirty-eight

In the two minutes it took to follow Ariel out into the street, Adam has lost her, as if she has been absorbed into the evening. The sidewalk is empty, and he cannot believe that she could move so fast on those heels. Or that it had taken him longer than he thought to get himself down the stairs and out. He waits, listening to the pounding of his heart in his chest, trying to decide which direction she might have gone. She doesn't know the neighborhood, doesn't know the area, can't possibly have known in what direction to turn to get to the subway. But *he* does, and heads that way now, jogging, saving himself for a full run once he spots her.

Reaching the station, Adam swipes his Charlie Card and darts toward the inbound platform. Lots of dark coats and short skirts. Not so many blond girls. Then he spots the back of a blonde leaning against a stanchion. Although she is inches shorter than Ariel even without the boots, he tries to convince himself that it is she; that this recent awareness of her mature height is a delusion. Surely she is still small enough to fit in his lap. He makes himself quiet his breathing, moves toward the figure slowly, casually, hopefully. But, of course, it's not Ariel.

Ariel has either gotten lucky and found a cab or had already planned on meeting friends with a car. He goes to fetch his Lexus and make his way to Cambridge. He'll find Ariel if he has to knock on every dorm door, walk into every frat house. There is no way he's going to lose her. He keeps calling her cell phone, his finger on the speed dial. He knows she'll just keep letting it go to voice mail, but he wants her to know he's coming, that his phone is in his hand.

Even as he sails down Memorial Drive too fast, Adam thinks about the frat parties he's been to and realizes something that Ariel, in her high school rebellion, doesn't know. No frat party starts this early. The best start at nearly midnight, not at seven-thirty. So, where will she go? Who will be with her? Maybe he has time to find her and get her home. He begins to relax. Sterling probably has the cell number of that wretched Courtney or one of Ariel's other friends. As a last resort he'll make that call. Right now he has a plan.

Adam pulls into the Trader Joe's parking lot, gives Ariel's phone another try. When it automatically goes to voice mail, he wishes that he'd added text messaging to his cell-phone package, six cents per message be damned. No answer. "Ariel, I want you to meet me at the student center. I won't embarrass you in front of your friends, but I'll take them home, too, if they want. No questions, no consequences."

He believes that, at heart, Ariel is sensible and will come.

This is not the student center of Adam's experience. This is a mall, and instantly he realizes that amid the food venues, bookstore, game room, he might wander all night and never find Ariel if he's not specific about location. He thumbs Ariel's number once again. "I'm in the first-floor seating area. Watching the Mass Ave entrance."

In the student center, Adam feels like a voyeur, or, at the very least, a middle-aged man sitting in a place that makes him suspect. Everyone else looks young, and those who aren't young look appropriately professorial, a little bleary, books tucked under arms, top-loader briefcases in hand. None of them looks like a deranged father on the hunt for a truculent daughter. Adam has swallowed enough coffee to stay awake all night and he's not sure how long he can sit here like a homeless man, observing every girl who walks by in her tight little skirt and her skinny tank top, before a campus cop comes over and strikes up a conversation.

None of them is Ariel. He really thought that she'd be here. That she'd listened to his message. Maybe he's left too many, all with the same invocation to call him, so that she never bothered to listen to the last one with orders to meet him here. Or never listened to any of them.

Adam had been to enough U Mass frat parties to know the damage the young can do to themselves with the heady freedom of supervisionless living. He had seen couches tossed over balconies and set on fire; had witnessed the dumping of an alcohol-poisoned girl at the door of the local hospital. It wasn't that long ago that a student died right here from that. It's a quick progression to thinking about date-rape drugs. His daughter and the sexual predators lurking around every corner. These thoughts send ribbons of anguish through him and his hands shake as if he's been drinking all night. Ariel is his responsibility and he's lost her. The time on his cell phone screen reads 12:30. The student center seems less now like a concourse of activity than a midnight bus station, those still around bent over books or asleep on the couches, satchels and backpacks making up rough pillows or footstools.

He dare not take his eyes off the door. He dare not give up hope. He dare not wait here any longer.

The first student Adam approaches is a big African-American guy wearing a sweatshirt emblazoned with Greek letters he can't identify. He carries a laptop case over one shoulder and has a weary look, as if he's been awake for days and can't wait to fall into bed. He is plodding toward the exit, shoulders hunched and head down, a bull-shaped man who does not look particularly approachable. He looks a bit like the punks who stopped Adam on the street to ask about Chance—his big sweatshirt, his crisp white athletic shoes. If it wasn't for the Greek letters on his chest, Adam would have looked for someone else.

"Can I talk with you a moment?"

The kid stops, altogether surprised to find Adam blocking his way. "I guess." He straightens up, imposing in his height and bulk. He is not hostile, just annoyed. He could brush Adam away with one hand and he knows it. Instead, he waits to hear what Adam has to say.

"I'm trying to find my daughter. She's at some frat party and I have to find her. She's seriously underage." The young man looks at him with some genuine concern and Adam feels that ribbon of anxiety tickle. He is right to be afraid for Ariel.

"Hard to say. There's always something going on. Might even be in Back Bay. Lots of Greeks over there. Are you sure it's at a frat?"

Adam feels the hopelessness of finding Ariel in this city of students.

"But, hey, lemme give a couple of friends a call."

Adam is amazed that the kid's massive thumb is so dextrous, but within a moment he's chatting up someone. "Hey, dawg, yeah, man, look, anything going on at your house?"

The kid looks Adam in the eye and shakes his head, thanks his friend, and snaps his phone shut. "My buddy says there might be something going on at TDC on Memorial."

"Thank you. You've been very helpful."

"Hey, wait, man. What are you going to do?"

"Crash a party."

"Good luck." The big kid in the Alpha Psi Alpha sweatshirt sets his cap on his head, careful to twist it into a fashionable tilt, and heads out the exit.

Adam follows, gets his bearings, and heads off at a jog toward the frat house. The late-night air chills him. He pulls the collar of his coat up higher, regrets that he hadn't taken his scarf out of the car, where it lies on the front seat. Clumps of students bump past him as he goes along the street, oblivious to the solitary man making his way through the Saturday-night crowd. He wants to ask if he's going in the right direction, whether he is getting any closer, but none of these students so much as glance at him. They are safe in their numbers and unconcerned with a harried-looking middle-aged man in a too-light jacket, a man who is trying hard not to be frantic.

The young men who stop him at the door are polite about his request to look for his daughter, and one offers to scout around for him. He will not stay, as told, at the bottom of the stairs, but forges on ahead with his chaperone, looking into every room they pass, despite the guy's assurances that no very young woman would be allowed in on a night for "over twenty-ones." Adam bites his tongue, not mentioning that he doesn't believe that rule for one minute. "She's very mature-looking; she can fool anyone."

"We check IDs. Every now and then some freshman tries to get a high school girlfriend in, but we're pretty diligent." He asks if Adam knows whom Ariel might be visiting.

"No." Courtney Bevin's cousin's friend. Adam thinks as hard as he can, trying to remember if Ariel has mentioned any specific names, boy or girl. What comes to him is the depth of her silence toward him. The lack of any insight he has into her life, despite his interrogations on her visiting days. He has asked, and Ariel has belittled his attempts at piercing the barrier she has built around herself as his daughter and as an adolescent.

The music is deafening; bodies are crammed together in the lounge. A black DJ is scratching records while a hip-hop tune plays for the predominantly white crowd. The ceiling fixture has been fitted out with a strobe light, and the dancers' faces are frightening with a here-there-gone dizzy flicker. Adam strains to pick Ariel's face out of the gyrating group, but the strobing lights make it impossible to fix on any one face.

The smell of vomit rises from the floor. In another room, a table is set up with plastic cups, which someone is filling from a keg. In another, there is an apparent contest to see who can swallow a twelve-ounce cup of beer the fastest. Three young men are already on the floor, and Adam can't tell if they are even breathing. Should he call 911? A small room off to the left holds two men, who are silent over a chess table, oblivious to the racket in the house.

"Upstairs? She could be upstairs with someone."

"I can't let you go up there, man. Privacy."

"This is my sixteen-year-old daughter we're talking about. Anything happens, you and your brothers are up shit creek. Frats have been closed before."

The frat-boy bouncer looks to his partner, who just shrugs. "Okay, but no knocking on closed doors. Open ones only, and I never took you up there."

They wander the length of all the floors, checking into any room with a wide-open door. Most of these have students in them, and Adam's presence startles several into hiding a hand behind a back, or slamming a door. A few are empty.

The hip-hop beat seeps into Adam's bones and he feels as if all of this searching is being done to a rhythm, a weirdly choreographed dance in which he is the soloist and can't remember the steps. "Ariel!" Adam cups his hands around his mouth at every floor and bellows her name.

Adam is back on the street. The boys have suggested a nearby dorm, and one after that. The magnitude of his search is daunting. He can't possibly get to every dorm and frat house on this far-flung campus. He is searching for someone who doesn't want to be found. Adam sinks down on the top step of the old brownstone frat house. He puts his head in his hands. He has to call Sterling, see if she has any ideas about whom Ariel might know here. Suffer her anger and take the well-deserved blame. He takes out his cell phone to call his ex-wife. The missed-call message is on the screen. He didn't hear it ring when he was in the frat house, the hip-hop drowning out any other sound.

His pulse is in his ears as he presses the key to identify the caller. In the instant it takes to see who it is, Adam knows that he is praying, making deals with a God he has all but forgotten. A vestigial belief in a merciful God burns through his heart as he squeezes his eyes shut and waits for the call to connect.

Chapter Thirty-nine

The campus police station is on Vassar Street, not all that far from where Adam is. He can barely remember where he left his car, so he walks the distance, taking the time to reel in his emotions, catch his breath, straighten up. The streetlights dog him. There are only a few people on the streets now: stumbling co-eds, arms linked together, giggling their way back to the safety of their dorm rooms; a lone bicyclist speeding down the center of the street, unthreatened by automotive traffic. A man walking a large dog comes out of the shadows. Adam thinks that he's going to go home to a mess. Poor Chance, abandoned without a backward glance.

Recently, Adam has found himself talking to Chance as if he's a sentient being. At first, he felt silly, embarrassed to think that he'd grown so used to the dog's presence that he'd begun to feel like a pal. "Did you see that play? What was he thinking?" he'd ask. But he didn't stop. It helped, this voicing out loud his train of thoughts, getting nothing more back than a sideways look or a big blocky head in his lap. Once in a while, the dog vocalized a little *rroorr rroorr* sound, agreeing that it was a boneheaded play or concurring with whatever Adam had said. He slipped his arm across the dog's sturdy shoulders when he did that and was rewarded with a quick lick on the cheek. Then they'd both sit back, assured of their masculinity.

Ariel is waiting for her father in a hard-backed chair across from the duty officer who made the call to Adam. She stands up at the sight of him coming through the door. Old tears already blotch her face, and the scent of vomit clings to her. A thin streak mars the perfection of her lambskin jacket. Her panty hose are torn above her boots, as if she'd stumbled and fallen down on her knees. Her hair is tangled. Her expensive purse is gone.

"Mr. March, your daughter is a very lucky girl. She was mugged but not assaulted. We found her alone on the street, although she says she was with friends."

"Ariel?"

"Daddy." It has been years since she's called him that.

"What happened?"

"I'm all right."

"Where are your friends?"

"I don't know."

"What happened?"

Ariel wipes her mouth with the back of her hand. Her nails are chipped and the palms abraded. "I fell down."

"Did someone push you?"

"No. We were going to another party, and I was a little behind everyone because they were moving so fast. Then I tripped. I don't think they knew I was down, because they kept going. They didn't hear me. Then this guy, this guy out of nowhere, was standing over me. I thought he was going to help me up, but he didn't. He swiped my bag. I was so scared, afraid that he'd hurt me, that I just let him. When I got up, I got sick. And then I was alone on the street with no phone and no money and I didn't know what to do."

"How did you end up here?"

"A cop found me. Brought me here and called you."

"And you were drinking?" He can see that she would like to deny that she was, but the evidence is obvious.

"Yes."

"Like the officer says, you were very lucky. You have no idea—"

"I do. You don't have to tell me. Lesson learned." Her tone is sardonic, as if the only lesson she's learned is to expect a lecture from a worry-fraught father.

Her face is tear-streaked and dirty, but she is dry-eyed now. She walks out ahead of him into the predawn darkness. Adam knows that there is more to this story, details that he'll never hear. This is a mishap that she has survived and that will become part of her life story. And maybe someday, when her own child does something equally rebellious, she'll suddenly understand how he feels right now. The panic may have subsided, but the memory of it will last forever.

The gray light of day has faded the long night as they reach Adam's building. The newsagent's door is propped open as he retrieves the bundles of newspapers dropped on the sidewalk. Adam thinks of all the sleepless nights he's spent, waiting for that door to open, those lights to come on. He is nostalgic, although grateful that he no longer awakens in the dark.

One Good Dog • 221

Beside him, Ariel is dozing. She's unhurt, except for her scraped knees and bruised ego. For this, he remembers his deal with God and breathes a prayer of thanks. The old words *by the grace of God,* come to mind as he looks at his sleeping daughter. He'll let her keep her nightmare night to herself, as he will. She doesn't need to know the anguish he experienced as he hunted for her. As long as he knows that it was only an injury to her pride and not something more dire that led to her being hauled off to the campus police station, he's satisfied. A lesson learned. Don't hang out with friends who will abandon you to puke in the bushes alone and leave you vulnerable to purse snatching, and be glad it wasn't anything more dire.

Adam wonders if Veronica ever learned her lesson.

Adam rejects the idea that his father could not race after his sister because of him. He could have taken Adam with him, or dropped him with a neighbor—they lived on a street with three family homes; surely some woman would have been willing to watch a little boy while a frantic father chased after a rebellious daughter. Adam knows that he would never have given up looking for Ariel like his father had given up on Veronica, and then on him.

Ariel stirs as Adam shuts off the engine. The short nap has already faded the nightmare result of her defiance toward him. She looks at him with embarrassed contempt. Gone is the "Daddy" of her rescue. He is, once again, the Nameless One.

"I want to go home."

"You're going to bed. I'll take you home when I'm ready to."

Ariel stomps off to shower and Adam snaps the leash on his

dog. They pound down the stairs and Adam feels every tense muscle in his spine and legs revolt. Chance has contained himself and hasn't greeted Adam with anything but gratitude. Adam walks him as far as the empty lot, but he doesn't let him off the leash. He's had enough of runaways already.

"Are you going to tell Mom?"

"Do you want me to?"

"Duh, no." Ariel isn't looking at him; she's looking out her window as the verge along the highway speeds by, guardrail posts spooling out the miles as they head to Sylvan Fields. "Besides, she'll blame you anyway. Save yourself the trouble."

"I can't say you're wrong about that. So, let me get this straight. I protect your butt from your mother, and I benefit somehow. And you've learned . . . what? Not to mix vodka with wine?"

"She's dating, you know."

"She has that right."

"He's a creep. He's younger than she is and she only likes him because he's got a really big . . ."

"What?"

"Portfolio." The corner of Ariel's mouth twitches into a little smile.

The resemblance to Veronica is so vivid that Adam pulls off the road at the next rest stop. "You have an aunt. Her name is Veronica. When she was your age, she disappeared. Ran away. I never saw her again and I have no idea what happened to her. She was just like you. Beautiful and headstrong."

"I'm not running away."

"You did run away."

"That was just to go to a party. I wasn't going to vanish forever."

"Maybe that's what Veronica thought, too."

Adam puts the car into gear and gets back onto the highway.

Chapter Forty

They didn't even have the common decency to call him and tell him over the phone. A fucking e-mail. "Sorry to have to cancel with you, but we've decided that we need to change consultants." Blah, blah, blah. New focus. Different direction. "We really can't take a chance on you. You should have told us. . . ."

His clients have bailed on him. A check will arrive in the mail. Time spent. Maybe two hundred bucks. They've seen his CORI. They've discovered his error. Just like Gina. His criminal offender record information sheet will list A&B—assault and battery. They won't care that he's been sentenced to community service. The lone woman in the group has probably kicked up a fuss. Who would want a consultant like him? A man who has been accused of being a danger to women.

Adam opens up the first draft of the business plan, stares at it, admires how he would have brought the dream to those spineless neophytes, and then deletes the document.

"Mornin', Artie."

"Mornin', Adam." As has become his habit, Artie wordlessly slides a dog biscuit across the counter, never looking at the dog or at Adam, keeping his eyes on his puzzle. The cookie disappears into Chance's satchel mouth.

"He says thank you."

"If I had one like him, I wouldn't need you know what." Artie waggles his bushy eyebrows, intimating that he has illegal weaponry stowed out of sight.

"Where were you when I was trying to find him a home?"

"I like my freedom. No pets."

Adam and Artie have had this conversation before. In the year or so that Adam has walked through that door seven days a week, Artie has always been on his stool behind the counter, cigar clenched between his teeth, newsprint streaked on his forehead and crossword puzzle under his hand. Adam seriously doubts the man has any freedom at all. If Artie thinks he's unencumbered, it's his delusion.

Adam fills his travel mug, snags a couple of packets of cheese crackers, a *Globe*.

"That's four and a quarter."

Adam hands Artie his last ten, pockets his change, and wonders how soon he'll get his kiss-off money from the skateboarders.

A second dog biscuit comes across the counter. "That's for later."

Gina is unlocking her door as they walk out.

"Morning, Gina." Adam nods to her, is rewarded with one of her smiles. Which he knows is for the dog.

"Hi, Adam. How's it going?"

"Could be better." He just doesn't have the energy to play at civilities with his unpredictable neighbor.

"You look a little ragged. What happened?"

Such small courtesies, a short lifeline tossed in his direction. Although he's certain that she'll snap it back, Adam decides to grab it anyway. "You want a coffee? It's a long story."

Chance is straining against his leash, trying to get closer to Gina. Adam steps forward, loosening the tension. Gina bends to stroke Chance's head, runs her hand along his back, scratches his rump, and then stands up. "Sure. I've got time."

Adam hands Gina the leash and his coffee, goes back into Artie's to get another one for himself. He's smiling and he doesn't know why. His pulse is just a little stronger, as if he's already downed sixteen ounces of dark roast.

The parrots squawk their greeting to Gina, who opens their cage and puts in a breakfast of seed and fruit, changes the water, feeds each one a tidbit by hand. She leaves the door to the cage open, eyeing Chance and wagging a finger at him. "Leave it." Chance wrinkles his brow and flops down on the floor, heaving a great sigh, like a bellows emptying.

Gina sips from her coffee cup while moving from tank to tank, scooping debris, sprinkling in food, checking temperatures as Adam spins out his tale of Ariel and her Saturday-night adventure.

He won't talk about his stillborn consulting job; it would force him to reveal too much about himself that she shouldn't know. It is too shaming.

She says nothing, but her activity doesn't suggest inattention. It's easier to talk about Ariel's attitude toward him, her defiance—her similarity to his sister in looks and attitude—without Gina looking at him. Adam finds himself telling Gina more than he should about his strained relationship with Ariel, and about his sister's more permanent rebellion.

"So where is she now?" Gina's done with the chores and now moves behind the counter.

"I took her home yesterday morning." His coffee has gone tepid.

Gina sets the canister of fish food back on the shelf, hesitating a moment longer than the task should take. She turns to him. "I mean your sister. Whatever happened?"

"I have no idea. She walked out that door and that was it." Adam clears his throat, sniffs a little to suggest that this fact no longer has the power to hurt him. "My father never went after her."

"Well, you did the right thing, going after Ariel."

"What else could I have done? Sat home waiting helplessly? As it was, I was helpless and I did wait helplessly, but at least I was near to hand when the cops called."

"She knows you were looking for her. She knows how much you care."

"I'm not so sure."

One of the parrots has emerged from its cage and has worked its flightless way to where Gina leans against the counter. Cocking its head right and left, it finally launches itself to her shoulder, where it begins to pull gently on her hair.

Adam remembers the packets of cheese crackers in his pocket and pulls one of them out. "Can Polly have a cracker?"

"His name is Fred, and yes. He loves that kind. Just break a piece off for him."

Adam offers the orange-yellow cracker to the bird, who

runs his beak against it, then gingerly takes the offering, keeping his tiny bird eye on Adam while he does this.

"Did you tell Ariel's mother what she did?" Gina lifts the bird off her shoulder and onto her hand.

"Not yet. Sterling wasn't home when I dropped Ariel off, not back from her weekend with her new paramour. The thing is, if I do, they'll both hate me; if I don't, who knows. Maybe Ariel will learn to appreciate my silence."

"I'm sure she appreciates what you did, or tried to do. If not now, she will eventually."

"I hope so." Adam offers another piece of cracker to the parrot. "It's been really hard lately to get the women in my life to cut me some slack." Their eyes meet over the head of the cracker-crunching parrot. In Gina's he sees a flicker of something, something she's keeping back. As if she knows something about him. "What?"

"Nothing." A slight flush touches the apples of her cheeks. He thinks of reaching out and laying a finger on those cheeks to see if they feel warm to the touch. The thought is so compelling that he raises his hand. Suddenly, Gina steps backward; the parrot flaps clipped wings to keep his balance.

"Are you all right?"

"Fine." The warm flush is now scarlet. "Just fine."

And then it hits him. Gina knows about Sophie, about his episode. She's Googled him. There is no burying past sins anymore. Anything and everything is laid out there for public consumption. Newspaper articles and the infinite discussion on blogs all there for the mere typing of his name on a search engine. Potential employers, potential friends can find all the dirt on you. The most personal of stories writ large across the electronic concourse of the Internet.

Adam is powerless. His reputation has been sullied forever by his loss of control that day, that moment. The grinding ambition coupled with the misleading message, exacerbated by hunger and an incipient, if phantom, attack of angina, topped by his personal assistant's increasing and unrepentant ineptitude had triggered a breakdown. A self-immolating act of breathtaking nihilism. He's paid for that error. But all the press or blogs or watercooler conversations ever recall is the act, the unforgivable act, of slapping Sophie.

He sees himself in Gina's eyes and is horrified. To her, he is a man who acts upon a baser impulse. She can't know that it's one driven up from the dark reaches of his background and upbringing. The raised hand. He's watched other foster children younger than he put into closets. He's sat hungry while others ate. He's seen the belt slide out from under the belt loops, the snap of it, halved and threatening. He's been struck. All in the name of good behavior, manners, respect. Mistakes.

But he has conquered this, pulled himself up out of the morass, bettered himself. He has denied himself the self-indulgent practice of remembering the darkness, recalling in his rare stories only the two foster mothers who were kind to him, and even their kindness was of the practical kind. Marge and Mrs. Salter. He's never gone back to see them, these two out of seven. He's pushed them and their kisses on his forehead into the same closet as the five who treated him as a piece of inventory.

Adam wants to tell Gina all of this, to explain himself to her, to get her to stop looking at him with these wary eyes. Eyes that tell him no matter how civil she is to him, how impressed that he's taken on Chance, she will always be aware of his single self-destructive act and judge him by it. The lifeline snatched from his hand.

"I'm not the person you think I am. What happened was an aberration. I'm much better than that. I don't . . ." He is about to say "hurt women," when he hears the anger in his own voice, the rising volume of frustration. Adam startles the dog out of his doze. "Come on, Chance." He leaves his cold coffee and newspaper behind.

Chapter Forty-one

The jagged edge of panic slices through Adam. Daylight demons, far more insidious than those of the night, circle his mind.

With his record, he won't even be able to get a job at McDonald's. He can't even get his old job of bus driving back. He's going to end up in line with the men at the center, being served, not serving.

The savings that the court allowed him to keep, out of which he's been paying child support and every other court-determined expense of his estranged family, has diminished to a laughable amount. He's got maybe three months' worth of rent and car insurance money. When he hears those "get out of debt" commercials saying if he has more than ten grand in credit-card debt, call today, he sometimes thinks he should make the call. He has never been so out of control of his finances. He gets the irony of it. He lost control; therefore, he is out of control. The man for whom the platinum credit card was invented, who had never allowed a balance of two dollars owing at the end of the month: unemployed, unemployable.

Despised by his daughter, his ex-wife. And the woman that he finds he thinks about, whose good opinion is being withheld because of his control issue. A woman who is so unlike Sterling. Who is comfortable with herself, content with her life as it is. Whose ambitions have been realized in the owning of a shop filled with fish and a home filled with rescued dogs. He would call her a simple person, but that would suggest mediocrity. Gina is anything but mediocre, and he feels her disdain more powerfully than even his family's. If his life had been different, if he'd pursued a less ambitious course, he might have found someone like Gina and settled down. Lived his life worrying only about fuel prices, not corporate takeovers. Accepted his rough beginnings and improved on them by being a good husband, a good father. Chosen to get his satisfaction from his family, not his career. Chosen a wife who loved him for who he really was, not for his potential success.

Adam sits on the edge of the futon and puts his head in his hands. He should call Stein, he knows this, knows he needs a voice other than his own in his ears. He needs someone to tell him that he is going to be all right; that this is the dark time, but the light will come.

Absent a comforting voice, Adam's thoughts sink deeper. If he were to disappear, who would miss him? Disappear like Veronica? Unlike his sister, he has no sibling to wish he would come back. His family might even be relieved to have him gone. Adam knows that *disappear* isn't the word for what he's thinking. Oblivion. Release from this black hole that he inhabits. How painful it is to think that his death might bring only a momentary regret to those who know him. *Too bad about Adam March.* Sterling could enjoy a social notoriety as an ex-widow. Ariel would get time off from school. Compassionate leave. Sympathy grades. His life insurance is paid up—a policy that he bought a week before they were married, and then proudly adjusted to designate their newborn daughter as a beneficiary along with Sterling. Adam has the unoriginal thought that he is literally worth more dead than alive.

So it has to look like an accident.

Unless his ultimate revenge is to leave Sterling and Ariel without that money. A slap in the face for their treatment of him, for their rejection of him as a man who is, at heart, not a bad man.

Adam thinks of Sophie. How glad she might be if he were dead. He'd be doing her a favor.

The bottle of scotch has appeared at his hand. The glass is empty. How much scotch would he have to drink to die of alcohol poisoning? There must be a formula. If he weighs 160—okay, maybe 170—and is six feet . . . He's not up to the math. Can he do it with the half liter left in this bottle, or should he run out and buy some more? Would vodka be more efficient? Add a little Tylenol PM?

Adam pours another half glass of scotch. No sense rushing things and vomiting up all his hard work. He has all day. Oops, no, he hasn't. For the first time in his adult life, Adam calls in sick. Rafe takes the call with good grace, "Take it easy, man. Don't worry about it." Rafe's swallowing his story of 'feeling like crap' adds an additional helping of guilt to Adam's quota.

No note. That would screw everything up. Unless he left

one in an unobvious place, to be found later, after the inquest. After the insurance is paid out. After his sorry body is cremated and his ashes are scattered. Or not. He'll probably get left in a box in Sterling's closet, eventually to be discarded with other out-of-fashion possessions. Or left at the crematorium. Unclaimed freight.

This is such a good plan. He has been forcibly disconnected from the world, and now he'll make the disconnection permanent. There is no one who cares about him, or needs him. Or will notice for five days that he's missing. Except Big Bob. Well, that's good. They'll find him before he starts to stink.

Chance walks up to Adam and sits down, lowers his big boxy head and drops something out of his mouth: the tennis ball that Gina gave them, which Adam hasn't seen since that day a month ago. The ball bounces; the dog pounces, scrambles around as if the thing were alive and worthy of capture, then returns to sit in front of Adam. He drops the ball again.

"Who taught you that game?" Adam kicks the ball across the room with his toe.

The dog's tail end is in the air, the ball between his paws. He noses it in Adam's direction, where it clunks up against the scotch bottle. Adam retrieves the ball, tosses it in the air, and catches it a couple of times, then flings it against the opposite wall where it hits with a dull thump. The dog plunges after it ecstatically, tail wagging, barking at Adam to keep up the game. He drops the ball at Adam's feet, looks at him with eager eyes, eyes that declare he is the one who will care. A dog will be the only one to miss him.

And what would happen to Chance if he died? Back to the shelter? Back into the hands of the boys who fought him? Would Gina take him?

Like a rust-stuck wheel, Adam's thoughts begin to loosen and turn. He is the hub of the wheel, his thoughts spokes leading to the faces of Ariel and Sterling. Sophie. Their voices connect to him with the rivets of scorn and accusation. He has failed them; he has frightened them. He has damaged them. They have reacted to him—his behavior, his temper, his unresolved issues.

He is unredeemed, despite the punishment of community service. Loss of job, loss of status, wife, daughter, friends. Most of all, he's lost his humanity.

This conversion from victim to villain is stunning to him. Guilt, embarrassment. Shame. "This isn't who I am." This is what he's said to Gina, and yet it *is*. The person he has become, the person so tightly wound that he can be undone by a minor misunderstanding. The person no one wants to be around. A pariah.

Until and unless he makes amends, he will never regain his humanity. He will never find redemption.

Chance drops the ball. He makes his little *rrooorr* sound, but this time it sounds like speech. This time, it sounds like approval. The dog shoves the damp tennis ball against Adam's closed fist. The two, man and dog, stare at each other for a moment, the man taking great comfort in the reflection of himself in the dog's brown eyes—the only eyes that don't look at him with disappointment.

Chapter Forty-two

Who knows where the tennis ball–playing gene comes from. All I knew was that this object fell to the floor from the counter—perhaps a mild earthquake, or perhaps I nudged it when I was reaching up to snag a half-eaten sandwich from the countertop. At any rate, the ball fell and I hit upon a great way to get my man out of his self-indulgent slump.

He was sitting there with his hand wrapped around a glass and his eyes fixed on the floor, just like the day he sat with his eyes and nose running and first touched me—the first time he acknowledged that I lived alongside him, and from then on it was much better being in this crib. I admit it. So now the sharpish scent of the fluid he was knocking back worried me. He hadn't been indulging in this as much lately, which meant that he'd had more time for me. I was alert to the fact that he was agitated, pacing around, sitting, banging his fists against his skull. Drinking. The odor of his beverage began to seep out of his pores, mingled with an amalgam of fear, anger, grief. He reminded me of a dog I'd known in the cellar who chewed himself with a self-destructive obsession until his skin was a bloody mass of scratches and sores.

I watched him for a long time while he drank and muttered, sinking deeper into a state of anxiety. Even as I grew increasingly fretful about him, I wondered why I was wasting my time observing him, worrying about him. This wasn't something that I came to naturally, this concern about a human. Yes, I knew all about dogs who did, who saved Timmy from the well. But I am not that kind of dog, I told myself firmly, reminding myself that once I was a professional fighter. All along I have been telling myself that I am not a *pet*. My plan had always been to book it for greener pastures in the spring, or early summer at the latest. Not to get attached. If the door opened right now, I reasoned, I would leave. Sayonara, pal.

I had been kind to him once before, but that didn't mean I was a permanent fixture in his life. I was not going to be part of one of those pathetic bonded pairs, man and dog, that I'd been observing a lot lately. Watching the dogs in the park play with their people—undignified romping, tails upright and wagging like out-of-sync metronomes. Happy looks on their faces—dog and man. Lavish face licking. For what? Nothing more than I had right here, a bowl of water, although mine was empty right now, and a twice-a-day meal of dry, crunchy bits and pieces. An occasional pat on the head. No no no. I'm an independent creature, a creature of self-possession, a dog who belongs to no man.

It was nearly dark, and I thought that if I could get him to take me out now and let me off the leash at the empty lot, then maybe it was time to go. To bid farewell to this solitary human.

Even as I thought it, I knew that I wouldn't go. He was talking, but clearly not to me. His speech was slurry, equivalent to the low moan of a defeated champion. I felt a twinge in my heart, a clenching against independence. I went over and stood in the bed that we'd taken away from the woman who liked to give me cookies. Although I frankly preferred the futon, this cushiony substitute curled nicely around my back; snuggling into it felt like a return to puppyhood. This time, I couldn't get comfortable, so I went back to stand and stare at him, urge him to look at me and remember that I had needs, too.

I took a deep sniff, filling my nose with his scent. Beyond the odor of his emotions and his drink, I could still detect the underlying essence of him. For the past days or weeks, or whatever the artificial enumeration of time is for these people, I had been feeling something beyond a normal thanks-for-the-kibble gratitude. Thanks for not hitting me. Thanks for not handing me back to those boys. I was grateful for the times we sat on the couch together and he let me rest my head in his lap. I was grateful that he talked to me, not for his scintillating conversation, but for the sound of companionship. That's the scent that was being overwhelmed, the odor of calm, of partnership, of connection. I was afraid that something very powerful had hold of him, something that mere companionship wasn't going to scare off.

Then the ball dropped. I picked it up and forced him to look beyond his trance to see me. Could I get him to play with me? Could I remind him that I needed him? *I needed him.*

At first, he looked at me as if with someone else's eyes. Me, a critic of play, I urged the ball forward with my nose until it jammed between his feet. Looked at him with a silly dog grin and waited. Something slid away from his eyes and at last he saw me, saw the ball and picked it up.

He threw that ball hard against the wall, where it bounced crazily around the room until I trapped it. Over and over he smashed that ball against the wall, and over and over I pounced after it like some demented retriever until we both collapsed on the futon. I was panting, and so was he. Then he picked up his glass and, with the same violence as throwing the tennis ball, he flung it against that long-suffering wall and it smashed into a thousand shards. I flinched; the sound hurt my ears.

He reached an arm around my shoulders and dropped his head against mine. We might have been littermates snuggling. "Good boy."

I knew then that I might never again entertain the notion of leaving him. Not as long as *he needed me*. I raised my muzzle, lifting my head backward until I could reach his face with my tongue. My own version of "good boy."

Chapter Forty-three

The insistently repeated rhythm of his cell-phone tone pene-trates the haze of alcohol-induced sleep. It is an annoying sound that has periodically entered his dreams as voices or objects or touching. Coupled with a full bladder, the sound of his phone ringing finally brings Adam awake. He fumbles for the teeny-weeny button but misses the caller. His missed calls function identifies a number he doesn't recognize. Tossing the instrument on the coffee table, Adam extricates himself from the gravity of the futon and stumbles to the bathroom.

Chance is waiting for him in the kitchen, the empty water bowl an indictment against Adam. He hasn't seen to the essen-tial well-being of this animal. Adam rinses out the bowl, pours in fresh water, and watches as the dog laps up half. Which re-minds Adam of his own thirst. Downing two glasses of water and a handful of aspirin, Adam becomes fully conscious of a new day. He looks at the shards of glass and the yellowy streaks of scotch that finger down the bland white wall.

"Ready to go out?"

Rrooorr says the dog, and Adam takes that as an okay.

The dog needs to go out. He needs to start his day. This new day.

Gina's store is open, the parrot sign turned to WELCOME. Adam walks in, Chance at his side. The parrot named Fred squawks a greeting, or an alarm. Gina holds a bucket of water and her window-washing pole. She sets both down, stands still. She doesn't smile at him, and her left hand goes to her throat, an unconscious gesture that makes her appear nervous and at the same time demure, persuadable.

"You've checked me out, haven't you? On the Internet."

"Yes. I was curious. I mean, after I realized who you were, I just wondered why you were living here, why you weren't at Dynamic anymore."

Adam is pleased that Gina isn't denying her curiosity. "Why didn't you ask me?"

Gina's supple mouth purses. "Wouldn't be polite."

"Ask me."

"Will you tell me the truth?"

"What I'll tell you will jibe with what you've read, only it'll be my side of the story. Can you accept that?"

"Yes." Gina locks eyes with Adam. In hers is a glistening of something that urges him on: a desire to believe him, to reconcile the two Adam Marches, the one she's found on the Internet and the one who stands in front of her.

Adam picks up the bucket and the squeegee. Taking Chance's leash, Gina follows him outside. He wrings out the sponge into the warm water, then wipes it in broad strokes across the rainbow and the dancing fish. As he draws the rubber blade down the window, smooth lines of water rushing ahead of the edge, he begins to talk.

The story he tells her spools out from deep within. He hasn't rehearsed, and so his story comes out in chunks, in truths that he has never before voiced. She knows a little bit about his sister, but he tells her about his childhood among strangers, about his father. As he talks, he finds himself elaborating, bringing old memories up from the depths of his subconscious. Stein would say that he was free-associating. He not only tells Gina things he has yet to speak about in therapy; he tells her about therapy. About Fort Street. About his anger at being assigned to serve food to the homeless and now his dependence on that place as the center of his days.

He feels no compunction about discussing a marriage that was more corporate partnership than love affair. About painful and abiding love for a daughter who detests him. About Sophie, what he'd done to her. And why Veronica's sudden reintroduction into his life had triggered his downfall.

"A nervous breakdown?"

"My shrink can't quite fit me into a diagnosis. I'm not quite a conduct disorder, not quite a depressive. A little of both. So we agree only that I had an 'episode.'"

Gina's olive eyes scan his, needing clarification. "But you say that you ran your departments, or divisions, with a firm hand. You were no one's friend. Even choosing your wife was a calculated measure. Everything was about the power."

There is a softening in his chest, a loosening up of the tightness he's felt for months, maybe years. It's as if the urge to cough has suddenly gone away. "Yes. And I now know that you just don't get to control everything. It's not sustainable. I'm not that man anymore."

He is done with the window washing and they go back in-side. She takes the bucket of dirty water and disappears into the back room. The fish tanks burble gently, a soothing perco-lation. Chance wanders around, the leash dragging behind him, sniffing at the chew toys and bottles of homeopathic rem-edies, stuffed animals and ceramic kittens. Adam leans his el-bows on the counter, facing Gina, who has come back but stays behind this barricade.

Gina looks at him, her mouth set in a way that suggests her doubt. She realigns the dozen charity jars. "I don't think that people can change that much just because they want to."

"With practice, you can." Adam lays a palm on the top of the jar designated for the shelter where he found Chance. "I've already changed into a dog owner."

"Why are you telling me this?" Although her words are sharp, Gina's eyes have begun to soften toward him. He can see that she wants to believe him. "Is this some kind of AA task where you have to go around making amends?"

"No. Although AA might not be a bad idea." He thinks of the shattered glass, the streaks of scotch on his wall. The dark terror of failure that plunged him into a soul-deep vortex must not happen again. Despite his proclamation that he is a new man, Adam knows that the vortex is only one bad mo-ment away. Every thought, every action from now on has to keep him from that edge. He likens it to exercise: Every day he will strengthen. "I had a waking nightmare where I was vis-ited by the ghosts of my life as it has been thus far. But today I have awakened to a new day. A new life. You represent the Bob Cratchit of the story, the humble clerk who understands that the good things in life are beyond price."

Adam watches a single tear slide out of the corner of Gina's eye, its contrail glistening in the morning light. He reaches across the counter and touches it, erasing its journey with a thumb. Gina reaches up and cradles the hand touching her face. She leans in and their lips meet over the divide of the counter.

Adam needs to go; Gina needs to get on with her day. He's got to head to the center. "Thanks for listening."

"Can I ask you one question?"

"Of course."

"Your sister. Do you ever wonder why she ran away? What she was running from?"

"I guess I've always believed that she was, like Ariel, rebellious. Maybe a boyfriend."

"Running from your father?"

Adam shrugs his coat on over his shoulders. "Maybe. I don't know, maybe running from me. From the responsibility of a little brother."

"You should find her. Ask her."

Even with all the resources of his former life, Adam has never considered searching for Veronica. She has always been so deeply embedded in a past he had disassociated himself from that the very idea was out of the question. Until now. Until Gina ever so gently has made the idea live.

The parents' waiting area at the barn is empty except for Adam. He sits down on the lumpy couch, pats his knee, and invites Chance up beside him. Asleep on a pile of empty grain bags is a cat. Chance, before jumping up, gazes at the recumbent feline. "Leave it," Adam orders the dog, and is pleased when Chance jumps up onto the couch instead of going after the small animal. Lately, Adam has been devoted to watching Cesar Millan on TV instead of Judge Judy. They are both forthright.

Beyond the viewing window behind him, Ariel, who cannot see that he is there, is jumping a course in the indoor arena. The jumps are not high, but set up so that she has to practice her takeoffs and tight turns. Adam leans against the back of the sprung couch and waits for Ariel to finish. This is not their regular Saturday. He's not here to pick her up, but to corner her into a conversation that is way overdue.

Adam almost dozes off as Ariel goes around and around, the steady thud of Elegance's hooves a melodic tune in four-four time. The little spaces of silence as she leaves the ground are like rests in a musical score. He snaps awake as he hears Ariel's coach call it a day.

In the main aisle of the barn, Ariel is untacking her mare. She sees Adam and doesn't stop what she's doing. She tosses the saddle over the half door of the stall, grabs a curry comb, and sets to work scrubbing the saddle marks off the bay mare.

"Hello, Ellie." Adam runs a hand down the long neck of the horse, something he's never done before; like Chance's, her coat is as soft as silk to the touch. The mare noses his hand for treats, then turns away, disappointed.

"Don't call her 'Ellie,' " Ariel says, but she's giving him a puzzled smile. "And watch that dog."

"He'll be fine."

"Why are you here? I drove here myself. You don't need to pick me up."

"I know. I want to have a conversation and I knew you'd be here."

"If it's about that night, I'm sorry. I said I was and I am. And I'm grateful that you didn't tell Mom."

"It's a little more than that."

"Okay. Just let me put her away."

Adam goes back to the waiting room. Ariel takes so long that he begins to fret that she's slipped out the back and driven off. It seems so odd that his little girl is driving. He's never even been in a car with her at the wheel. He's somehow missed the traditional bonding of parent and child over learner's permit driving hours.

The connecting door to the barn opens and Ariel comes in, flops down on the couch, with Chance between her and her father. She begins to stroke the dog's ears, the good one and the half. "What do you think happened to this ear?"

"I have no idea." Now that she's here, Adam is stumped at how to begin.

"So, what's up?"

"I'm going to let you decide when and where you see me. I'm not going to insist anymore. You're sixteen; you have your own mind. When you want to be in touch, I will always be there for you."

"Dad. Why?" To Adam's complete surprise, Ariel looks hurt.

"Because I can't take the cold shoulder anymore. I think that if it's your idea, you'll come to want to be with me. Why should we both suffer?"

"Are you trying to use reverse psychology on me?"

"No. I'm apologizing for being a crappy, absent, preoccupied, errant father." From somewhere in the barn, a horse whinnies. The sound is piercing, plaintive. "I thought that I could buy your love, but I can't. All I've paid for is contempt."

"That's not true. You don't have to buy me stuff. I thought you liked to."

"If I had the money, yeah, sure. But I don't. And you don't need anything, Ariel. You have more than two-thirds of what anyone else in the country ever gets. The men I work with have nothing, not even a home. And they don't complain. They don't lament their lives; they come up to the serving counter and they thank us. Thank us for serving them the only hot meal they're going to get in a day." Adam is aware that he's lapsing into a polemic, so he shuts up.

"Do you like working there?"

Chance squeezes out from between Adam and Ariel. He walks over to where the cat is still sleeping, gets close, but not too close, sniffs, and then flops down on the floor, leaving a gap between father and daughter.

"I do. I like it very much."

Ariel slides over so that their thighs touch, his in blue jeans, hers in cream-colored breeches. Adam takes her hand. Ariel rests her head on her father's shoulder.

"Tell me about my aunt. About Veronica."

"She looked like you. Or maybe I should say you look like her. I haven't seen her since she was just a little younger than you. She and my father had a fight one day and she walked out. I was little. Around five."

Adam and Ariel sit on the lumpy couch, the dog snoring lightly on the grain bags, and Adam tells Ariel his story.

Chapter Forty-four

Sophie Anderson stands in the cereal aisle of the Stop & Shop. Adam is surprised to see that she is pregnant. When did she get married? Did she marry that guy with the black T-shirt and the tattoos? She could do better, he thinks. She's a smart girl, if a little careless.

Dr. Stein has helped him break the barrier of restraining orders. He's made a phone call and gotten other phone numbers. Introduced the topic to Sophie's lawyer, to her shrink, to her. Sophie has said no, no meeting, however brief and public. She will not give Adam the chance to say he's sorry. Now Stein is cautioning Adam against pushing it. "It's almost enough, Adam, that you know you want Sophie to forgive you. You don't actually have to hear it from her."

Adam disagrees. Unless he gets to ask for her forgiveness, in person, there will always be that unresolved issue haunting him alongside all the others. It's a simple thing to ask, and withholding from him the opportunity to say those words,

"I'm so sorry," is almost as much a punishment as anything else he's suffered.

Stein is proud of him, and encouraging. But Adam isn't going to be put off.

If he's an easy Google target, so is Sophie Anderson. A simple address lookup. Her phone isn't unlisted, and despite the common name, he's able to pinpoint where she lives. If it's quite a distance from where he lives, it's still not inconceivable that he might find himself in that town. He isn't stalking; he's just putting himself in the area, patronizing establishments that she may patronize. Like the Stop & Shop. He needs dog food. He needs milk. It is purely by chance that they both need cereal. It's purely by chance that he's timed this casual drive to coincide with the end of the day at Dynamic, when so many employees who live in this suburb do their errands on the way home. Like Sophie.

"Sophie." She is studying the nutritional values on the side of a box of sugar-coated cereal. Adam speaks softly, gently, so as not to startle her. The way a man might wake up a woman. "Hello, Sophie."

His voice does startle her and her mouth drops into a little O of surprise. Her eyes immediately dart around, looking for someone, anyone, to prevent this meeting. "I said I didn't want to see you. Are you stalking me?"

"No. Not at all. See?" He holds up the bag of dog food, the half gallon of milk. "I just spotted you and . . ." Adam knows he has seconds to make his case. "Sophie, I only want to say how sorry I am for what happened. That's all." Adam bows his head a little, like a courtier to a queen, and turns away, the sound of his athletic shoes squeaky against the flat gray surface of the linoleum floor.

"Mr. March?"

He stops. He is flanked by cartoon characters shilling their confectionary breakfast foods, their leering smiles beckoning. Adam keeps his back to Sophie and waits.

"I know you are."

Adam's shoulders relax; he shifts the weight of the dog food to the other arm.

"But would you be as sorry if you hadn't lost everything?"

It is a crystal moment. Adam is thrust back into the seconds before he picked up the pink memo slip, read the words that triggered his breakdown. If he could go back to the life that he had worked so hard to achieve, a life of long meetings and high anxiety, late nights and a semi-estranged family that wanted ever more from him, go back to doing things that people like Gina despised, all in the futile hope of burying his past deeper and deeper, would he? Adam is unsurprised at the answer that bubbles up. No, he would not want to go back to that life. It no longer appeals to him. He is not that man anymore.

So Adam tells Sophie the truth. "Yes, no matter the outcome."

He walks briskly to the checkout counter. He smiles at the cashier, pulls out his last twenty. In the car, his dog waits for him. It's staying light later now and they'll have time to go to the park on the way home.

Chapter Forty-five

In typical New England fashion, summer has descended abruptly. The wet, cold spring shrugged off the stage, opening the way for the three H's: hazy, hot, humid. The kitchen of the center is a furnace, and Adam works in a clean white T-shirt and Dockers shorts. His apron comes to the bottom of his knees, so from the front, it looks like he's wearing a dress. A blue bandanna is banded around his forehead like Cochise's to keep the sweat from pouring into his eyes. They are all dressed in some variation of this, fighting the heat that comes from outside and within, feeding men who continue to wear their year-round wardrobes, impervious to the swelter.

The air conditioning in Adam's apartment has been broken for a week and his super has yet to replace the antique unit with a new one. The dog is an as-yet-unacknowledged interloper in the apartment complex, tolerated by the neighbors who have seen him, overlooked by the super, who will no longer be able to pretend the dog doesn't exist if he has to enter the apartment while Adam is out. Hence, Chance now comes to the center with Adam. Adam has cobbled together a lean-to shed in the backyard, which is fenced in already. The shed offers shade even at midday, and Rafe offers scraps. Chance seems happy enough out there, and when Adam looks through the back window at him, the dog is usually asleep in the shade. Occasionally, one of the smokers goes out and sits on the back steps and the dog sits with him, making Adam just the tiniest bit jealous. He wants Chance to be friendly but still remain a one-man dog.

Adam is putting in extra hours at the center. Not volunteer hours, but compensated time. He has been given a small stipend to research grant opportunities. Fluent with the language of finance and comfortable with the intensive application questions, Adam has crafted two successful grant applications in the last four months. His pay isn't much, but it keeps Chance in kibble and himself current with his rent. The rest still hangs over him like an anvil, but it's a step in the right direction, and the work is curiously satisfying, gentle as it is.

It is late by the time Adam shuts down Big Bob's computer, pulls off the bandanna, and changes his sweat-soaked T-shirt for a clean one. Chance is doing his "happy to see you" tap dance on the steps, his front legs pumping up and down, his big head swinging side to side, tongue lolling, eyes squinting up at Adam. "Ya wanna go home, big boy?"

Unhnnn unhnnn.

In whimsical moments, Adam thinks that the dog is teaching him a new vocabulary. Different sounds for different occasions. *Unhnnn* meaning "I sure do." *Rrooorr* meaning "I hear you, man." Or "Let's eat." Or maybe "What did you think of the game?"

Adam and Chance emerge onto Fort Street and head east.

The sultry part of the day is past and a slight breeze is coming up off the water miles away. Shadows spike across their path, street signs and buildings, abandoned shopping carts, wheels off, their shadows casting Jurassic figures before them. The sounds of traffic and the commuter train block out voices and birdsong as they walk along. Adam feels more than hears the low growl, telegraphed through the leash to his sweaty hand. He looks down. Chance's hackles are upright, forming a cox-comb of fur between his shoulders. There is no other dog in sight, nor is Chance yanking at the leash. No full-throated barking, just this low growl and the pressure of Chance's body leaning against his legs. There is only an old man stand-ing at the bus stop in front of them. Then Adam realizes that Chance is looking backward.

Without their puffy jackets, Adam isn't sure if these are the same boys he'd encountered before, but Chance's behavior speaks of familiarity. They approach Adam, keeping enough distance that even if he let the leash go slack, the dog wouldn't reach them. "You still got my dog, man." The slenderer of the pair accuses him, pointing at Chance, then at himself. "He's my dog."

"Not anymore." Adam will not be intimidated by these punk kids. In broad daylight, without their massive coats, he realizes that they are just kids a few years older than Ariel. They have no power over him. He's a lone white man in their neighborhood, but, by God, he's got the big dog. He stretches to his full height. "You want him? Try to take him."

The boys look at each other as if daring themselves to reach out and grab the leash out of Adam's hands. They look at Chance, who is snarling and barking, his tail whipping from side to side with the force of aggression. It is all Adam can do to keep his hold on the dog. Part of him wants to keep taunting, "Come on, come and get him." But they aren't going to take Chance; they can't get close enough. They're punks, two kids who act all tough because that's what's expected of them. He was a tough kid once himself. Had to be in order to survive. Maybe his streets weren't as mean as these, but mean enough. Maybe these kids don't have intact families, either. Maybe they are foster kids. Maybe he has more in common with them than the desire to own this dog. "He's my dog. Not yours. Maybe once, but not now. Nuff said?"

The boys simultaneously plug in iPods, turn away from Adam, and disappear.

"Guess we told them." Adam reaches down to touch Chance, calm him down, assure him that everything is all right.

Chapter Forty-six

At first I was a little put off by being left outside to cool my heels in the backyard of the building where the man goes in smelling like himself and comes out smelling like food and other men. I guess I was getting a bit puffed up with myself, what with my status as house dog. Why should I be left out in the backyard like any common cur? Then I realized that being just outside the window where all those good food smells originated was pleasant. Plus, I had the bits and pieces of meat ends and the occasional shinbone to enjoy, courtesy of the man in the big hat. And there was no one around to threaten my possession of such treats. Just me. It was very pleasurable to lie in the shade of the shelter my man had constructed, water bowl topped off, shinbone beneath my chin. Pigeons skulking around, burbling and mating. If there was a fence keeping me in, it also kept out the street dogs that might wander by. Being a dog, I really can't say how long I'd been living this life of leisurely unemployment, but it seemed to me that a whole new generation of street dogs had come of age. In other words, I knew no one. So I acted all territorial about this square of yard defined by a man-made structure. I yarked and growled. Lifted my leg on my fence. Acted all fierce, protective. Sometimes, bitches in particular, they'd ignore my bad manners and come to the fence anyway. A chain-link fence is an obstruction, but not impenetrable, and noses met greeting areas. I wagged my tail in apology. They were all right. Most of them.

There was this one dog. Big fella. Didn't have the look of a fighter, but clearly not someone to be messed with. His tail had been lopped off and he kept the vestigial end of it poked straight out, as if there were a lot more to it. He became a frequent visitor, but he never got over his wanting to challenge me. We'd growl at each other over the fence, him taunting me about my captivity, me throwing back insults at him. *Man, if that gate was ever left open, I'd show you a thing or two.* He was the only one who wandered by that provoked me. I was forced to check the sturdiness of the gate by throwing myself against it. Usually someone came out of the building to put a stop to it. Then the coward would run off, that poky short tail flung down to cover his anus. *Guess I told you, didn't I?*

Most days some of the men in the building would come out and sit with me. Lighting up those sticks that burn, they'd group around the back stairs and puff away. I didn't much like the scent, which reminded me too much of my time in the basement with the boys. They'd often reeked of this odor, or one similar to it. But these guys liked it if I joined them. Once in a while, only one of them might come out. If I sat beside him, the guy might throw an arm over me, talk to me, tell me things I was fairly certain he kept to himself most of the time. These men reminded me a little of the man I lived with. There was a certain fragility to them. The soft voices that they used with me immediately rushed into gruffness whenever someone else came out, as if they were embarrassed to be caught talking to a dog. When they sat with me in a pack, they betrayed none of that fragility. Sometimes on the street, you meet a dog that isn't supposed to be a street dog. He might be lost, or his people lost. Those dogs often make fairly good street dogs, but there is always this core of disbelief that they have ended up this way. That's what these guys were like.

I'd seen the boys more than those times with my man. I'll give him credit: He stood up to them, growled in a very professional way. Good man. What he didn't understand was how much they wanted me back. I don't mean to brag, but I was a top dog for them, a winner. Which made them happy, which meant they wanted to continue to fight me. So when they showed up, leaning against the fence that surrounded the backyard of the building where my man had left me to slumber away the summer days, I got nervous. Which meant that I barked. Which meant that someone from inside looked out and the boys skulked away like half-grown pups lookin' cool.

So every day that he left me in the fenced-in yard, I grew more nervous. I liked the job I had now, giving aid and comfort to the street men, being my man's singles partner with the tennis ball. I just couldn't see myself back in the pit. I was a pacifist now, not a contender. I admit a tiny bit of embarrassment at that admission, but truth isn't always pretty. I once was powerful and feared. Now I was loved. A much bigger deal.

Chapter Forty-seven

Adam has two weeks before his final hearing with Judge Johnson. Labor Day is past; the streets are filled in the morning with schoolchildren. He waits at crosswalks manned by crossing guards who eye a childless man with a fierce-looking dog with a wary expression. He smiles at them, says good morning. Hitches Chance closer to his side. He has been assured of a good report from Big Bob, a real testimony to good behavior and going the extra mile. He has proven himself a tractable volunteer and will keep on with his grant writing even as his time will be filled with his new work.

Even better, Adam has been hired as a consultant for a firm downtown. This one isn't an Internet start-up, or a pie-in-the-sky scheme by recent college graduates; this one is a long-established business looking for someone to head a special project. He sat with two of the three partners and gave them a brief "need to know" about himself. Then hawked his skills so well, they shrugged at the confession. They were getting a very skillful executive at a very reasonable price; his personal failings were his own.

Dr. Stein is pleased with Adam's recent progress, too. And his report will reflect that.

Adam comes out of Stein's building and drops another coin into the meter. There's a gourmet cheese shop nearby, and suddenly Adam has a longing for Wensleydale. They also sell gourmet dog biscuits, and Chance deserves a treat. He deserves a treat. The fresh, dry air ruffles his hair. Tomorrow he'll stop in at the local barbershop for a trim. No more haircuts that cost as much as a car payment.

All the way down the street, across the road, between buildings, Adam looks for Jupe. Jupe has been absent for several weeks. Maybe he's back in a hospital, or maybe he's hitchhiked to Manhattan. Bob doesn't know, but with continuous good weather, he's not all that concerned.

Adam doesn't know why he should be so concerned about Jupe. The old man hasn't spoken to him since the failed dog search, since he tried to give Chance to him. He cuts Adam dead anytime their paths cross. Jupe is one of those who won't go into the backyard and sit with Chance.

Adam understands that in Jupiter's tortured mind, he's responsible for Benny's disappearance because he'd failed to keep the promise the old man exacted from him to find the dog. Jupe can't accept the truth that the dog was doomed the moment he was hospitalized. It wasn't that Adam didn't find the dog; he simply no longer existed. But, like a promise spoken to a child, or a man with a child's grasp of the world, that promise to find Benny was a bond that had no alternate reality. No excuses. But Adam knows how he feels. If anything ever happened to Chance, he'd be devastated. He has become, in a very short time, one of those people who would stay in his house during a nuclear attack if his dog couldn't be evacuated with him.

So now Adam tends to look for Jupe when he's in this area, where Jupe alone or with Benny most often lingered.

Adam decides not to tell Gina yet that he's hired a private investigator, although it was the first impulse he felt after his decision was made, before he'd even met the man in a Denny's to discuss exactly what he wanted to find out, and how much he was willing to pay. To finally act on this lifelong disappointment came with an unforeseen reaction: relief. It was a relief to think that sometime soon he might be able to stop wondering about Veronica, about what had happened to her, and where she'd ended up. He's not even anxious to get the news. He doesn't even try to imagine a reunion, even a nervous phone call to say, "Hi, I'm Adam."

He knows that it could take awhile, and maybe even that the detective will be unable to come up with any results, but that's okay. The important thing is that Adam has taken charge of the situation. Just like problems at work, the first step in handling them is to begin doing something. Inertia is a weight that presses down; action is the removal of that weight.

"Mornin', Adam." The litany of everyday living.

He's not late today. He's been up since dawn, preparing the outline for Stryker, Royal and Martin. He's already taken

Chance around the block. The coffee is brand-new. He's in sweatpants but has shaved. His business clothes are laid out.

Adam fills a second cup, sugars it, dribbles just enough low-fat milk in to suit Gina's taste. He makes his purchases, gives Artie an answer to 46 down—archetype—and goes out the door.

The impeccably dressed businessman is headed his way. Late, unusually late. Adam smiles and steps into his way, armed this time with his name. "Good morning, Mr. Martin."

Augustus Martin of Stryker, Royal and Martin, snaps his head around, his expression one of alarm: How does this bum know my name? Then recognition sets in. Embarrassment. "I thought you looked familiar at that meeting."

Adam thinks, What bullshit. The guy has never looked him in the face in all the months that they have crossed paths on a daily basis. He would put out a hand, but both are occupied. "You, too. Out of context, right?"

"Yes, out of context. I didn't realize you lived in this area. I thought that . . ."

"I know what you thought. Appearances can be deceiving, after all." Adam sips from his cup, decides to let the guy off the hook. In the glory days when he was in Martin's Cole Haan shoes, he would have treated a shabbily dressed, unshaven early-morning stranger the same way. "I've got some ideas on paper to show you at our meeting. I think that you'll like them."

"I'm sure I will."

There is a moment of awkward parting. They do not know each other at all, but there has been such a long period of morning encounters with prejudice that they don't quite know how to say good-bye.

Gina is washing her front window and watching this little pas de deux between Adam and the man she, too, recognizes from his daily route past her store. She scrapes the squeegee left to right, winks at Adam, and then draws the rubber edge right to left.

"You look pleased with yourself." She scrapes the moisture off the blade with a paper towel.

"Yes, I am."

Gina hears something in his voice and sets down the squeegee and toweling. "Why?"

He tells her about his detective.

At first, Adam doesn't recognize the number illuminated on the screen of his cell phone. He almost lets it go to voice mail, then remembers that the 978 area code belongs to his private investigator. It's been only a week. Surely not enough time, even in today's overexposed electronic Big Brother world, to find someone missing for forty years. Someone who maybe has never wanted to be found, someone whose youthful identity has been made over by marriage or alias into something completely new. Someone Adam has always—and don't ask him why—believed was now on the West Coast, as far away as she could get from her New England beginnings.

"I have some news. Can we meet?" The PI is a small, round man, but on the phone he sounds imposing.

"Can you give it to me over the phone?"

"In person. Denny's, in an hour?" The solemn voice prohibits argument.

Adam swallows against a swirl of nausea. "Are you afraid I won't pay you?"

There is a heartbeat of insulted silence. "I prefer to give my reports in person."

Denny's is mostly empty at eleven o'clock on a workday, just past breakfast, too early for lunch. The lone occupied table has an old couple sitting in silence, mulling over their plates of eggs and red-tinged home fries. It is the perfect backdrop for hearing news of his missing sister, with its massive plastic-coated menus, the slightly sticky tabletop, a garish interior design based on the color of egg yolks. The geometric pattern of the industrial carpet makes Adam feel unsteady on his feet as he follows the middle-aged waitress to his seat. Ron Pascal joins him almost immediately, handing his menu back to the waitress and asking for black coffee. Adam does the same.

"Can I getcha some home fries or a order of toast or somethin'?"

Ron Pascal meets her eyes, "No. Just coffee. Please." The waitress moves away from the table. "You know why I hate missing person cases so much?"

"You never said that you did." Adam has a packet of sugar in his fingers; he's rotating it around, as if measuring the sides.

"'Cause it almost always isn't good."

"You're telling me . . . what, exactly?"

Ron pulls a thin file folder out of his briefcase, sets it on the table between them. "This is what I found."

The file has a neat green-bordered label on it, VERONICA MARIE MARCH typed in all uppercase Times Roman letters. Solid, real. Not like a missing person at all, but like someone who should have lived enough life to fill this folder. A folder so thin, the edges touch. Thin enough to hold one piece of paper.

"Your sister passed away six weeks after she left home." Ron flips open the file folder; the death certificate is facing Adam, but Pascal knows the line he's looking for. "Cause of death: massive internal injuries consistent with being struck by an automobile."

"Hit by a car? Veronica was killed?"

"I'm afraid so. The two paragraphs of press coverage state that she was either hitchhiking or crossing the street at around two in the morning, when she was struck and killed by a hit-and-run driver." Pascal pulls the newspaper clipping out from under the death certificate, along with the one square inch of obituary.

Adam feels dizzy. He doesn't take the articles from Pascal. His hand is shaking as he reaches for the handle of the coffee mug the waitress has set down in front of him. He's afraid to lift the mug to his lips. It's not that he hasn't steeled himself, considered the idea that Veronica might be dead. It's always been a latent possibility, one that he has from time to time talked himself into expecting. The shock is that she's been dead all this time; that his every childhood dream of how she would someday come rescue him was beyond fantasy, was impossible, an impotent hope. Should he be grateful for not knowing? How could he not have known? Why didn't anyone tell him? He imagines a giant conspiracy of silence keeping the most important fact of his childhood from him. Was it a misguided kindness? Don't say anything and he'll forget all about her?

If he had known that his sister was dead, throughout all those years of foster homes and pullout couches, of bullying, of loneliness, he would have had no hope at all.

Adam pushes himself out of the booth. His knees buckle as he staggers toward the men's room, getting inside just in time to vomit.

"Why didn't my father tell me?"

"I guess you'll have to ask him." Pascal snaps shut his briefcase, pulls a wallet out of his back pocket, and drops a couple of dollars on the table.

"I can't." Adam lifts his eyes from the folder containing his sister's death certificate and looks Pascal in the face. "I have no idea if he's even still alive. I haven't heard from or spoken to the man since I was nine."

Pascal opens the folder again and points to a yellow Post-it Note stuck to the inside. "That's his address and phone number."

Chapter Forty-eight

Because of his unscheduled appointment with Pascal, Adam is an hour late to the Fort Street Center. He's called ahead, gotten Big Bob's dispensation without having to give him any excuse. He's never been late before, a fact that only today occurs to Adam. He's treated this enforced do-gooding as he treats all his responsibilities—with professionalism. Someone should be proud of him. It's not like he's been working for a merit raise. He's just applied his hard-coded work ethic to this situation, exactly as he has always done in all of his positions in his rise up the ladder. Automatically doing his best as an involuntary volunteer.

Adam stops by the apartment to leave the car, get Chance, and walk to the center, despite already being late. His pulse is still pronounced from the effects of his conversation with the investigator and he needs to slow it down, to force the twin facts of his sister's untimely death and his father's unlikely survival into some form of neutral territory, assign them someplace in his mind where they are harmless. He has to make the basic facts lie down and be still. Instead, his mind cavorts with the unanswered questions.

Gina is in her shop, but Adam can't tell her yet. He needs to digest this new truth on his own. He can't speak out loud, can't make the words come out in a way that will make sense to himself, much less to another. He needs time to adjust his entire concept of the past.

Adam latches the gate behind him, unsnaps the leash, and runs cold water into the dog's bowl from the outside faucet. With a quick pat on the head, he leaves Chance to entertain himself for the next few hours. Chance lumbers over to his lean-to and flops down in the shade.

Ishmael is behind the steam table, ladling out the day's soup. Adam grabs a clean apron and a paper toque and settles into serving the main course of pork chops and mashed potatoes. Everything looks gray to Adam, the chops, the gravy, even the soup. Shades of gray, like they say dogs see. Nothing is sharp.

"You okay, man?" Ishmael asks.

"Yeah."

"You seen a ghost or somethin'?"

Adam shakes his head, tries to smile. "I'm okay."

"You sick, you shouldn't be here."

"Not sick."

"Sad." Jupiter is standing in front of Adam. After so many weeks, it is a surprise to see the old man standing in front of him, his watch cap pulled low, his eyes flinty, and Adam notices for the first time how pale they are, not like looking into eyes at all, but into reflectionless mirrors. "Too bad." Jupiter might be addressing them, or himself. His pale eyes flicker from Adam to the plate, then to Ishmael. "So sad your dad. *Sad* is the loneliest word in the world." Adam vaguely recalls that rhyming can be a symptom of some mental disturbance, but he doesn't recall Jupe ever doing it before.

"You want gravy with that?" Ishmael slides the plate across the stainless-steel surface.

Jupe takes the plate, squinting at Adam. "Now you know. Now you know."

Ishmael raises an eyebrow at Adam, mouths, "Woo. Woo."

"At least he's back." Adam lifts the now-empty soup tray out of the steam table. At least he knows where Jupe is. One less disappearance to worry about.

Chapter Forty-nine

I was alone in the backyard, tending to my nethers, waiting, hoping that the man in the hat would come out with a treat, wondering if something interesting might be on the docket for later. Maybe a ride in the car, a walk in the park.

"Hey, boy."

I stopped my ablutions to stand and appraise my visitor. It was the man who once hung around with my former mentor. I hadn't seen him in a long time, not here and not on the street. I sniffed the air. He smelled ripe—of the street, of the untamed, free life. I drew closer.

"Good boy."

Two words of their noisy language that I knew, and agreed with. He wasn't in the yard with me but standing outside the gate. I trotted closer, anxious to meet him, breathe in more nearly that sweet scent of street. Obligingly, he opened the gate. Then he walked away.

The gate swung itself three-quarters shut. Not enough to keep me in. I sat. I am a dog; I do not usually wrestle with the ethics of trust and obedience except as they suit me. My man has trusted that I not jump out of his car if he leaves the windows open. I trust that he will feed me, scratch my belly. That's about as far as I go. This open gate, this invitation to walk out onto the street like a free dog was like a gift from some bountiful deity. Who was I to say no? But I sat. Waited. I have no capacity to debate right and wrong, or the moral dilemmas of faithfulness. I had never been told to stay. Neither did I have any excuse to go.

I was waiting for a reason to push that open gate wider. And along he came, that mutt who loved to challenge me as long as he thought I was behind bars. Boy was he in for a surprise.

Chapter Fifty

Adam has moved in a fog all afternoon. The last time he'd felt like this was after his episode at Dynamic, the light-headed feeling, the sense that his hands are attached to his wrists by thin threads, his feet blocks of stone. Adam goes through the motions of helping Rafe, of serving lunch, of running the dishwasher, of listening to Ishmael's chant of "You want gravy with that?" over and over, until the five words hummed in his head like the catchphrase from a B movie or the chorus to a country-western tune. You Want *Gravy* wi' That? Gravy. Wi'. That? What Do You Want? Ishmael even pushes a little rhythm to the words. Sing along now. Follow the bouncing ball. Where did that come from anyway? Funny how the references faded after a generation or two but the phrases lasted forever.

The last man has been served. The tables are nearly empty. Mike has folded up most of them, letting the stragglers bunch together at one, the other meant for the staff. Right now the smell of food is making Adam queasy. He'll just skip it today.

Get his dog and go home. Big Bob will understand; sometimes a guy just isn't hungry. But when the others grab their plates and cutlery, Adam finds himself joining them. If he goes home, he'll just sit and think. At least the conversation here will provide a slight distraction; maybe he can even summon up the verve to add his two cents to the inevitable discussion about the Red Sox. Anything to avoid thinking about Pascal's report. About Veronica. About the fact that his father is still alive and living within a scarce two miles of him. All this time. All this time she's been dead and he's been alive. It's not that Adam's ever thought about the old man being dead; it's more that he's cast him so far out of his life that he cannot conceive that his father still exists. The pain in his sternum twinges and Adam presses a hand against it.

Rafe drops onto the bench beside Adam. "I got some scraps for Chance. How come you didn't bring him today?"

"I did. He's out back."

"No he ain't."

Adam extricates himself from the fixed bench, banging his knee against the table, nearly kicking Rafe in the process. "Are you sure?"

"Gate's open, man. No dog."

"Fuck." Adam starts for the back door, and suddenly Jupe is in front of him.

"Excuse me." Adam doesn't want to touch the old man, but he's desperate to get outside. "I need to get by." *Some idiot has left the gate open.*

"Now you know." Jupe doesn't move. "Now you know."

Adam has been here for three hours, and he knows that he was careful with the U-bend latch. No one is supposed to come in by the back door, Big Bob's rule, but someone did. Or left that way. The staff are all here; he was the last one in. So which of the men slipped out, careless with the gate, careless with Chance? A panicked notion: His dog may have been on the loose for two hours by now. He could be miles away. Or dead from running in front of a car. Adam pictures Chance running, confused, dismayed. His former street dog panicked like anyone's coddled purebred. Alone.

There is no time to lose, and this old man is in his way. Adam tries to get past Jupe, but Jupe is determined to be in his way and nimbly blocks Adam's route.

"I said, now you know what it feels like." Jupiter grins at Adam, grins and holds his Swiss Army knife at chest level, the blade extended. "Sad. Sad."

"Whoa. Okay, Jupe. Hold on there." Adam hears Big Bob, feels his bulk just behind him, a bulwark against this madness. "You need to put that down."

It's not a very big knife. Not a long blade, but the light touches it in such a way that it reflects a dull shine, an ancient patina, lovingly sharpened. The tip is tilted just so, like a woman's smile. Adam steps back. Jupe follows, a pas de deux. Big Bob, Rafe, and Ishmael circle the dancers.

"You killed my dog."

"No I didn't. I just didn't find your dog."

"Don't engage him, Adam. Just hold on." Big Bob is slowly working his way around behind Jupe. "Mike's calling for help."

Jupe is more dangerous than a man who knows how to use a knife. He slashes wildly, pokes and thrusts the short blade with a jerky rhythm—up and down, from side to side. A manic sign of the cross. The sharp little blade is poking out of the handle like a serpent's tongue.

Adam backs away. Jupe is too fast and too erratic for Big Bob or Rafe or Ishmael to attempt to knock the knife out of his hand. The group moves as one into the middle of the dining room, until Adam feels the bench of the emptied table behind his knees.

"Look, Charles," Adam hopes that using the guy's real name will shock him back into reason. "I'm sorry about your dog. I know how much he meant to you."

"But you tried to foist a fake on me. You didn't know what he meant to me. You think one dog is like another. Didn't even look like Benny."

"I do know what it's like to lose someone you love. I do know. You can't replace them. They aren't interchangeable."

"You promised me."

"I shouldn't have. I didn't know it would be impossible to keep that promise."

Jupe is suddenly still. His flinty, pale eyes are rimmed in pink, the sclera yellowish, and they bore right into Adam's eyes, making him think that this isn't a man they're dealing with at all, but a demon. There is nothing human in those eyes.

Adam forces himself to stare into those eyes. "And now I want to go find my dog. Before it's too late."

Jupe's right hand, the one with the knife in it, begins to relax. It's like watching the demon leave a soul as the flinty look is replaced with confusion, with a mildness. An awakening. In the distance, a police car's siren. Adam thinks that he can ask for the knife, that the demon is gone and Jupe, the man, can be disarmed. That maybe Jupiter has returned to being Charles. Adam puts out his hand, waggles his fingers as if encouraging a small animal to come to him. "Will you give that to me?"

Jupiter lunges.

Chapter Fifty-one

Here I was, on my unexpected ramble, practically intoxicated with the world of street scents, enjoying my leashless freedom, and—wham—trouble. I was as naïve as a newcomer to the street life. My months on the end of a leash had dulled my instincts for self-preservation. For too long I'd been led around, not using my own brain, relying on a human to tell me where to go and how to get there.

After chasing off the poseur, I snuffled along the sidewalk of the neighborhood I had ended up in, a little disoriented, since I had paid no attention to landmarks while I chased the bastard off into traffic, so I was exploring what seemed to be new ground, which, I have to admit, was great fun. Until I hit on a scent that tickled the memory keys in my brain. I imaged the scent, searching for the visuals that would tell me what my nose was trying to. Cage. The filthy backyard redolent of feces. The scent of dried blood. I had somehow ended up on the street where I got my start. This was definitely not in the plan, so I raised my nose, trying to discern the scent of my neighborhood—either the one I shared with the man or the one with the backyard—from the myriad threads that make up the world. Maybe that way? Was that the scent of the coffee place he likes to sit outside? Or that way? Do I smell the street men gathering? Nothing. Nothing I could get a line on.

I was well and truly lost. I'm dog enough to admit it. My fanciful thinking that I'd play a little hooky and be back in time for our walk home turned into being lost. Well, I may have been lost, but I wasn't stupid. Retrace my steps. Logical, huh? But I'm a dog, a male, and one who had clearly challenged the other dogs in these neighborhoods in that I had announced myself on every post, hydrant, and rear tire. Every one of my own markers had been covered by someone else's. And not the same someone. Eventually, I found myself right back on the same block of my former life.

"Looky here, dawg. You b'lieve it?" Since I'd been gone, the fine distinction between potential and corruption in these almost men had disappeared, and in its place, was sheer hostility. They reeked of it. They reeked of dog, of smoke, of malice. Of pizza and beer. Of the blood on their shoes. Of their own fear, which masked itself as anger. I hadn't realized before that they were much like the dogs in their cellar, guided by forces outside their control. Victims of their breeding.

This time, there were four of them. The two I'd known, and two who were bigger, older, and distinctively powerful. Men.

I snarled, snapped, spun around, not wasting my breath on sound but putting it all into action. But I was surrounded. I ducked, made for the gap between legs covered in baggy jeans. The kick hurt; I stumbled. I had never used my teeth on a human before, but I wasn't going to go down with a whimper.

But, of course, they knew how to handle a snapping dog. The last thing I remember is the quick grab of a rope around my muzzle, squeezing my jaws together, then nothing as one of them brained me with a break stick.

I awoke in a cage, my old cage. Deep in the corners, it still bore some trace of me. My parents were gone, replaced by another breeding pair. She eyed me with dull curiosity. He growled. I didn't respond. I wasn't about to get into a shouting match. I was just relieved to have my mouth open, and I drank from the shallow puddle of water in the bowl in the cage. Here I was again, right back where I'd started. I wondered how soon I'd be back in the pit.

Chapter Fifty-two

Adam holds a large, thick square of absorbent material against his face, the ER staffer having taken away the kitchen towel that Rafe had given him to stanch the bleeding. Big Bob sits beside him in the waiting area, thumbing through a dated *Popular Mechanics* magazine and drumming his leg with sausage fingers. Adam had fought the idea of racing to the emergency room, wanting only to get out on the street and look for Chance. Every hour that goes by, and they have been here for over two, means it will be harder to find him. How far can a dog get? By the time Bob and Rafe had convinced Adam that he was well and truly injured, he was faint from the searing pain of a short-bladed slice in his face and was willingly led to Big Bob's car.

Adam gingerly pulls the pad away from his cheek. Has it stopped bleeding? He turns his head to see Big Bob, and feels a fresh drizzle of blood. He'll give them ten more minutes and then he's going to leave, despite his blood-soaked shirt and bleeding face. He's got to find Chance.

"You don't have to stay."

"'Course I do. You got hurt on my watch."

"I'm fine. You should go home." Ten minutes, as soon as he can convince Big Bob to leave, he'll bolt. "Really. Go." He can see Big Bob's temptation to get out of this depressing place, to go home, versus his good nature working against that temptation. Adam pushes. "Face wounds bleed worse than serious wounds. I'll be all right."

"You have anyone to call? Anyone who can come get you?"

"I'll grab a cab."

"Adam, I'm not going to let you do that."

"I need to find Chance."

"You need to get stitched. The dog's fine."

"Gina. Gina DeMarco." Give Bob a name and then get him out of here.

"Okay. What's her number?" Bob, ignoring the NO CELL PHONE USE sign, pulls out his Nokia.

"I don't know."

"Not a close friend?"

A slight dizziness, as if he is standing on the roof of a tall building and looking down. "A neighbor."

"Listed?"

"Try DeMarco's A to Z Tropical Fish."

Bob's massive hand fondles his cell phone and he speaks first to an automated voice, then to a real person. "Okay."

A nurse scowls at Big Bob and he walks outside to make the call. She then beckons Adam.

Gina is sitting by herself in the waiting area when he comes out. Her hand goes to her own cheek in spontaneous reaction to the sight of him, face swathed in bandage and surgical tape, bloody shirt and pants. "Oh sweet Jesus, what happened?"

"Chance is gone. He got out. I need to go look for him. Now." Adam shoves his discharge papers into his back pocket and grabs Gina's hand. "It's almost dark. Can we please start looking?" Adam has inadvertently made a good choice in giving Bob Gina's name. Of all the people he knows, she is the only one who understands his frantic desire to drive around the mean streets of Boston with half of his face numb, looking for a half-eared pit bull.

They drive in slow squares, block by block, radiating outward from the Fort Street Center. As they drive, Adam talks. "It's all tied together; Jupe's attack and Chance's disappearance are two sides of the same coin. Because I failed to find Benny. No, not my failure to find Benny. It was my lack of understanding as to how much the dog meant to the man, that one dog is not like the next. I just didn't get it, and the poor guy has been mourning—" Adam's voice catches with a sudden and powerful dismay.

Gina takes her right hand off the wheel to place it over Adam's. "We'll find him. There are plenty of good ways to locate lost dogs. We'll keep looking until we do."

As dark descends, making the search well nigh impossible, the lidocaine begins to wear off and suddenly Adam's face feels like he is being seared with a hot poker. The pain distorts his thinking, overwhelms him, and he lets Gina take him home. As they make the corner, he prays that his brindled dog will be sitting on the steps, *Lassie Come Home*. There is nothing there. No dog waiting for him.

Adam dreams of Sophie, of his hand on her face, but somehow it is he who feels the pain of the slap. He wakes. He is given only a split second before the pain and worry return.

His face aches with the seventeen stitches that form a neat crescent from the corner of his eye to the corner of his mouth on the left side of his face. He knows that he is lucky. Jupe's blade missed his eye and didn't penetrate through his cheek. The slice is deep, but his plastic surgeon has promised that he'll look piratical, not disfigured.

The hollow space under his ribs aches with emptiness.

Deep in his heart, Adam fears that Chance's fate is going to be the same as Benny's. His breed will be his demise. The prejudice toward his type: the automatic death sentence for animals like him in some cities. A dog can wander a long way, and he may be well away from the Animal Advocate shelter, which has his photo and his description and his tag number. Adam deeply regrets not getting around to microchipping him. Even though there is a better than even chance that no shelter would bother to run a reader over a brindled, half-eared, scarred pit bull.

The hollow place is filled with panic. He keeps losing those he loves. Veronica. Ariel. Now Chance. He presses on his sternum, willing the panic to subside. The panic begins to diminish. He is breathing too hard for someone sitting in a chair. He concentrates on slowing it down. He's back where he started. Alone. The leash hanging on the door mocks him, tells him that he was soft and stupid to let emotional well-being be dependent upon the presence of a mere animal. Animals die; they disappear. Veronica disappeared. She died.

The bolus of grief may be for Veronica; it may be for Chance. It is indistinguishable, these two losses, and he feels guilty about that. He should mourn his sister more, but it is the dog he misses. He is alone again.

Alone with the thought that his father, his abandoning father, lives two miles away.

Adam wasn't even ten when he last saw the man who had turned him over to the state. The visits had winnowed down to once a year, usually in the fall, so that returning to school, usually a new school, became synonymous with being made to dress in too-short dress pants and a short-sleeved dress shirt. A tie would be clipped at his throat. A knock, or sometimes the doorbell. This last time Adam had shot up so much in the previous year that he nearly reached his father's chin. They were almost eye-to-eye, a fact that clearly startled his father. "You've grown some." Adam couldn't read the look in his father's face. Was it concern or pride? His father wore a gray jacket, like the kind mechanics wear. He smelled of cigarettes, his fingertips stained with nicotine; his hair was still dark, slicked back, giving him a wolfish profile.

As usual, they walked to the nearest McDonald's. All around them were families with small children, teenagers banded together, and senior citizens sipping endless cups of coffee to kill the empty hours. "You want a Happy Meal?"

"No. Quarter Pounder with cheese."

"Please."

"Please." Once a year, and his father had to correct his manners.

Adam doesn't remember much of what they talked about. His father asked the usual litany of questions an adult asks of a child he barely knows: school, friends, sports.

School was fine, he told him. He had a couple of friends. He played baseball and basketball.

Just like his exchanges with Ariel. Brief and unadorned.

This time, Adam ate quickly. Did not want to prolong the

interrogation, had nothing to ask of his father but one thing. "Will I see you again?" Meaning, "Are you coming back into my life?"

"Sure. Soon."

The last words his father ever spoke to him. For the first time, Adam wonders why he never asked his father any questions. Why hadn't he asked the important ones? He knows now that by this time Veronica had been dead for four years. Why hadn't he asked about her? Had he known but not known? Suppressed the knowing? Certainly by this time, Stein would have weaseled that out of his subconscious. Along with why he never thought that his father was still alive. That after all these years, he's never imagined him as still alive. And yet he'd never truly imagined that Veronica was dead.

A knock on his door, purposeful. At once, Adam jumps up; the hopeful grin hurts, as he wants to believe that someone has found his dog, maybe someone in the building who has been generously quiet about the illegal tenant in 3A. Adam wrenches open the door. Gina stands there, a gentle, empathetic smile on her face. A mourner's smile. She carries a casserole dish, a carry bag full of bread and cheese and all the comfort food that she will press on him.

Adam wants to take her in his arms; instead, he goes into hers. The panic is gone. The hollow place is slowly filled as he tells Gina about Veronica being dead all these years, about his father living almost in the same neighborhood where Adam has been living since his expulsion from Sylvan Fields. She sits with him, holding his hand, rubbing his back. He doesn't know if she'll stay in his life, but right now, she's here, and he is so grateful.

Gina is slowly knitting Adam back together. She takes care of his wounded face, applications of vitamin E and gentle cleansing. She feeds him, turning his inadequate kitchen into a source of delight. She lets him hope. She lets him howl. She lets him talk. She lets him be silent. She finds his phone, which has fallen behind the futon. She makes up a list of shelters and calls in her animal-activist troops. She promises that if Chance is to be found, they will find him.

She calls Ariel for him, recruits his daughter into helping. Day by day, they scour the neighborhoods, the good ones and the bad, hanging lost-dog posters, making calls. Ariel holds Adam's hand as they walk the streets. Maybe it's the fact that she's simply growing up a little that has changed the dynamic of their relationship to something that, if not perfect, at least has the seeds of hope in it. Sometimes Adam thinks that, even absent, Chance has brought them together.

Ariel has Photoshopped a picture of a brindled pit bull into a reasonable resemblance of Chance. Adam can't bear looking at the picture. Sometimes he wonders how he ever came to lay so much human emotion at the feet of a dog. Wonders if this is normal. Gina has lent him a plaque from her store with Rudyard Kipling's poem "The Power of the Dog," the last line of each stanza warning against giving your heart to a dog to tear.

Chapter Fifty-three

The only light that works its way into the cellar is a thin border of gleam surrounding the cardboard squares set against
the rectangular windows. I can judge day from night only by
the strength of that thin line as it goes from bright sunshine
to dull streetlight glow. I'm not taken outside even to defecate.
My cage grows ever smaller as I try to keep the mess to one
side. I am fed, watered. Talked to in low mutters, but not the
kind that means sweetness, but which indicates a surliness at
my mess, at having to feed and water me. All too clearly, I
understand what is coming. I'd left this place a champion;
now I'm the underdog. Upstairs, the sound of toenails on linoleum. Men's voices, challenging each other. Laughter. A
sharp bark followed by the sound of a hand on flesh. Shaddup.

The cellar is divided into two spaces—the space where we
live and the space where we fight. When I hear the sound of
feet on the stairs, I look at the other two dogs in residence.
The male lowers his head, his eyes barely reflecting in the
dim light. He raises a lip at the scent of the challenger. This is

someone he knows, someone he's fought. A soft growl. *He's a tough one. Lost to him last time.* The female circles three times and lies down. This isn't her game.

I am on my feet. The idea of impending battle sends the adrenaline coursing through my body. I fill the room with my voice. *Hey, pal, you just wait and see. Better look to your hind end.* All sorts of flimsy challenges. Bravado. The truth is that I no longer want to obey the orders of these boys. The game that I once was compelled to play, that once was my job, has been supplanted by a new and better job. I am no longer a gladiator. I am a pet, a leash dog. I miss my man. I didn't think that was possible, but that is the image that fills my mind, my man. Why hasn't he come to get me? What is taking him so long? I stop barking and start howling.

One of the boys pokes me with a break stick to get me to shuddup. In one smooth action, he opens my cage and slips a muzzle over my mouth, then a pinch collar over my head. Good. Let them take me seriously, let them understand that I'm a danger to them, and maybe they'll let me go. He doesn't have to drag me from the cage; I leap, roaring and twisting in an attempt to intimidate him into letting go. He just laughs, and the pinch collar obstructs my breathing until my roar is squeezed off into a pitiful choking sound.

I will not be dragged. I pull against the one holding the short chain attached to the pinch collar, pull him toward the other half of the cellar. Pull toward the pit. Okay. Let's do it. I may be out of shape, soft from good living and affection, but I'm still a dog. I'm still a fighter. Maybe a lesser challenger than this mass of muscle on feet in front of me, but I am. Woe betide the gladiator who doesn't understand that there is a better life away from this pit. I want that life back, and the only way to it is through this moment. Then the boy not holding my chain, he does it: wraps my jaws together with silver tape. I am not a fighter; I am bait.

I will not describe what happens. A dogfight is best left to the imagination. Suffice it to say that it will be my last fight.

Chapter Fifty-four

It has been a very long time since Adam was with a woman. Even longer since he touched one who didn't counter his efforts with instructions, with time limits, or with conditions. Adam knows that comparisons are madness, yet he can't help but compare the soft curves of Gina with the exercise-hardened ridges of his former wife. Gina isn't self-conscious about the shape of her hips, or the full, swinging weight of her breasts once released from her brassiere—breasts that are natural, unaugmented, soft and sweet. She doesn't make excuses; she makes love.

In the end, Adam feels as though he's been borne away.

They have left a side lamp on in the bedroom and have dozed beneath its gentle light. They wake and nuzzle and Gina reaches over to turn off the lamp. The streetlights outside his bedroom window keep the room flooded in a pale light; he hadn't pulled the curtains, too hurried when they slipped into his room, drew back the heavy corduroy bedspread, and lay for the first time together. It wasn't inevitable, this act. Like their friendship, this moment has never been a foregone conclusion.

Adam flops backward on the mounded pillows and pulls Gina to him upside down across his lap. He's told her so much about himself, his life and troubles, that he's ashamed he's asked so little about hers. She's come to him whole, not in pieces, and that's how he imagines she's always been. But that can't be true. There are photographs on the shelf in her store; an elderly man and a set of twins—her grandfather, with whom she lived from the time she was seventeen, and her siblings from her mother's second marriage, no longer little kids, now young married people themselves. There are other people in her life. Certainly other men. Surely, Gina would have had someone besides lovers, surely someone better than damaged goods like him. "So why hasn't some smarter guy than me snapped you up?"

Gina raises a hand and touches Adam's face gently, tracing the route of his fresh scar. "I was married for two years. A long time ago."

Adam begins to stroke Gina's hair back from her face. Waits. He wants to know that she isn't grieving for a lost love. "What happened?"

"I told him to get out."

Adam shifts a little under Gina's weight. "And did he?"

"Went without a protest. Easiest thing I ever did."

"You are a very strong woman." Adam bends and kisses her on the forehead.

Gina moves off him, sits up, and takes his face in her hands. "So are you, a strong man, even when it hurts."

They lay quietly for a time, until Gina moves away from

him, turning in the bed to look at him, putting her hand on the cheek without the slash. "Adam."

"Yes?"

"You're doing the right thing."

Chapter Fifty-five

Adam has chosen his clothing carefully. Chinos, not jeans. A light blue dress shirt, but one that has been retired from business, demoted to weekend wear. No tie. A golf jacket, not a sports coat. On his feet a pair of Reeboks. At first, Adam thought that he'd wear his best suit, his most expensive shoes, his favorite understated tie, but when he took them out of the closet, they looked wrong, formal wear at the diner. The statement he wants to make needs to be spoken, not bespoke.

Adam has circled the block twice, ostensibly looking for a parking place, but there are several to choose from on this residential street. He finally parks directly in front of the house.

The three-decker house looms over an empty lot on one side and a more recent two-family house on the left. It is painted in graduated shades of brown, tan, and yellow, so that the third floor seems less substantial than the first two. A double driveway takes up the space between the houses, a thin grass strip of border between them; a light gold Marquis sits alone on the right side. The porch steps lead to twin front doors. He knows that one will lead to a stairwell, the other to the first-floor apartment. Adam checks the address in his hand—42 A, first floor. A fence encircles the property, rhododendron bushes softening the chain link. Adam opens the gate, careful to replace the latch. There is a small round table on the porch, tucked into the corner, a citronella candle full of dead matches in the middle of it. The last few nights have been cold, and a pair of chairs are folded up, leaning against the porch rail as if done for the season.

The door on the left is the one he wants. A brass plate with *March* written in script adorns the doorbell. All Adam has to do is push the white button. He shoves one hand into his jacket pocket, runs the other through his hair, over his face, forgetting that his cheek is quite tender even though the stitches are out. Adam feels a light scrim of sweat prickle against his exposed neck, beneath his arms. This is ridiculous, he thinks. He's performed far greater acts of courage in the business arena, boldly facing down naysayers and enemies to prove his point. Asking Sterling Carruthers to marry him; asking for her hand from one of the most powerful men he's ever known. Adam suddenly realizes that he'd either better push the damned doorbell or retreat before someone notices him standing out here like some anxious adolescent on his first date.

None of the other brave moments of his life ever felt so fragile. All the other times, he was absolute in his vision of the outcome. This time, this once, he has no idea what resolution he wants.

Adam presses his forefinger into the bell. Twice.

A woman opens the solid wood door, leaving the storm door latched. The screens are still in, and she looks at him through the fine mesh. She studies him, looks past him to determine if he's alone. "You're not a Jehovah, are you?"

"No." Adam has forgotten to rehearse what he might say, fully expecting his father to be the one to answer the door. He hasn't considered this, that there might be a wife.

They study each other through the door.

"I'm Adam March. John's son."

She nods slowly, considering this bit of information. "Yes. Yes, you are. Come in." She unlatches the storm door and stands aside to let him in. The small foyer with an empty hat stand leads to the front parlor. He can smell something baking, brownies or maybe a cake, the aroma coming from beyond the parlor. The room is tidy, uncluttered. Old-fashioned furniture: a sofa and matching wing chairs, a mahogany occasional table with a pair of silver candlesticks on either end, a Revere bowl in the center. "Wait here." She doesn't invite him to sit.

He looks around the room but remains standing in the middle of the Oriental area rug. The pattern is worn in the center, but still beautiful in reds, blues, and yellows. Adam realizes he's looking for something, some item that will connect him to this home. He walks over to the fireplace, where there are three matching silver frames. He studies the photos: a wedding picture, a baby picture, and a family group.

He is still studying the photo when the woman comes back into the room.

"That's my family. My son, Carl, his wife, Jennifer, and their kids." She doesn't take the picture down, doesn't touch it. "I'm Bea. John's wife."

"I'm Adam. And this is awkward."

Bea March smiles at him. "I know it is."

"Is he here?"

"Yes. I'll take you to him. I have to warn you: He's not well. Bedridden." She looks away, studies the pattern in the rug. "It's lung cancer. Couldn't get him to give them up." Bea pulls her gaze from the floor to meet Adam's eyes. "I don't want him riled up, and he's already riled up knowing that you're here. You probably have a million questions, but if you can keep it to a few, that would be best. I won't have him tired out."

"Just one. Just one question."

"Okay. One question."

Bea leads Adam through the dining room and down a short hallway. The scent of baking is now mingled with a mild pungency beneath an overlay of air freshener. She knocks on the door with a single knuckle and Adam can see how nervous she is. "Johnny, he's here."

There is a sound, a hissing susurration of air accented by an audible blip, like the sound made by someone clearing a piece of tobacco off his tongue. Bea doesn't wait for an answer, but swings the dark-stained door open to let Adam in. John March is in a hospital bed, the head cranked up so that he is sitting at an angle, the foot bent slightly so that his legs are elevated. A white sheet is pulled up to his waist, folded down, and straightened over an orange thermal blanket, and Adam knows that Bea has just tidied him up for company. The gray face that looks at him is hollow-cheeked, a nasal cannula fitted under the nose. The eyes, deep brown, stare at him, assessing him, quite obviously reconciling this man with the boy he last saw nearly forty years ago. The boy he left behind, the boy he gave to the state. Adam swallows. The shape in the bed raises a hand, reaches out. That hand is shaking, trembling with nerves or with palsy. Adam can't tell which, but his own hand is equally tremulous. There is a folding chair placed beside the bed. Bea touches Adam on the shoulder and points to it, then walks out of the tiny, claustrophobic room and shuts the door behind her.

Adam is close enough now to see the places where Bea has missed when shaving his father. His hair is steel gray, slicked back from his forehead and longish in back. Adam remembers that his father always wore his hair in what used to be called a pompadour, a style that required an application of Brylcreem. He remembers the tube on the sink in the bathroom, the smell of it. It comes back to him in a flood of recollection. His father, standing at the bathroom mirror, black comb sweeping this way and that. His dark brown hair turned jet black, glistening from the hair cream. He'd sing the slogan: "A little dab'll do ya." Adam would sing it, too, ask for a dab of Brylcreem.

It's the first time he's thought of that, ever. All the thoughts he's ever had about his father have been of his temper, his fighting with Veronica, of her leaving. A little dab'll do ya.

"Hello, Dad."

His father smiles, and over the sound of the oxygen machine, his own voice a breathy susurration, he answers. "Hello, son." He taps the covers with a hand that is bruised from the permanent line in his vein, and Adam wonders if he's supposed to take it.

Adam gets one question, if he's to play by Bea's rules. One question after a lifetime.

John March licks his dry lips. "How you been?"

His father's first question after a lifetime.

"Why, Dad? Why did you let me go?"

His father reaches up for the cannula, pulls it away from

his nose. "I had no choice. I was alone." He puts the cannula back but misses one nostril.

"Why didn't you come back? When I was old enough? Why did you leave me in the system?" Adam reaches over and helps replace the tube.

"Complicated."

Adam knows that he's used up his allotted question, and he still has no answer. The old man is struggling to remove the cannula again, and Adam presses his hand away from his face. "I know it is. I just don't understand why you stopped contacting me even once a year. But you know what? I managed. I succeeded. I have a daughter. You have a grandchild. You missed knowing her. You missed knowing me."

There are tears in the old man's eyes, but they seem less like tears of regret than tears of defiance. Adam sits back, taking a deep breath that is filled with the smells of illness and old man. Two eight-by-ten framed photographs sit on the bureau. For a moment, Adam thinks that one is a picture of Ariel that has somehow come into his father's possession. The long blond hair, the angle of the chin to eye, the closed-lip Mona Lisa smile. Veronica. The other is of him, a gap-toothed five-year-old with a crew cut and wearing a plaid shirt. Sears portraits. The photographer had him hold a toy train. Adam remembers this. And the swoop of recognition, of memory, threatens to force him to run from the room. His father has kept those studio portraits, taken weeks before Veronica was dead and he was placed into the foster system.

"Why did you—" Adam stops. There are no answers to his questions. None that he wants to hear; none that will make forty years of anger go away. He stands and opens the bedroom door. "Good-bye."

John March raises his hand again, struggles against his disease to speak. "Will I see you again?"

Adam is aware of the irony. He has turned the tables on his father; he has the upper hand, the ability to choose to see him or not. The choice to get even. The last time he asked his father that question, "Will I see you again?" his father had said, "Sure. Soon." And then he disappeared from his life. The hurt, the anger, the grief eventually mellowed into a dissonant memory. Adam turned his sights to a future that he would have control of. That he thought he had control of. One that turned out to be beyond his control.

"Sure. Soon."

Beatrice March is waiting for him. She takes him into the kitchen, despite Adam's protests that he has to go. She sits him down and puts a cup of coffee in front of him; a plate with warm brownies cools in the middle of the kitchen table. She is wearing an old-fashioned apron, the kind that slips over the shoulders and crisscrosses in back. She doesn't sit down, stands to one side instead, her hands busy with wiping the counter, her back to him. He feels like a little boy waiting in a neighbor's kitchen. Waiting quietly for a parent to return to fetch him, or a pal to burst into the room. Waiting for an adult to take over the moment.

"He told me about you." Bea wrings the sponge out into the sink. She doesn't look at him as she says this. "About having a child he had to give up. Broke his heart. I will tell you that."

"If it broke his heart so badly, why didn't he keep in touch with me? He did, you know, for a few years. Come see me, take me out to lunch. Then, when I was maybe ten, he didn't come. No contact. No one ever told me why. I began to assume he was dead."

Bea turns to Adam, pulls out the chair opposite, and sits down. "No one ever said what happened?"

Adam's heart does a tricky little quickstep. "No."

Bea presses her hand to her forehead. "Men don't admit failure easily. John doesn't admit failure easily. He'd failed with poor Veronica. He was adrift with a five-year-old, couldn't work enough hours to make a living. Right after Veronica left, he was offered a job doing long-distance trucking. It was good money, but he knew that he would never be home. He had no prospects of being able to offer a kid a consistent home life. It was the best choice he could make at the time. To put you in state care. He wanted you to have a family, to be adopted. As painful as that was, it's what he saw as the best choice for you."

"You're excusing him."

"Damn right I am. The first thing he told me about himself when we met, and we've been married twenty-five years, is that he'd lost his family. And how it had been his fault. He's rarely spoken of it since. It's too painful."

The quickstep has settled into an arrhythmic thumping.

"Then they told him you were unadoptable as long as there was a parent in the picture. He wanted a better chance for you, a chance at a stable home. He had no family to help. He thought that if you were adoptable, you'd finally have that stability. He anguished over it until he finally gave you up."

"And I was never adopted."

"He never knew that. The belief that you had a happy home was all that cheered him when he got despondent about the past. The belief that you had ended up with a better life than that of the son of a transient."

One Good Dog • 299

"He doesn't look very transient to me. You've got a nice home. You raised kids together."

"No. I raised Carl, in this house, by myself. I met your father after he retired. Course, he wasn't a trucker anymore; he retired as a mechanic, so, yes, he wasn't transient anymore. He lived next door. Rented from the Garritys. Turned their backyard into a vegetable garden. I used to watch him from the kitchen window. I knew who you were in a minute because you look just like he did back then. Handsome." Bea covers her mouth with one hand, then reaches for her coffee cup. "Since he's been sick, he's been talking a lot about you. Wondering about you."

"Did he never imagine that I might have wondered about him? About what happened to Veronica? I've only just found out that she was killed. Why didn't anyone tell me that?"

Bea shakes her head. "People weren't so—what's the word nowadays? Up front with kids. Some things weren't meant for little pitchers' ears. They believed that ignorance was bliss. I'm sorry. If I'd been around then, well, it would have been different. I'm sorry you never knew that the poor girl was run down like a dog in the street."

A dog in the street.

"I have to go."

Bea nods. "He hasn't got long now. It would be a wonderful thing if you'd . . ." She puts her hand back over her mouth, unable to say the words.

"Forgive him."

Adam lets himself out of the house.

Adam sits in his car, which still smells faintly of Chance. A leash is on the floor on the passenger side. He hopes that Bea

March isn't looking out the window, seeing him still sitting there as he waits for his heartbeat to level off, waits for the shaking in his hands to subside. His phone is in the console, and he picks it up out of habit, checking to see if anyone has called while he was in the house. Two missed calls. He goes to voice mail.

The first is Ariel, calling again to see if he's found Chance. As if she wouldn't be the first call he'd make once he does. If he does. In her message he hears a faded optimism that someone will spot Chance, that miracles do occur. The only good to have come out of Chance's disappearance, besides Gina, is that Ariel has found her way back to being his daughter.

The second message is brief.

"Mr. March, this is Dr. Gil at the shelter. I think we may have your dog."

The expression "emotionally overwrought" comes to mind as Adam copes with the juxtaposition of his strained reunion with his father and the joy of getting Chance back. In one hour, he has been emotionally flayed alive. Every feeling has come into play, but right now he is enjoying the pounding heartbeat of hope. If Chance is back, then things will be all right. That bugger, how could he disappear like this for so long? He'll take him right over to Gina. Get him some new chew toys. This is ridiculous thinking. He's a grown man. Why is he weeping with relief over a dog?

There is one parking space left near the shelter and Adam pulls in, drops quarters on the sidewalk in an effort to feed the meter, and bursts through the shelter doors, trotting to the reception area. "I'm here for my dog."

The receptionist looks a little puzzled.

"The dog Dr. Gil called me about. The brindled dog, half an ear?"

"Oh. Right. Let me get the doctor."

The scrubs are green today, the Crocs lime-colored. Gil's ponytail is slightly askew. "March, okay, man. Here's the thing."

Gil goes on to describe the dog: mauled, crushed bones, loss of blood. Found in an alley, dumped. Except for the fact that Adam had been pestering the shelter for ten days, Gil would have euthanized the animal immediately. The half ear was the only resemblance to Adam's description, and it was then that Gil remembered him, remembered the unorthodox adoption and put two and two together. "I'm asking that you not be alarmed. And that you make the right choice."

Adam hasn't said a word. He's listened to the doctor and begun to pray that this poor battered animal isn't Chance. He wants to call Gina. To have her opinion. To have her hand on his shoulder.

"All right."

The swinging door leads to the hallway of doors. This time, the vet takes Adam through one that leads to the infirmary. The walls are stacked on two sides with cages, one up and one down. Some are small and contain small sleeping animals; others are occupied by silent creatures looking like science experiments with bandages and tubes. Other cages are doubled for larger animals, and all but one are empty. Gil leads Adam to the cage and squats. "Hey, boy."

Adam kneels beside the cage, fingers looped through the wire mesh. Inside is a brindled hulk. White gauze interrupts the brown striping. The hulk's head is swathed, one foreleg is splinted right down to the end of the paw, making it look like a prizefighter's hand wrapped for the glove. It lies with its back toward the front of the cage, so Adam cannot see its eyes. Nothing moves. Adam looks at the veterinarian. "Is it too late?"

"He's been given a little happy juice."

"I don't understand."

"Something to make him rest. Not too much. Not until you say so."

"Can I have a minute?"

"Take as long as you want." Gil rises to his feet, presses a hand on Adam's shoulder. "As long as you want. I'll be in my office when you're ready."

Adam unlatches the door, reaches in and strokes Chance along his shoulder, between the lines of gauze continents. "Hey, buddy. It's me." Adam doesn't feel self-conscious whispering to the recumbent dog. His knees hurt a little against the tile floor, so he sits, leans in awkwardly, and rests his scarred cheek against the dog's side. He can hear Chance's heartbeat. "You wouldn't believe who I met today. My father. My absent father. He's as banged up as you are, but from the inside out. He's dying, too, and there's no one who will put him out of his misery. Are you miserable? Do you want to die? Do you want me to do it? To say 'Do it'? I've missed you. The place is pretty empty without you, except that now Gina is there. Oh Chance, where have you been? How did you get into such trouble?"

Adam feels the dog stirring under his sore cheek. He lifts his head and two sets of brown eyes meet. A tail thumps against the cage floor. *Thump. Thump. Thump.*

Rroorr. Chance puts his head down and is still.

Chapter Fifty-six

Bea has filled in some gaps in his father's life, things that have helped to move the old man from contemptible to comprehensible in Adam's mind. A man with a high school education and few prospects; a suddenly single dad with no living relatives; a man who had grieved for a wife lost to cancer. Circumstances that had made his father seem an angry man, a man whose temper lost him his teenage daughter, lost him his son.

It's too hard for John to talk, so Adam does. One day, he brought pictures of Ariel to show his father. Now he has brought her to meet the grandfather she never knew she had. They don't stay long, he and Ariel, and at the end Adam feels washed out, drained of the substance that has been keeping him upright for years. Most of his life has been spent in defiance of his upbringing. He sits with the fragile shape that was once his powerful and angry father and understands that he is just like him. But Adam knows that he has been given a chance, a chance to regain the happiness lost by his own actions. Maybe not regain what he once believed constituted happiness, but to appreciate a simpler, more profound contentment with what has become his life.

Judge Frank Johnson stares at Adam's face for a moment longer than is polite. "Bob told me what happened. Tough."

Reflexively, Adam touches his cheek, touching the groove that is still carmine. Gina insists vitamin E will soften the scar. "It's all right."

"He also told me that you've done well." The judge motions toward a side chair. "Sit."

This time, Adam is confident that his sentence is complete, that his term of community service has been served, and he is no longer nervous that the judge will tack on more time. As long as he doesn't ask if Adam has learned a lesson. That would be too paternal for Adam's taste. And yet he isn't embarrassed to admit that, yes, he has learned something. Adam takes a seat, runs his slightly sweaty hands against his legs. "Frankly, it's turned out to be a very good thing."

The judge slides his Buddy Holly glasses to his forehead. "You've taken on grant searches. Are you going to keep doing that?"

"I am. I've found a couple of foundations that award funds to purchase needed equipment, like a new computer, and one whose grant will allow us to bring in a visiting nurse once a month."

Johnson sits back, squeezes his chin with one hand. He nods slowly. "Good. Case dismissed."

And just like that, Adam March is a free man.

. . .

Adam is startled awake by his cell phone playing the overture to Rossini's *Barber of Seville*. He answers the phone, then leaves his bed to go to his father's house.

Adam and Ariel stand in the cemetery, arms linked, the first real chill of fall nipping at their ungloved hands. "She was my age."

"Yes. And just as rebellious."

Ariel shoves him a little, her shoulder against his arm. "Not quite. I haven't run away lately, but I will if Mom marries that a-hole Troy."

"She has a right to be happy."

"Can I come live with you?"

"Yes. But not out of anger. You have to come live with me because I'm your favorite."

"Okay."

They have just buried his father. The rest of the mourners have already gone back to Bea's house for refreshments—her son, Carl, and his wife and kids, the neighbors, friends from church. Adam and Ariel have hung behind so that he can tell her what happened to Veronica. And more about her grandfather, who has been in her life only briefly and is now gone. It was painful to see his father's eyes light up at the sight of this girl who resembles the long dead Veronica so completely that she is a gift.

"Why did she run away?"

"I don't know. I asked my father, mostly because I wanted to blame him, but he didn't know, either. She was looking for a better life." Adam squeezes Ariel's hand. "I always thought that she was running away from me, from having to take care of a little brother when she was just a young woman, ready to start her own life. Wanting freedom and fun, not be a house-keeper and surrogate mother."

"That's so cheesy. I'd never do that."

"You've never been responsible for a little brother."

They are quiet for a moment, both lost in their own thoughts.

"I've been thinking about taking a year off between high school and college and doing City Year."

Adam slides his arm around her shoulders, surprised that she comes up to his shoulder. "That would be fine with me."

"Mom's flipping out."

Adam smiles at the image. "You have to do what you feel is right for you."

"It does feel right. I've been listening to you talk about Fort Street and it got me to thinking. You went back even though you didn't need to anymore."

"It's a lot nicer volunteering than being ordered to do good works." Once his face no longer pulsed with every movement, the hole in his days was deep, and he'd missed the structure. He'd gone back a few weeks ago. With a second consulting job, he is finally able to make ends meet, and that is enough. Jupe, med-icated, more Charles than Jupiter now, has apologized to Adam. Strings were pulled and he is living in a halfway house nearby but still takes a noontime meal at the center. He wants Adam to go with him to the animal shelter to find a new companion.

Ariel pulls the sleeves of her cashmere sweater down over her hands. "I'm cold. Let's get out of here. Do we have to stay long at Bea's?"

"You don't. Just come through and have a nibble. I'll make your excuses."

Adam and Ariel link hands and walk to his Lexus. Despite their flawed history, Adam is deeply saddened by his father's passing. These last few weeks have been hard and yet the sweetest that he has known. Reconciliation. Renewed affection. Recovery. A new love.

Gina, wanting Adam and Ariel to have some private time, waits for them in the car.

And in the backseat, boxy chin resting on the open window, Chance waits for them, too.

Epilogue

I walk with the swagger of a champion, but I know that is only because I limp. My foreleg aches on cold mornings, a reminder of the long weeks in which it was splinted, the miserable days of wearing that ridiculous plastic cone over my head. There were moments when I was crazed, mad to chew that splint off and lick the multiple wounds along my chest and on my belly that itched and ached simultaneously. My man scratched them for me, allowed me a brief respite of coneless sleeping when he was around. He gave me canned food to accommodate my sore mouth. He fed me bits of cheese that he pretended didn't contain sharp-tasting pills. He carried me downstairs to do my business, and carried me back up.

They say that a dog cannot know about its own death because it doesn't really know about its own existence, but I can tell you that simply isn't so. I knew that I was headed for oblivion as I lay drugged in that hospital cage. One cage is much like another, the one in the cellar or the one in the shelter. They both restrict and protect. The one in the cellar had been a prison, but the one in the shelter a haven. I was waiting for the moment when I could let go of life. It isn't something you can do at will; you have to be patient. I'd had a good run. Adventure, travel, a little romance. A good man. As I lay there, I realized that I wasn't just waiting for my end, but for him.

As I lay dying, I thought about him, about how I knew his kind said "Adam" when he was called. That he depended on me to keep him happy. I lay facing my death, and if dogs can wish, I wished that he would come to me, to be there as I let go of life.

And, lo and behold, out of my too-deep sleep, I awoke and found him there.

I pushed the desire for death into a corner as his face pressed against my side, his voice rumbling into my center. I could feel the slow moistening of the tears he shed and I knew that his crying wasn't for me alone. A profound sadness transmitted itself from him into my racked body. I'd awakened with the thought that now he was there, I could let go. Join my ancestors, give up the ghost. But when I felt those tremors, heard his raspy voice, I realized that I was still needed, maybe as much as ever. I had chosen this one and I owed it to him to see him through this new pain. It's my job; I'm a pet. We're a pack of two.

So I wagged my tail.

Acknowledgments

If it takes a village to raise a child, it certainly takes a team to write a book. This book could never have happened without the guidance, insight, crystal-ball gazing, and friendship of Andrea Cirillo. Thanks, too, to the gang at the Jane Rotrosen Agency, who patiently read every iteration of this book; and, to my copy editor, Carol Edwards, who smoothed things out.

To Jennifer Enderlin, who had the vision and imagination to see this as a "big" story—thank you isn't saying enough.

To Jane Rotrosen Berkey and Bernice Clifford, CPDT, of Animal Farm Foundation, who opened my eyes to the charms of the much maligned pit bull. Thank you.

Thanks Kevin, for being my non-pro, yet eagle-eyed, reader.

Bonnie, Hunter, Sprout—you are all good dogs.

1. What explains Adam March's outrageous attack on Sophie?

2. Why do you think the author used the first person in telling Chance's story?

3. There are two protagonists in this story. How would the reading experience change if we saw only one side?

4. What is Adam's initial attitude toward Chance?

5. How does that attitude reflect his attitude in general and the situation he's in?

6. When Adam breaks down, what motivates Chance to approach him?

7. What does Chance think of his "career" as a fighter?

8. Should Adam forgive his father?

9. What role does Gina play in Adam's personal growth?

10. Describe Adam's relationship with his daughter Ariel. Does his childhood impact this relationship, and if so, how?

11. Does Adam relate at all to the boys he encounters on the street? How so?

12. What are Adam's three sins and does he overcome them?

13. In this story, men are living on the streets as well as dogs. Are you more likely to support animal shelters or homeless shelters?

14. Conventional wisdom believes that fighting pit bulls cannot be rehabilitated. In many cities, a dog that has been known to fight is automatically put down. Do you think that a character like Chance is realistic? Does he change your mind about pit bulls?

15. In the end, has Adam been redeemed?

For more reading group suggestions, visit
www.readinggroupgold.com.

A
Reading
Group
Guide

St. Martin's
Griffin